FALLING FOR A WOMAN

"Mistress," the Kook said to Alexis, "I have concluded that your arguments are sound enough to overbear those against them. So command us, and we shall obey."

"Then grab that man!" Alexis commanded, pointing straight at Salazar.

The Kook bodyguards approached Salazar, who gripped his knife and aimed an underhand thrust at the nearer Kook with a lunge that would have disemboweled a Terran opponent. But before Salazar's thrust sank home, the Kook's scaly hand gripped his wrist and stopped his attack. Another Kook seized his other arm, while the first assailant twisted the knife out of Salazar's grip.

Then the Kooks were dragging Salazar toward the crater to throw him into the volcano. Salazar could hear Alexis calling to him.

"Good-bye, Salazar! No hard feelings!"

D1022615

By L. Sprague de Camp
Published by Ballantine Books:

THE ANCIENT ENGINEERS

THE PIXILATED PEERESS
   (with Catherine Crook de Camp)

The Reluctant King
Volume One: THE GOBLIN TOWER
Volume Two: THE CLOCKS OF IRAZ
Volume Three: THE UNBEHEADED KING

THE HONORABLE BARBARIAN

THE VENOM TREES OF SUNGA

THE
VENOM
TREES
OF SUNGA

L. Sprague de Camp

A Del Rey Book
BALLANTINE BOOKS • NEW YORK

A Del Rey Book
Published by Ballantine Books

Library of Congress Catalog Card Number: 92-90617

ISBN 0-345-37551-3

Manufactured in the United States of America

First Edition: November 1992

Cover Art by Darrell K. Sweet

To Caleb B. Laning, Rear Admiral, USN (Retired)

Contents

Note

This story is a semisequel to my wife's and my science-fiction novel *The Stones of Nomuru* (Bluejay, 1988). That is, it is synecumenal with (laid in the same world as) the previous novel, but a couple of decades later and with different characters. Among the less obvious pronunciations, I suggest:

Akbar	as	UCK-bar
Feënzuo	as	feh-en-zwaw
Gueilin	as	gway-lin
kyuumei	as	kew-may
Oöi	as	aw-oy
Seisen	as	say-sen
Sungao	as	soong-gow

"Shiiko" rhymes with "pekoe"; the "singh" of "Mahasingh" sounds like "single" without the "le."

I.

The Ship *Ijumo*

The steamship *Ijumo* wheezed and puffed its way to the pier at Sungecho, on the island of Sunga, on the planet that Terrans called Kukulcan after an Aztec god. Kukulcan was a satellite of the star Epsilon Eridani. Kirk Salazar stood with his parents' friends the Ritters at the rail.

"That's Sungecho," said Hilbert Ritter, graying and stoop-shouldered. "A lot of Terran riffraff have collected here; not a good place to explore alone at night."

On the bridge the Kukulcanian skipper, Captain Oyodo, bawled orders in the Sungao dialect of Feënzuo. He spoke in the harsh, rasping voice of his species, like the screams of an angry macaw.

"There's Alexis," said Hilbert Ritter, pointing.

"Where?" said Salazar. "Oh, you mean the redhead beside the armed Kook?" Terrans called the civilized reptiles of Kukulcan "Kooks."

"Yes. I think the Kook is a cop, though I can't quite make out his insignia."

The paddle wheels ceased their thrashing; the ship drifted up against the bumpers. Longshorekooks snubbed hawsers round bollards. The gangplank slammed down like the crack of doom, and a rush of Kook porters came aboard.

Kukulcanians were slender bipeds of vaguely dinosau-

1

rian appearance, taller and leaner than most Terrans. Their horny mouths gave them a turtle-beaked appearance, while their scaly hides bore painted symbols in a rainbow of colors. Otherwise unclad and displaying no visible organs of sex, they wore a harness of straps, whence dangled pouches and sheaths in lieu of pockets. They attacked the pile of luggage and marched back up the gangplank, each bearing a load that would have strained the broadest Terran back.

After the Kooks, Salazar and the Ritters clustered around the plank with others of the Patel Society's field trip. Lanky, graying Igor Tchitchagov, the director, stood at the base of the plank, waving his group ashore. As the Patelians shuffled up the plank, Salazar touched Ritter's arm and pointed, asking:

"Hey! How does Cantemir get ashore ahead of us? He's not a Patelian."

He pointed to a squat, stocky, ruddy, robust-looking man with bushy blond hair and beard, just stepping from plank to pier. Ritter sighed.

"George Cantemir does as he damn pleases, and he gets away with it because he's a flunky of the Reverend Dumfries, and Dumfries is in cahoots with High Chief Yaamo. By God, I think he's headed for Alexis!"

"He'll probably proposition her," said Suzette Ritter. "He's done it to every woman on the ship under a hundred and fifty—including me." She gave a little sputter of laughter.

"That's not funny," growled Ritter. "Least of all to me."

"Jealous, Hilbert?" said Suzette.

"Damn right! Now he's introducing himself, all smiles and smarmy charm. That Kook policeman has disappeared."

"She'll take care of herself," said Suzette.

"What I don't understand," said Salazar, "is why, if the reverend is such a puritan, he puts up with George's womanizing. After all, the Bible has some nasty things to say about fornication."

"That's Saint Paul," said Ritter, stepping from the gangplank to the pier. "My preacher friend thinks Paul was not a celibate, as most suppose, but a married man who hated his wife. In the Old Testament they took a more relaxed attitude, allowing concubines—"

"Oh!" exclaimed Suzette.

Whatever Cantemir had said, Alexis Ritter backed away from him with an expression of fury. Salazar could not hear the words, but they must have been pungent. Cantemir moved a step towards her.

Salazar hesitated. He wanted to protect the Ritters' daughter not only because the Ritters were family friends but also because of a subliminal chivalrous drive to which he would not have admitted. On the other hand, in a rough-and-tumble with Cantemir, he would have all the chance of a snowball in the crater of Mount Sungara. Although like Cantemir he was of average height, the latter had half again his weight.

Kirk Sheffield Salazar was young and slim with rounded features, a toothbrush mustache, and a small chin, which led some unkindly to liken his face to that of a rabbit. Most Terrans knew how rabbits looked, although there were no rabbits on Kukulcan, thanks to the Interplanetary Council's rule against the importation of exotic species.

As the dispute between Cantemir and Alexis Ritter seemed about to explode, Salazar lengthened his stride. For two paces, fear of looking ridiculous kept him from breaking into a run. Then he thought, To hell with dignity, and ran towards the couple.

"Hey, George!" he called.

Cantemir turned his jowly face. "What is it, Kirk?"

Salazar spoke to the girl: "You're Alexis Ritter, aren't you?"

"Yes. What—"

"Is George giving you trouble?"

"He—"

"Damn it, Kirk," said Cantemir, "mind your own goddamn business and go away!"

The girl said: "He made a—"

"Look," said Salazar, whose heart pounded between fear and combativeness, "this is the Ritters' daughter. You can't—"

Cantemir's ruddy face reddened further. "Didn't you hear me? I said bugger off!"

"Who the hell are you—"

Stepping closer, Cantemir brought up a fist. Salazar had an instant thought: Oh, Lord, now I shall get the shit beat out of me in vain!

Cantemir aimed his punch at Salazar's jaw. Salazar jerked his head back, but the blow glanced off his cheekbone with enough force to stagger him.

Behind Cantemir, Alexis swung her handbag in a swift circle. The bag struck Cantemir on the side of his head with a clank, audible above the noise of wind, wave, and disembarkation. Cantemir stretched his stubby length on the splintery planks of the pier.

The older Ritters hastened nigh. Hilbert Ritter demanded: "What's going on here?"

Salazar faced Alexis, seeing a pretty, slightly plump young woman of stocky, muscular build in well-filled shirt and slacks. She received him with a toothsome grin. "Thanks! You gave him just the distraction I needed."

"Nothing very heroic, I'm—"

Hilbert Ritter said: "Alexis, this is—"

"I know," said Alexis. "You're the Salazars' boy Kirk, aren't you?"

She extended a hand. Salazar shook, receiving a crushing grip. He knew the appearance of plumpness was deceptive; she was all muscle.

"How did you know?" he asked.

"Don't you remember my fourteenth birthday party?"

Salazar thought. "Oh, yes. You're the one who pushed me off the roof! Lucky you didn't break my neck."

"But you had such a funny expression on the way down! Hey, the slob's reviving!"

Cantemir hauled himself to his feet, felt the spot where the weighted bag had struck him, and with an angry growl started toward Alexis Ritter and Kirk Salazar. As he approached, he fumbled in a trouser pocket and produced a small pistol.

"George!" said an extraordinarily resonant, penetrating voice.

Cantemir instantly ceased his advance. Alexis, who had been swinging her bag in small arcs, let its motion dampen out. Salazar, who had suffered an instant of stark fear, looked at the speaker, the Reverend Valentine Dumfries.

The preacher was a tremendously fat man; he was also, a rarity among Terrans of his day, bald. His round, clean-shaven features bore a wide mouth beneath a blob of a nose and blue eyes beneath two bristly bushes of gray eyebrow. He had a way of screwing up the inner corners of his eyelids that gave the effect of a hypnotic glare. He wore a transmundane, the usual semisafari suit adopted by most Terrans for going about a foreign planet. But Dumfries's suit, instead of the usual khaki, was black. He leaned on a massive, crutch-headed walking stick as he rolled slowly forward like something risen from a Mesozoic swamp.

"Look, Val," began Cantemir, "this red-haired floozy—"

"I saw it all," rumbled Dumfries. "I've warned you."

The Kook policeman, identified by the symbols painted on his scaly hide, reappeared, unslinging the rifle strapped slantwise across his back. Salazar noted that the firearm was a breech-loading repeater instead of a muzzle-loading, single-shot musket such as a few years before had been the island's most advanced native weaponry. He had heard of High Chief Yaamo's efforts to modernize his armament.

Several Terrans from the *Ijumo*, drawn by the disturbance, followed the Kook. The reptilian officer hissed like a teakettle, and a quarter-meter of pink forked tongue flicked out and in. He said:

"Troubre iss?" Terrans unused to it could not understand it.

"No, nothing I cannot control," said Dumfries. Cantemir quietly returned his pistol to its pocket. Alexis said:

"Now *you* bugger off, Mr. Cantemir, or I'll have you run in!"

With a wordless growl, Cantemir turned away. He and Dumfries walked off, talking heatedly in undertones. Alexis Ritter said to the Kook in good Sungao:

"The trouble is all over, Officer."

As the policeman departed, Ritter asked: "What happened, Alexis?"

"The usual," she said. "He put it more politely, but the gist was 'How about a nice, quick fuck?' You'd better go claim your baggage."

Two nights before, after the final show of passengers' night on the *Ijumo* had ended and Kirk Salazar had washed off his makeup, Hilbert Ritter had said: "Hey, Kirk, come have a drink with us!"

Seated at a bar-lounge table, he continued: "Quite a show you put on, your burlesque mahatma act. All that bilge about resuming the triad in unity, engendering the cosmic tetrad. You made it sound as if it really meant something."

"I got a stitch from laughing," said Suzette Ritter. "You even got a discreet smile or two out of the Reverend Dumfries."

Ritter continued: "You surprised me. You seemed like such a quiet, shy little fellow—" Salazar winced at the word "little" "—but on the platform you became a real spellbinder, with a hypnotic delivery. You could probably lead a cult and make ten times the money you get as assistant instructor at the U."

Salazar waved a dismissive hand. "Oh, I was in the

drama club as an undergraduate, and the patter I got from a couple of occult books. Speaking of cults, I heard something of your daughter's being involved in one.''

Suzette sighed. ''That's our particular problem.''

''Oh, I'm sorry,'' said Salazar. ''Didn't mean to bring up a sore subject which is none of my—''

''That's all right,'' said Suzette. ''We don't mind talking about it, especially since you'll probably run into her where you're going.''

''Then are you two on this safari to look at zutas or to—ah—rescue your daughter?''

''In a sense, both,'' said Ritter, ''though anybody who thinks he can rescue Alexis when she doesn't want to be rescued has his work cut out for him. At least, we hope to make her hold still long enough for a reasonable discussion. You might say we're in the Patel Society under false pretenses, but Igor won't mind. He's an old friend, and we've paid our dues up to date. We leave the main group at Amoen.''

''I suppose I'm a faker, too,'' said Salazar. ''I joined because I could get to Sunga cheaper on the group rate. The university makes us take such field trips on our own; say they've already committed all their grant money for the year.''

''If not to identify zutas, then why are you going to Sunga?''

''Bucking for my doctorate. My thesis is on the kusi-nanshin problem.''

''Tell us,'' said Ritter. ''I'm in xenanthropology, and Suzette's in linguistics, so we wouldn't know.''

''All right,'' said Salazar, seeming to expand in size and stature as he started in on his specialty. ''You know the kusi, the omnivorous, semiarboreal relative of the hurato? Well, the stump-tailed kusi, *Cusius brachiurus*, lives in the forests of Mount Sungara. Some colleagues think it's a living fossil, like the common ancestor of the Kooks and the rest of the Pithecoidea.

''This species has a peculiar adaptation. The main tree

on the upper slopes of Mount Sungara is the nanshin or venom tree, *Pharmacodendron saitonis*, though it also grows elsewhere in the highlands. If you brush against it, it sprays corrosive venom from its needles, like little hoses. The stuff eats holes in your skin if not quickly washed off. But the stump-tailed kusi lives in the nanshin's branches without apparent damage. I'm supposed to find out how it does it.''

"How," asked Suzette, "will you do that without getting holes in your skin, too? Wear a fireman's suit?''

Salazar shrugged. "I shall have to see when I get there." His speech held an audible trace of his father's down-East accent, from the elder Salazar's youth on the coast of Maine, on Terra.

Ritter asked: "What if, despite precautions, you get some on your skin?''

"They say sodium bicarb neutralizes it, or at least limits the damage.''

"Are you doing the whole job yourself?" asked Ritter.

"Not quite. A Kook at the U, a Gariko scholarship student, recommended his cousin Choku as a helper. This Hakka, a Shongarin, was, I suppose, as close to a personal friendship as one can have with a Kook.''

"I know," said Ritter. "Those cold, reptilian minds don't seem to know friendship in our sense. That inflexible formality becomes a bore.''

"That's not fair, dear," said Suzette. "They have excellent qualities. You can rely on their word more than on a Terran's.''

"True, my dear. They're honest, truthful, logical, and literal-minded. Also humorless, hidebound, and pigheaded, like our daughter. If I had to jump into a river to save a drowning man, I'd rather hand my wallet to a Kook to hold than to a Terran, but I could never have so good a time with one as with a Terran friend—or with you. Go on, Kirk, about this helper.''

"If I can find this Choku in Sungecho, I shall at least

have someone to haul the heavy baggage. It's no imposition, since they are much stronger than we. And I'm to inquire after my former roommate, Jean-Pierre Latour.''

"The one who disappeared?''

"Yep. The kusi problem was originally his.''

"I've heard rumors of others' disappearance on Sungara. When they send someone to investigate, all they find is a mob of naked naturists running around and saying they know nothing.''

"Is your daughter's cult on Sungara?''

"So they tell me.''

"Then I ought to talk to your daughter. She might be helpful in getting me into the kusi country.''

"Well, watch yourself. She's the most willful, bullheaded person I've ever known, quite different from her brothers. Besides, we don't know what the Reverend Dumfries is cooking up, and he wields a big stick on Sunga. He may disapprove of her cultists' going bare-arse naked and send the lot packing. Is the kusi problem the basis for your thesis?''

"Yep. If it's accepted, there'll be another unread Ph.D. thesis on the university library shelves.''

"I don't know about that,'' said Ritter. "Remember the dust-up your father's friend Firestone made with his scholarly book on population statistics, showing that the two civilized societies on Kukulcan were on a collision course? He thought that births should be managed, which made the natalists howl.''

"And since he was wrong,'' said the resonant, penetrating voice of Valentine Dumfries, who had come up silently behind Ritter, "it was the duty of those who know better to correct him. My dear friends, if someone were to go around preaching that the planet Kukulcan was flat, wouldn't you—''

"Just what was wrong?'' said Kirk Salazar loudly enough to break into Dumfries's flow of speech.

"On several counts,'' said the fat clergyman. "In the

first place, he put human beings on the same level as Kooks, as if each had equal rights.''

"But Kooks are reasoning beings—'' began Salazar.

"If you will permit me to finish,'' said Dumfries, holding up a hand. Such was the commanding note in his voice that Salazar, not easily silenced, broke off. Dumfries continued:

"So are Terran dogs and cats reasoning beings, within their limitations, but we do not put them on a par with us legally or morally. See first Genesis, twenty-eight. God—that is, the Terran Demiurge to those who understand these things—gave man dominion over the fish of the sea and so on. In other words, over the animal kingdom. And Kooks certainly belong to the animal kingdom.''

"Oh, come on!'' said Salazar. "Do you believe that God paraded samples of Terra's several million species before Adam—''

"That is second Genesis, nineteen and twenty,'' said Dumfries. "It is a later and more mythologized version. We must understand these things in the light of modern discoveries.''

"I don't believe Genesis mentions other worlds,'' said Suzette Ritter.

"Next,'' continued Dumfries, ignoring Suzette's point, "Doctor Firestone proposes the limitation of births by any means available: contraception, abortion, or—he hasn't actually proposed infanticide, but wait and see. It is such degenerate practices—''

"Come off it!'' said Ritter. "Even the Pope has come around to admitting—''

"I cannot help it if the great Catholic Church has fallen into error,'' said Dumfries. "If the possibility of conceiving a child is artificially deleted from the conjugal act, couples shut themselves off not only from the Terran Demiurge but also from the Supreme God whose will is that they be fruitful and multiply—''

"And replenish the Earth," said Ritter. "But he didn't say what to do *next*."

"It is obvious, my dear professor," said Dumfries. "Since the faculties that the Demiurge gave man have enabled man to be the first species to attain space travel, it is the Supreme God's will that man go out and conquer other worlds where conditions permit human life and where the native inhabitants show no sign of spiritual enlightenment and must therefore be classed with the lower animals—such as our lizardlike friends." Dumfries jerked his globular head toward a table at which a quartet of Kooks were drinking a native beverage.

"How about Krishna?" asked Ritter.

"That is not yet decided. The Krishnans have evolved impressive theologies and are possibly groping toward that degree of spiritual advancement whereat their Demiurge will send them a Redeemer, as ours did to Terra."

Dumfries looked at his poignet and added: "I should like to carry this interesting discussion further, but I find I have an appointment with some of the enlightened. So, dear friends, excuse me for the nonce."

As Dumfries departed, Salazar said: "Somebody ought to expose that guy for the nutty troublemaker he is."

"Been done," said Ritter. "Didn't stop him; didn't even slow him down. The kind of people who believe in him would say the exposé was just persecution of their messiah. Too many of our fellow anthropoids fall for his kind of thing; we belong to an incredibly credulous species. And don't underestimate him, either. He's dangerous."

Salazar mused: "I'm told he's completely sincere, even if that Gnostic Gospel is, as my father thinks, a forgery."

"No doubt he is sincere in his way. That only makes him more dangerous."

In the customs shed, the fishy smell of Kooks was strong. Each zuta watcher had claimed his or her own baggage and passed inspection. Drumbeats and the wail-

ing music of the chief Sungan instrument, like a hybrid
of zither and clarinet, announced the approach of Yaamo,
high chief of the Sungarin. Tchitchagov fussed about,
getting his charges in line. He said:

"One knee, remember! Two knees would be an invitation to cut off your head. Ready? Down! Down! *Vniz!*"

The Terrans sank to one knee on the planking as Chief
Yaamo strode forward, resplendent in symbols of gold
paint spangling his scaly skin. A golden disk hung round
his neck on a golden chain. Nodding politely, he said in
barely understandable English:

"Weycome, member of ze—de Patey Society! Rise,
prease!"

"Is all well with your Highness?" asked Tchitchagov.

"Aw iss wey wiss my Highness. Iss aw wey wiss
you?"

"All is well with us. Is your Highness's health good?"

"Sanks to our ancestors' spirits, our hess iss good. Iss
your hess good?"

"Thanks to the Universal Law, our health is good. Has
your Highness lived a tranquil life?"

"Sanks to ze Great Spirit Shiiko, we have rived a very
tranqui' rife. We trust you wi' have a successfu' visit.
But you mush—muss make ze most of your time here,
because zis may be ze wast—rast such expedition to
Sunga."

Society members stirred and muttered. Tchitchagov
spoke to the chief in Sungao, which Salazar could follow:
"How means your Highness?"

The chief replied in the same tongue: "It is the price
of progress, honorable Tchitchagov. The Adriana Company, represented by their vice president, the honorable
Mr. Cantemir, and the chairman of their board, the Reverend Dumfries— There they go now!"

The chief glanced around as the fat cleric and the
stocky Cantemir walked past the line of zuta watchers,
nodded casually to Chief Yaamo, and went on without
further ceremony. Yaamo turned back, resuming:

"As—as I was saying, the honorable Cantemir has made me an offer for the timber on Mount Sungara. He has come hither to render our agreement final. When cutting begins, we cannot have other Terrans running about the mountain, getting in the way of Mr. Cantemir's machines and belike being injured or slain. A part of the contract whereon we have agreed ordains that to avoid possible lawsuits, all Terran visitors to Sunga be barred from the mountain and the surrounding area whilst lumbering be in progress. His company has already brought in the necessary machinery."

Tchitchagov translated for the benefit of such Patelians as could not follow Sungao. Society members burst into cries of dismay, like people who had bought a ticket to one place and found themselves in quite another. Salazar muttered:

"Bet it's really Yaamo who's afraid of lawsuits. Kooks abominate Terran litigation, which they think a plot to steal their lands."

"They may not be far off," replied Suzette Ritter.

Tchitchagov said: "But your Highness, the Patel Society has field trips to Sungara planned for two years in advance! We have already paid your deposit!"

"That," said the chief, "were no obstacle to the proposed agreement, honorable Tchitchagov. When the treaty is signed, the society's payments would be as naught compared to the Adriana Company's royalties. Your advance against the next year's fee would be refunded, and you would have to revise your plans. Zutas flit all over the mainland."

"Your Highness," said Tchitchagov, "this is a serious matter. I doubt whether Mr. Cantemir has presented both sides of the question. May I, therefore—"

"Come to the residence as soon as these formalities are completed and your people settled, and present your arguments. Now, pray introduce your zuta watchers!"

Tchitchagov said to the Patel Society members: "Step forward singly or in couples, please, starting with that end of the line. Bow and give your names as you greet him. Do not fear his offer of a handshake; his claws will not hurt you.''

The zuta watchers lined up. They were Terrans of both sexes and a wide spread of ages, with a slight preponderance of women and a tendency toward mature years, getting on but still fit. At that period, modern medicine had more than doubled the normal human life span, so that human beings far into their second century were still active and two-hundred-year-oldsters were not uncommon. The common cliché was that legends promised eternal youth, but in fact medicine had given eternal middle age.

The Terran population of Kukulcan was dominated by three ethnic groups—the Chinese, the Russians, and the Anglophones—but other strains, much mixed, were also common. This group of zuta watchers was mainly Anglophone with a sprinkling of others.

Kirk Salazar found himself behind the Ritters in line. The Ritters advanced, bowed, and shook the chief's scaly, clawed, four-digit hand. Ritter introduced ''Dr. Suzette Ritter, my wife.''

Salazar in turn stepped forward, saying: ''I am Kirk Sheffield Salazar of Henderson.'' He switched to Sungao. ''If I may take the liberty, knows your Highness aught of what befell my colleague, Jean-Pierre Latour?''

The spines on the Kook chief's neck rippled in a way that signified startle. An experienced Terran could infer a Kook's emotions from the movement of those cervical bristles. Since each Kook thus bore a built-in lie detector, this feature might have accounted for their unhuman honesty. Yaamo replied:

''Nay indeed, honorable Sarasara. Naught beyond the fact that this Ratoo went up Mount Sungara and failed to come down again. Belike he remains with the wiseman Seisen.''

''Permit me to ask: Who is the wiseman Seisen?''

''He was a teacher in that advanced school which Empress Gariko established in Machura. On retirement he came to Sunga, ascended the mountain, and settled himself to think.''

"Do people consult him?''

"We human beings do, aye, but Terrans think they know everything already.'' For "human being'' the chief used the Sungao word *konohto*, with the "h'' pronounced, which Kukulcanians employed about their own kind in exactly the same sense that Terrans referred to themselves as "human beings.''

"How does one consult him? By bringing an offering of food?''

Yaamo's neck spines rippled in the Kookish equivalent of a chuckle. "Nay, he raises his own. The needed tribute, to hear his wisdom, is a book, either human—a boxed scroll—or the Terran kind, with all pages bound together at one edge.'' Yaamo fiddled with his golden disk of office. "Tell me, pray, are you kin to the Terran Sarasara who digs up the remains of ancient cities and burial places?''

"My father.''

"He is well regarded here. Are you, like him, connected with one of your institutions of Terran learning?''

"Aye, sir. I am a candidate for the degree of doctor.''

"Then you will, certes, find Seisen of interest.''

"I thank your Highness and will pursue the matter further.''

"That were a worthy course. I congratulate you on your mastery of human speech. Not once have I had to ask you to repeat!''

Salazar made a self-deprecating motion. "Just a quirk of mine, but it is useful in my work.''

"May your health continue good!''

"And may your Highness's health surpass even mine!''

"May your ancestral spirits preserve you . . .''

Yaamo finally broke off the exchange of formalities to speak to the next Terran in line. Salazar hurried after the Ritters, who walked leisurely toward the exit. Alexis Ritter had rejoined her parents. As a permanent resident, she did not have to go through the formalities that had greeted them.

When Yaamo had disposed of the last Patelian, he said: "And now farewell. Take utmost care of your health!"

Tchitchagov replied: "And may your Highness take utmost care of his health also!"

"May all your lives be tranquil!"

"May your Highness's life be as smooth as a mill-pond!"

"May your ancestral spirits be well disposed toward you!"

"And may your Highness's ancestral spirits sustain him in all ways!"

The Kukulcanian formalities continued as Tchitchagov and the high chief piled good wishes on each other. Then the chief stalked off, surrounded by bodyguards and followed by the musician playing a martial-sounding tune.

Outside on the cobblestones, members of the Patel Society stared at the slatternly town, more Terran than Kukulcanian. As a zuta fluttered overhead in pursuit of insectoid life, a Patelian exclaimed and pointed. At once a dozen pairs of binoculars swung up like the guns of a battery. Terrans across the avenue halted to stare at the zuta watchers.

The zuta looked like a small flying lizard or perhaps like one of the smaller Mesozoic pterosaurs. But its bat-like wings bore a colorful pattern like those of a Terran butterfly: gold, ruby, and emerald flashing in the light of Epsilon Eridani.

Salazar pulled out his glasses and followed the example of the others. Although the zuta was in plain sight, he could not seem to find it in the narrow field of the glasses. Mrs. Ramos cried:

"That's a *Nicterophis jacksoni*, I'll swear!" She marked a tally sheet.

"Right genus, wrong species," said Mr. ben-Yahya. "That's the *orlovi*."

"No, I'm sure of my identification."

The argument died as the zuta fluttered away and disappeared. Then another took its place, and again the binoculars swung. Beside Salazar, Hilbert Ritter murmured:

"On these field trips, Kirk, the one thing you can count on is a sore neck from staring up."

Tchitchagov puffed up with the mannerisms of a mother hen trying to govern a fractious brood of chicks. When he had caught his breath, he said:

"I—I have obtained transportation. We shall go to Levontin's Paradise Palace, down the main street beyond that mushroom-shaped tower." Tchitchagov pointed. "Do not, from the name, get exaggerated ideas of the quarters. But it is still the best in Sungecho, having what I believe are the only flush toilets on Sunga."

A pair of Kooks—rustics from the symbols spangling their hides—trotted past on jutens. The common riding animal of Kukulcan looked something between a medium-sized bipedal dinosaur and a featherless ostrich. Their large heads ended in hooked beaks like those of Terran birds of prey, and their coppery scales reflected the blazing sun.

The animals bore saddles but no stirrups or bridles. The riders held on with their clawed feet and controlled their mounts by voice, although each juten had a leading rope dangling from its neck. When a juten had been specially trained to carry Terrans, on command the animal grasped its rider's ankles in its handlike forefeet, obviating the need for stirrups. Salazar's father, Keith Salazar, had devised this system many years ago, before Kirk's birth. At that time, the older Salazar was courting his ex-wife, Kara Sheffield, who after their remarriage became Kirk's mother.

A pair of wagons driven by Kooks, each drawn by a kyuumei, a large, horned, reptilian, purplish-brown quadruped, called a "buffalo-lizard" by many Terrans, rumbled up. One wagon bore benches, while Kook porters loaded baggage on the other. Mrs. Eagleton said:

"Igor, why must we ride in these primitive vehicles when the Kooks have perfectly good steam cars?"

Tchitchagov said: "Because the only steam car on Sunga is High Chief Yaamo's personal auto. The Council of Chiefs argues furiously over letting more in. Opponents cite noise and smoke and have so far carried the day."

Salazar said: "Don't think there'll be room for all of us."

"How did you figure that out so quickly?" asked Alexis Ritter.

"We have twenty-three Terrans, counting Igor. The wagon has four benches with space for five butts each, provided none is so fat as the Reverend Dumfries. That's twenty places."

"Let's walk!" said Alexis. "You need the exercise after being cooped up on that little ship. Besides, there wouldn't be room for Hatsa and Hagii. Come on!"

She started off with an aggressive stride while the zuta watchers were still fitting themselves into places on the first wagon. A glance showed Salazar that Tchitchagov was perched atop a pile of baggage on the second wagon. As Salazar followed Alexis, walking fast to catch up, he became aware of two Kooks, each with a rifle slung across its back, following the pair. A glance told him that neither of the twain bore the painted insignia of the Sungecho constabulary; therefore, these had to be the Hatsa and Hagii she had spoken of, apparently bodyguards.

Alexis slowed her taxing pace. Salazar thought that Alexis was an athletic girl, too husky to be altogether cozy. Still, she was certainly one to arouse masculine lust, with the sun agleam on her coppery mop. He said:

"What did you hit George with?"

"Heft this!" She proffered her handbag.

"Jeepers! It must weigh over a kilo. What's in it? Lead sinkers?"

"Gold from the Kashanite treasury."

"Is 'Kashanites' what you call members of your cult?"

"Damn it, it's not a cult! It's a spiritual confluence of minds!"

"Sorry."

"But yes, we do call ourselves the Kashanite Society, after Rostam Kashani, our founder."

They walked silently for a few steps; Salazar had no wish to become entangled in a theological argument. At last he said:

"How come Dumfries and Cantemir walk in here with a mere nod to the chief, when the rest of us had to go through that kneeling rigmarole?"

"Dumfries owns the controlling stock in the Adriana Company and has the final say about paying the chief for his timber. Cantemir's just his flunky. I hear rumors of some big plan those two are cooking, but nothing definite.

"Not to change the subject or anything, but isn't there an odd story about your parents' having been divorced and remarried? It happened before my time, so I haven't any firsthand knowledge."

Salazar sighed; discussion of this quirk in the family history made him uncomfortable. He said: "Just one of those nutty things middle-aged men sometimes do—dump the spouse of their youth to run off with a much younger woman and then wish they hadn't. But it all happened before my time, too."

"Obviously," she said, "since you're the product of their second marriage. How are they getting along now?"

"They seem happy and devoted. She bosses him, and he spoils her; guess he's afraid she might trade him in on another spouse, the way he did to her. What's that structure?" Salazar jerked a thumb at the mushroom-shaped tower as they passed it.

"That's Mao Dai's revolving restaurant, or 'retsuraan'

as he calls it in imitation of the Kooks. If you stand still and watch, you'll see it turn."

"What's its source of power?"

"Look over that fence."

Salazar rose on tiptoe to peer. At the base of the tower two large kyuumeis, yoked to two of the four ends of a cruciform whim, walked the device around. A Kook leisurely walked outside the circle, now and then flicking one animal or the other with a whip. A pen beyond held two more kyuumeis, eating from mangers.

Salazar squinted up. Behind him the two wagons summoned by Tchitchagov rumbled past on the waterfront street. "I should estimate four or five revolutions an hour. That implies a gear ratio of—"

"You scientists! Instead of being thrilled by the novelty, your first thought is to turn everything into numbers. Let's move on. You'll want to clean up for dinner, and I'm expecting a—a friend.

"That's Doc Deyssel's clinic on our right. He's the only Terran M.D. on the island, and thank Shiiko he's competent. And there is the library. It has a fine collection of tapes and even some real books."

Salazar joined the three Ritters at the entrance to Levontin's Paradise Palace to walk with them back to Mao Dai's. As he approached, he heard Alexis growl:

"If that bastard has stood me up again . . . ."

"Maybe he broke a leg or something," said Suzette Ritter.

"Then he could have left word with Levontin . . ." She broke off as Salazar approached, and the four set out for the restaurant.

Mao Dai's servitors were all short, yellow-skinned, flat-faced, black-haired, slant-eyed Gueilin types like Mao himself. When the party had been plied with the Kukulcanian distillate that pretended, without great success, to call itself whiskey, Hilbert Ritter asked:

"Alexis, tell us about this cult of yours."

"Father! It's not a cult; it is a spiritual philosophy."

"Call it what you like. But tell me about Kashani. Immigrant from Iran, wasn't he?"

"Rostam Kashani was a man of great spiritual insight, in touch with intelligences other than those inhabiting visible bodies." Alexis stared into the distance, and her voice took on an oratorical quality, as if she were addressing a throng. Some of the other diners turned to look.

"Was?"

"Oh, didn't you know? He's ascended to a higher plane."

"Dead, you mean?"

"If you want to call it that. He sacrificed himself to Shiiko, the spirit of Mount Sungara."

"How? Diving into the crater?"

"Exactly. He held our mortal bodies of no account."

Ritter said: "Mine may be of no account from the cosmic point of view, but it's the only one I've got. Then who runs the cult—excuse me, the spiritual philosophy—now?"

"I do."

The jaws of the three other diners sagged. Suzette said: "You mean you're their high priestess?"

"If you want to put it that way. My official title is Supreme Choraga. I'm expected to set an example for my fellow seekers that shall give them an advantage in assignment to their next incarnations."

The older Ritters exchanged a long glance. Hilbert Ritter said: "Have you some sort of tract or textbook setting forth the theology of—"

"No theology, please!" Alexis interrupted. "We recognize spirits, those of our ancestors not yet reincarnated and spirits of places like Mount Sungara. But no all-powerful gods like those of—"

"Hel-lo, folks!" said George Cantemir, grinning with glass in hand. "Mind if I join you while waiting for my grub?'' When the four at the table stared stonily, he added:

"Now, Miss Ritter, I want to apologize for the misunderstanding this afternoon. I was just bein' friendly, not meaning to go beyond the bounds of polite intercourse.''

"Depends on what you mean by 'intercourse,' '' said Alexis. Salazar thought she gave the nearest feminine equivalent of a growl that he could remember hearing.

"I meant just ordinary good manners, miss. It was just a misunderstanding, and you came out of it better'n I did. I've still got a lump on my poor head. See, here? That's right, smile a little. Are you folks going with the rest of the gang to the Michisko Bush?''

"I suppose so," said Hilbert Ritter. "It's on our itinerary. We're to get up early tomorrow. But what we want is the straight goods on this deal between Yaamo and the Adriana Company.''

"Just normal lumbering," said Cantemir. "I've got some of our machinery at the base of Sungara now.''

"Are you planning to clear-cut the whole mountain?''

"Just the nanshin forest.''

"But still clear-cutting?''

"Sure. That's the most efficient, profitable way.''

Salazar asked: "How will you cope with the poison-spraying nanshin trees?''

"No problem. We'll wear protective suits.''

"But you'll wipe out the local biota, which I'm here to study!''

"Sorry about that, but we can't hold up progress while you superdomes take a century to study the situation. Yaamo wants to uplift and modernize his Kooks, to catch up with the mainland nations, and we'll pay him enough to make it possible. As the boss Kook here, he has the right, by their laws and ours, to sell that stand of timber if he wants. Our population is growing, and people have to live somewhere. The nanshin tree has the best wood for houses on Kukulcan.

"Besides, it'll provide jobs for the Terrans of Sungecho, which is a pretty seedy outpost of humanity. If you say we've got to put up a front for the Kooks so they'll respect us, they'd say: 'But look at Sungecho, with its gangs and crime!' "

Salazar asked: "Alexis, how will that affect your cu— the followers of your philosophy?"

She shrugged. "We'll adapt. We are one with nature now, but nature is always changing. The geologists say that millions of years ago there was no Sunga; it was all built up by the volcanoes. Then it was once connected with the mainland, until the sea level rose."

Hilbert Ritter said: "The Patelians may have something to say about your project. We're not without influence."

Cantemir smiled through his curly blond beard. "Go right ahead! Then we'll see who comes out on top. I know you are all red-hot environmentalists. If Terrans had felt that way a couple of million years ago, we'd still all be running naked through the woods and turning over flat stones for our dinners—a state of culture that, I take it, your daughter wants to go back to.

"Understand, I sympathize with your feelings, but business is business. And there are plenty of other places where you can watch zutas flitting about or kusis sitting on a branch and scratching. Don't take it personally. Just because we disagree don't mean we can't be friendly. Here comes my dinner, so excuse me!"

As Cantemir returned to his solitary table, Salazar leaned forward and said softly: "This looks like an ecological disaster for me as well as for Mount Sungara. If they start cutting the nanshins, the kusis will beat it to another woodland, just to survive. Those lumberjacks will be the kind whose idea of fun on an off day is to take a gun out and shoot something, no matter what. In any case, they'll bollix up my thesis."

"I agree," said Suzette. She looked after Cantemir, now seated and shoveling away. "That man must have a hide as thick as a tseturen's." The tseturen was a huge, massive, four-horned quadruped of the mainland.

"That's how he got to be a successful corporate exec," said Hilbert Ritter.

"Dreadful," said Suzette. "What can Skanda Patel do for his society?"

Hilbert Ritter shrugged. "He's as full of lofty ideals as an eggshell is of egg, but he's more talk than action."

Alexis asked: "Is he the man the society is named for?"

"Yes," said Ritter. "He's a modest fellow who didn't want the name, but the members insisted because he's the founder. He's never mobilized the members for political action. In fact, he looks down on politics and politicians, which didn't do the museum any good when he was director."

"I know Skanda," said Salazar. "He was my father's boss at the University of Henderson Museum until he retired. His wife is a holy terror, but she built up his money until he didn't have to work for a living. Now he just does an occasional dig when he feels like it. Do you know any useful politicians, Doctor Ritter?"

Both older Ritters answered at once, since both bore the title. Hilbert Ritter said: "Maybe I could pull a wire with Basil Aliprandos . . ."

Suzette said: "I know the wife of Representative de Sola pretty well . . ."

Dinner arrived. During a pause Salazar said: "You should help, Alexis. Set your naturists to raiding the lumber camp and sabotaging their machines."

Alexis smiled grimly. "You don't know what you're asking. Can you imagine fifty-odd naked, unarmed followers attacking a camp full of tough lumberjacks in hobnailed boots, armed with axes and probably guns as well? Besides, Cantemir will probably hire Kook guards."

"You don't wear clothes there?"

"Only when weather demands. The climate's mild, and this is the hot season."

"And unarmed, you say? What do you do if a fyunga or a pack of poöshos attacks?"

"We have a couple of heavy rifles, but so far it's been enough to keep a fire burning."

"Look, Kirk," said Ritter. "Your father's director of the museum, and he's as hot a conservationist as we are. He also wields a big stick politically. Why don't you get him to work on the legislature about this."

"I'm thinking," said Salazar. "It's not really his kind of dispute; he'd rather argue the order of kings of the ancient Nomuruvian Empire. But I'll write him."

"Couldn't you call him on your poignet?"

Salazar shook his head. "We're out of range of Henderson. I shall have to write, and it'll take several days for a letter to reach him by ship and rail."

Ritter leaned forward. "Kirk! The *Ijumo* sails at midnight. If you can get a letter aboard, it might make all the difference."

Salazar sighed. "Okay, I'll do it."

"Promise?"

"I promise."

Several other Patelians entered the restaurant during this conversation. When not greeting fellow zuta watchers with smiles and waves, the quartet discussed ideas for ditching the Adriana Company's project. They rejected many plans and by the end of dinner had not yet found a hopeful one.

Back at Levontin's, Alexis excused herself for a brief, whispered conversation with the innkeeper. Salazar heard Levontin say, spreading his hands in an expression of impotence: "Absolutely not, Miss Ritter! If there had been a message, I should have known it! My people are well trained!"

Salazar bade the senior Ritters good night and walked Alexis to her room. The girl was frowning and muttering expletives under her breath. She opened the door and turned to face him, looking him up and down as if he were a prize piece of livestock. Then she broke into a sunny smile. Without further ado, she slid her arms around his neck for a long, moist kiss. Salazar was so startled that he almost failed to respond, but he quickly pulled himself together. She said:

"How about coming in for a while, Kirk? We ought to get to know each other better."

Salazar's blood pounded in his ears. His own experience with women had been negligible. He had driven himself so hard in his studies as to leave little time for even the most innocent dalliance. He pushed himself because of a burning desire to equal or surpass his father, whom he vastly admired for his signal achievements and fair renown among the Terrans of Kukulcan. Keith Salazar was planet-famed for the discovery of the buried library of the ancient Kookish king, Bembogu of Nomuru.

If Keith Adams Salazar had become the planet's foremost archaeologist, Kirk Sheffield Salazar was determined to become the foremost biologist or perish trying. The older Salazar encouraged and supported his son's progress.

And now, unless all indications were wrong, Alexis was offering the utmost in female hospitality. The thought made him pant with anticipation, tempered by fear that he might not measure up. The nasty little thought also crept in that he was substituting for a truant lover of Alexis. Hesitantly he said:

"Look, I've got to write that letter to my father."

"Can't that wait?"

"I might miss the *Ijumo*'s sailing. I'll come back for a proper good night."

"Oh, all right, if you must," she said.

Back in his room Salazar dictated his letter into a small wire recorder, extracted the spool, put it in a pouch, addressed it in English and Feënzuo, and applied a United Settlements stamp to the pouch.

Kukulcanian postal service was still chaotic. He would have to pay the postal clerk on the *Ijumo*, hope that this person would put the letter aboard the right train at Oöi, and hope that the conductor would put it on the right connecting train at Machura to Henderson. When it reached the museum, assuming that it did, the elder Salazar would have to pay a whopping bill of postage due, owed to each of the carriers through whose hands the missive had passed. The wonder was that any letter reached its destination.

Salazar walked swiftly to the pier, where the *Ijumo* was getting up steam. He paid the postal clerk and was on his way back to Levontin's when lightning flashed, thunder roared, and rain came down in bucketfuls. He reached the inn soaked.

In his room he shed his wet clothes and hung them up to dry. Since they were drably durable garments for travel, he did not fear damage from wetting. But there was something he was supposed to do once he got the letter off. What was it?

Oh, yes, he must enter a record of the day's events in his journal while they were still fresh in his mind. If he did not faithfully discharge this task, then, when he later came to write up his expedition, dates and places would be jumbled.

He sprawled on the bed, holding the recorder near his mouth, and dictated a narrative into the machine. At the first reference to Alexis Ritter, he remembered that she was waiting for an assignation.

Kirk Salazar had a compulsion to finish any task he began before starting on another, despite hell or high water. Having commenced this job he was determined to finish it before letting anything distract him. Besides, it had only a few minutes more to go. He dictated as much verbatim conversation as he could remember.

He awoke to find that the time, by his poignet, was

nigh unto dawn. Then he remembered Alexis's invitation. Now, however, seemed hardly the time. He cursed
himself as an ineffectual incompetent.

In the morning Salazar entered the room where Levontin's staff served breakfast. When he sighted Alexis, he
started toward her with a cheerful "Good morning, Al—"

She saw him coming and turned her back.

"Hello, Kirk!" boomed George Cantemir around a
doughnut. He gulped *acha*, the Kukulcanian analogue of
coffee, and asked: "Sleep well?"

"So-so."

Cantemir drew Salazar toward a corner and lowered
his voice. "I saw your little byplay just now. What did
you do to get her sore?"

"Fell asleep."

"Huh?"

"Yep. She told me to come back for a proper good
night after I'd done some necessary work. But I fell asleep
on my bed, and when I woke up the sky was getting
light."

Cantemir shook with suppressed mirth. "No wonder!
You got her all horny, and then, when she expected a
royal fuck, you stood her up! If I'd known, I'd have been
glad to substitute."

"Sure that's what she wanted?"

"Oh, sure. I've asked around, and she's a hot piece.
Up in the hills, with her cult, she's holier than thou and
asks the same of her suckers. But every couple of sixt-
nights she comes down on the train for a good frigging
with some local. Named Peters, I hear. In fact, I think
that's him now."

He jerked his leonine head toward a large young man
with sandy hair and a snub nose standing near Alexis.
The young man was speaking in an earnest undertone,
with rapid gestures. Probably, thought Salazar, trying to
explain why he had not appeared for his date with Alexis.

"Better luck next time," said Cantemir, slapping Salazar's narrow back. "What work was so important you couldn't break it off for a good screw?"

"I had to write—" Salazar began. He almost blurted out that he was writing his father to use his influence against Cantemir's project when he realized what a bungle that would be. He finished: "I mean, I had to dictate my day's observations."

Cantemir grinned. "You've got some growing up to do yet, boy. No real man lets clerical work stand in the way of free cunt; only with her, watch out she doesn't hit you with a bag full of buckshot, like she did me. Going to look at the giant makutos in the Michisko Bush?"

"Yep. I'm told they're the only herd of them on this island."

"I'll ask Tchitchagov to let me tag along. I haven't seen them, either, and I want to before we kill them off. See you!" Cantemir walked off.

II.

The Michisko Bush

In the ruddy light of rising Epsilon Eridani, outside Levontin's Paradise Palace stood another wagon. Two purple-brown kyuumeis drew it, with a Kook on the driver's seat in front. Standing before the zuta watchers, Tchitchagov counted and said:

"Only nineteen? Where are the others?"

"Mrs. Ramos was tired," volunteered a member.

"Mr. Antonelli said he had seen all the makutos he wanted on the mainland," said Kirk Salazar.

"Mr. Mpanza isn't feeling well," said another.

"Miss Bedford wanted to shop in Sungecho," added still another.

"If she can find anything worth buying," said Tchitchagov, "I should like to know about it. At least I shall not have to find another wagon." He added in an undertone to Salazar: "Unless the Reverend demands to come along. He would fill two places."

Salazar said: "Igor, how did you make out with the chief?"

"I won a delay," replied the tour director, turning. "Hello, Mr. Cantemir."

Cantemir strolled up, accompanied by two armed Kooks. "Got room for me, Igor?"

"I fear there is not," said Tchitchagov. "All seats are occupied."

"He iss not velcome, anyway," said Herr Wille-brandt. "We know about his plans to—how would you say?—Mount Sungara to scalp."

"Just one of those ruthless exploiters," added Mrs. Long. "The kind that has made our Terra into a big, overcrowded, overregulated jailhouse. You have to get official permission to keep a pet parakeet lest it upset the balance between food production and consumption."

Cantemir grinned through his golden beard. "Now, ladies and gentlemen, is that any way to convert anybody to your point of view? You'd get further with flattery and soft soap. Igor, I can sit on the tailboard." To his two Kooks he added in Sungao: "Fare ye well, lads. Do naught that I would not do." The Kooks walked off. "Ready?"

"Not quite," said Tchitchagov. "Chief Yaamo is sending one of his people as a guide. Here it comes, now."

Salazar thought the Kook approaching was probably as much a policeman to keep a wary eye on the aliens from outer space as a guide. The newcomer's hide bore a painted pattern of green and brown symbols, and a rifle was slung across its back. From its lack of the small, spiny crest that distinguished male Kooks, Salazar inferred that the newcomer was a female. Perhaps she was an onnifa, a barren female filling normally male rôles such as soldier or mariner.

Approaching Tchitchagov, the guide spoke in Sungao: "Are you Chief Tchitchagov? I have been assigned to you as guide. I hight Fetutsi, forest warden third class."

"We are glad to have you," replied Tchitchagov in the same tongue. "This is an English-speaking group. Speak you that language?"

"A ritter," said Fetutsi. "Not very wey."

Conversing with Fetutsi was like talking with an intelligent parrot because of the differences between human and Kukulcanian vocal organs. Salazar knew that Kooks felt the same way about Terrans' efforts to imitate their rasping, cawing speech. Terrans trying to learn a native language complained that the sounds meant by letters used to transliterate Kukulcanian words bore only a faint resemblance to the Terran sounds those letters usually denoted.

"Where sit?" asked Fetutsi.

"On the tailboard," said Tchitchagov, pointing. The Kook nodded and heaved herself up, sitting with her back against the aftermost bench and with her feet dangling. Cantemir hoisted himself up beside her, while Tchitchagov climbed up to the little bench in front and sat beside the Kook driver.

"All ready?" he said, peering around. Then to the driver: *"Katai!"*

The driver released his brake and flicked the two kyuumeis with his whip. The massive animals ambled off; after them the wagon groaned and creaked. The wheels rattled on the cobblestones, shaking the passengers like one of those vibrating machines used to thin down overweight Terrans. As Salazar had noted before boarding, springing was of the simplest. Soon the paving ceased, and the wheels squelched through the mud of the latest rain. The vehicle lurched more but vibrated less.

The slatternly port drifted past, the houses becoming smaller and more widely spaced with each block. Along the street Terrans halted to stare, while the occasional Kukulcanian went about their business with typical indifference to anything but the task at hand.

The wagon staggered past the remains of a defensive wall that had warded the port before Yaamo's clan had established hegemony over the isle of Sunga, and on out into the country. They plodded past stretches of farmland until the patches of dusky green woodland grew larger and denser. Gradually the countryside changed from farmland with woodlots to forest with occasional clearings.

* * *

Salazar sat beside the Ritters, whom he knew the best of anyone in the group. He inquired: "Where's your daughter?"

Hilbert Ritter replied: "Gone back to Mount Sungara."

Suzette added: "When she found we'd come to try to talk her out of this cult business, she got furious. We had a frightful row, and she walked out on us. This morning, I hear, she's collected her two Kook bodyguards and taken the Unriu Express to Amoen."

"Sounds like a difficult offspring," said Salazar.

"You don't know the half of it," said Ritter. "Are you a family man?"

"Nope. Not married or even engaged."

"Oh?" said Suzette. "We saw you kissing a little blonde good-bye before the ship left Oöi. We assumed—well—"

"Just a friend, come to see me off," said Salazar. "She and I have been, I guess you'd say, going together. She's Professor Fisker's daughter, Calpurnia."

"Any future plans?" asked Suzette.

"If you mean getting married or even taking on a live-in arrangement, no. At least not till I get my degree and something more than a beginning instructor's pay."

"A careful man like your father," said Ritter with a chuckle. "One can be too careful, like the man attacked by a fyunga who called for help to his Kook companion but took so long getting his grammar right that the fyunga ate him."

Salazar changed the subject. "Will this—ah—disagreement with your daughter change your plans?"

Ritter grunted. "Looks that way. We were going to skip the zuta-watching trips from Amoen and spend the time deprogramming the girl. But after last night I think we may go on those field trips, after all. She said she never wanted to see us again; serve her right if we took her up on it."

Suzette added: "I doubt if anything we said would

make a difference. If she likes the power and pelf that comes from being a high priestess, why would she want to give it up?''

The conversation was broken by a cry in Sungao from behind the wagon: *"Keëkai! Keëkai!"* meaning "Move aside" or "Out of the way!" Two Kooks on jutens overtook the wagon, their animals at a full run. When the wagon driver paid no attention, the two riders pulled over to the grassy strip alongside the road and pounded past, missing the wagon by millimeters. A gob of mud thrown up by the jutens' feet struck Miss Shakeh Dikranian, the sultry-looking, black-haired, Oriental-seeming beauty, on the left ear. She cursed in three languages and, with help from Mr. Antonelli, wiped off the mud with paper handkerchiefs.

"Juten racing," said Ritter, "is the nearest thing adult Kooks have to sport. Otherwise they say games are fine for children, but they think Terrans touched in the head to go on playing them when grown up.''

Two hours later the wagon drew up on the rough, rutted dirt road that ran west from Sungecho. To the right rose the somber forest of the Michisko Bush. A substantial wire fence ran along the left side, where the forest had been cleared for farming half a kilometer back from the road. Beyond the fence, where the wagon halted, stretched a bare field, sparsely spotted with wild herbage and a few saplings. Salazar inferred that either the field was lying fallow or the owner had given up trying to raise a profitable crop there.

"We get down here," said Tchitchagov. "Follow Fetutsi. Do not get ahead of her and do not straggle. Do not approach any large wild animal closer than a hundred meters.''

The driver spoke in Sungao: "Honorable Tchitchagov, I shall take my team an *itikron* down the road, where there is good grazing.''

"Be back in two hours," said Tchitchagov; then to the Terrans: "Let us go!"

Fetutsi unslung her rifle and, holding it in one clawed hand, walked into the Michisko Bush. She turned her reptilian head to say: "You ay-yens, keep crose!" Her speech was even less intelligible than Chief Yaamo's. Tchitchagov brought up the tail of the column, herding stragglers along.

On either side rose huge trees, as thick as temple columns. Faint sylvan smells of rotting vegetation filled Salazar's nostrils. In this climax forest, little sunlight reached the ground, which was fairly free of underbrush. The gloom of the forest seemed to dampen the visitors' spirits, for there was none of the usual banter and chaff. When, however, a zuta with black and white striped wings flew over their heads, weaving among the tree trunks, some of the more dedicated zuta watchers whipped out binoculars and tally sheets.

"It's the greater chocho!"

"No; it's the *Saurophychus nesiotes*. That's another genus."

"Catch one and I'll prove I'm right!"

"It's gone now, damn it. It's listed in Parker's book . . ."

"Over there," said Tchitchagov, "you'll see the yellow-bellied gougebeak."

"Where?" asked Salazar, searching the forest in the direction indicated.

"On the left-hand side trunk of that V-shaped tree."

Salazar looked, but there seemed to be at least six V-shaped trees in that direction. "*Which* tree, please?"

"Too late; it has gone behind the trunk."

Fetutsi turned to say: "Prease keep move! And keep noise down. No roud noise, prease!"

The column got under way again. Salazar noted that George Cantemir walked a couple of paces ahead of him, beside Miss Axelson where the trail permitted. He was murmuring to the young woman, now and then bringing giggles to her fresh young face. Salazar thought, No doubt he is asking her for the same thing he tried to get from Alexis. Salazar also thought: Wish I had the guts to proposition every woman who came by—or even one of them once in a while.

An hour later the party entered an area of smaller timber and more undergrowth. A few charred, rotting trunks of larger size implied that this area had once, perhaps a century earlier, been swept by fire, and they were walking through second growth. Trees became sparser and more widely scattered, allowing longer views. More shrubs and saplings impeded their progress.

"Ouch!" said Mr. ben-Yahya. "That damn thing has thorns."

"Watch thorns, ay-yens," said Fetutsi belatedly. "You skin too soft." The Kook had brushed past the same thorny shrub without harm, her scales being proof against its spines.

A fallen trunk lay across the trail. Fetutsi put a clawed hand on the bark and, holding her rifle in her other hand, vaulted effortlessly over the obstacle. She said to the Terrans behind her:

"You ay-yens go round."

The Terrans straggled toward the butt end of the log, where a mass of roots stuck up to more than man height. Cantemir put both hands on the trunk and vaulted over, as Fetutsi had done. He came down with a loud grunt.

"What wrong?" said Fetutsi.

"Hurt yourself?" said Tchitchagov, hurrying forward.

"Just sprained my damned ankle," gritted Cantemir. "I'll cut a walking stick."

"Too bad Mr. Mpanza isn't with us," said Mrs. Nicollet. "You could borrow that blackthorn shillelagh he carries."

Cantemir limped off a few paces, chose a sapling, and pulled out a big sheath knife. In a few minutes he had cut a serviceable stick and was limping after the column.

Serves him right, thought Salazar, for showing off in front of the dame.

"You've put us behind schedule, George," grumped Tchitchagov.

"Sorry about that," growled Cantemir. "How much farther?"

"Maybe half a kilometer."

They plodded on. A wild tisai, looking like a slate-gray reptilian version of the Terran tapir, crashed away, followed by four spotted young.

At last Fetutsi held up a hand. "Ay-yens quiet. Makutos iss. Cameras ready."

Fetutsi advanced slowly, waving back the occasional wildlife enthusiast who tried to push past her. Salazar heard a subdued rustling and crashing ahead. A louder, prolonged crash, together with movement of the foliage, told of the overthrow of a smaller tree.

As the party neared the source of the sounds, huge dark bodies materialized through the trees. A herd of mouse-brown makutos was browsing in a comparatively clear area. Salazar heard gasps from some Patelians.

The makuto was a bipedal herbivore, larger than any he had ever seen. When they reared up, bracing themselves by their huge balancing tails, they towered as high as an eight- or nine-story building. Their hind legs were like the trunks of the larger trees, ending in huge splayed feet with massive toenails like small hooves. Their forelegs, though smaller, were still long enough to reach down branches with their clawed hands, like those of Fetutsi on a gargantuan scale. One of those hands, Salazar thought, could pick up a zuta watcher as easily as he, Kirk Salazar, could pick up a kitten. Their bellies rumbled like distant thunder, punctuated by explosions of vented gas like trumpet blasts.

Their snouts were prolonged into meter-long probos-cises, like dwarfish elephants' trunks. They pulled down branches to within reach of those prehensile organs and stuffed the greenery into vast pink maws.

"Pictures now," said Fetutsi in a low voice.

Cameras buzzed and clicked. Cantemir muttered: "Boy, if I had my fourteen-millimeter, I'd show 'em!"

"What would you want to shoot one for?" asked Salazar. "You couldn't eat it."

"What real man could see a good shot like that and not want a crack at it? Anyway, there are plenty more on the mainland."

"This is a subspecies, distinct from those on the mainland."

"Huh! They don't look different to me."

"Too roud noise!" hissed Fetutsi, flicking her forked tongue.

Salazar forbore to argue further, although as a biologist he took a poor view of sport hunting. For the next quarter hour the watchers quietly watched and photographed. Now and then one would whisper:

"I say, look at that one!"

"There's a couple of young, playing like puppies!"

"If one played with you, it would squash you like a bug."

"Don't they do anything but eat all day long?"

"I suppose they must copulate, though how they manage with those great tails I can't imagine."

"Standing face to face, maybe?"

"They must eat hundreds of kilos of green stuff daily."

"It takes a lot of fuel to power an engine that big."

"It would get pretty dull, just watching them just eat, eat, eat."

"You just bother one and it wouldn't be dull at all."

Fidgeting restlessly, Cantemir muttered: "Damn! Can't see right with all these trees in the way."

"Can't be helped," said Ritter. "They are—"

"I'm going up where I can get a whole one in my field." Cantemir set out, helping his injured limb along with his stick.

"Hey!" said Tchitchagov. "I told you—"

"What do?" said Fetutsi sharply. "Back, ay-yen! You come back!"

Cantemir ignored the command. He advanced to fifteen or twenty meters in front of the others, then knelt and aimed his little camera.

"Back!" said Fetutsi more loudly. "Animars angry!"

In fact, Salazar noticed, the nearest makuto had turned toward the Patelians. Its round ears, like those of an oversized mouse, swiveled toward the watchers, and its trunk was raised to horizontal, swinging right and left. It sniffed with a sound like a starting steam locomotive.

"Time to go!" called Tchitchagov. "Get back, George, before you get us stepped on!"

"Come back, George!" added Salazar. "Want us killed?"

More makutos turned toward the Terrans, bringing their bodies down to horizontal, balanced by their enormous tails. They moved agitatedly about.

"Oh, all right!" said Cantemir, rising and limping back to where the rest of the party was lined up.

"Let's go!" said Tchitchagov. "You lead, Fetutsi!"

"Damn!" said Cantemir. "Dropped my lens cap. Be right back." In Sungao he added to Fetutsi: "Cover me!"

He limped back to where he had knelt. After looking about for several seconds, he snatched up the lens cap and turned back toward the party, which was already hastening back along the trail.

The nearest makuto gave a thunderous snort, like the blast of a celestial trumpet, and started for the Terrans. After it came the rest of the herd, their footfalls shaking the forest floor.

"Tchyort!" yelled Tchitchagov. "I warned you! Grab his other arm, Kirk, and help me hurry him up."

With Tchitchagov on one side and Salazar on the other, they boosted Cantemir along. The lumberman made fair time by bringing his stick down beside his injured foot with each stride and putting most of his weight on the stick.

Behind them, the crashing of the makutos and the rumble of their footfalls told them that the herd was getting closer. Cantemir speeded up even more, uttering little grunts every time he put his weight on his injured ankle. Ahead the Patelians, strung out, ran after Fetutsi. Now and then one tripped and sprawled, but the crashing and thunder behind had them instantly up and running again.

They ran and ran until one Terran after another had to stop for breath. Then the approach of the herd sent them running once more. Tchitchagov and Salazar hauled Cantemir along at a slower pace but one that did not force them to stop.

At length they burst out on the road at the spot where they had left the wagon. The vehicle had not yet returned, since they had been gone for less than the two hours planned.

The crashing in the forest became louder. Tchitchagov said: "Across the field!"

The Terrans ran across the road and started to climb through the fence. Some became enmeshed in the wires until the others freed them. Among the last to reach the fence was Cantemir, who threw his stick beyond the fence and pushed through a gap in the wires. But the wires caught on projections of his gear, so that his struggles seemed only to entangle him further.

Tchitchagov had already cleared the fence and was running across the dusty field in pursuit of the other Terrans. Salazar said: "Hold still, damn it, George!" as he bent to untangle the wires. As he pulled the last one away from Cantemir's body, the lumberman crawled through, picked up his stick, and rose. Just then the first makuto loomed up between the trees across the road.

Being slim, Salazar quickly wormed his way through the wire. He caught up with the hobbling Cantemir, who paused to look back. Three makutos had come out of the forest and stood blinking in the sunshine, raising their trunks and loudly sniffing to locate their annoyers.

"Hell, that fence won't stop 'em," said Cantemir in a

despairing voice, "unless it's electrified. And if it was, we'd know it."

"Keep moving, idiot!" said Salazar.

"Hey, look! There comes Chief Yaamo's automobile!" cried Cantemir, pointing. "He's got the only steam car on the island."

The vehicle resembled a small flatbed truck with a tall, slender stack rising from the steam boiler in front. There were no seats, merely a rail running around the rectangular deck. On the deck, holding the rail in front, stood the driver and Chief Yaamo. Two bodyguards with rifles held the side rails. Kooks were indifferent to what Terrans considered necessary comfort.

The vehicle was passing in front of the makutos before any of those aboard it noticed. Then a guard pointed and cawed. The car speeded up, flashed past the makutos, and continued on toward Sungecho, leaving a plume of gray and white smoke from its stack and a cloud of yellow dust from its wheels.

The three makutos lumbered out of the forest and set off in pursuit. Seven others—two adults and five young of various sizes—erupted from the woods and joined the chase. Steam car and makutos vanished around a bend in the road.

The Patelians stood on the field or sat in the dirt, breathing heavily. Tchitchagov, who had lost his hat in the flight, shaded his eyes against the sun and peered along the road to the west.

"Here comes our wagon," he said, glancing at his poignet. "Right on time. Damn it, George, if you did not have that hurt ankle, I would leave you to walk back to Sungecho."

"Then my ankle's a blessing in disguise," said Cantemir with a naughty-boy grin.

"You may find it funny, almost getting us killed," said Tchitchagov. "Next time . . ." He waved to the wagon driver and shouted: "Zaiye! *Koko!*"

* * *

As the watchers straggled back to the road, the driver asked in Sungao: "What do you out in yon field?"

Tchitchagov told briefly of their adventure. Zaiye said: "I always knew that Terrans were crazy. I saw his Highness go past. But I am not fain to proceed toward Sungecho, honorable Tchitchagov. We might meet those monsters coming back."

"We cannot remain here," said the director. "I do not think they will long stay out in the midday sun. So go ahead; I will scout at bends in the road so that we shall not encounter makutos unawares."

"And if we do encounter them, what then?"

"Then we shall turn the wagon around and speed away."

"I hope the road prove wide enough," said the driver. Nevertheless, he flicked his animals, which set off pulling the now-laden wagon.

On the tailboard, Cantemir craned his neck to speak to Salazar: "Now, Kirk, maybe you'll understand why we've got to get rid of those things to develop the area for human settlement. They're not only a danger to any people who come near them; they're migratory. They need a huge area to roam over."

"I know," said Salazar. "We were lucky to catch that herd where it could easily be reached from Sungecho."

"Ah, but that herd will clean out everything green in that territory, then move on to another and eat it bare while the first area recovers. So you can't preserve them in a small park or refuge, because they'd soon eat it barren. So there's nothing to do but kill them. There won't be room on Sunga for us and them both. If we're going to kill them anyway, why not get some fun and profit out of it?"

"Your idea is to make Sunga into just one more Terran suburb."

Cantemir grinned. "Sure; why not? It's at least as natural a process as the makutos' migrations. At least *I* know what species I belong to." He turned away and engaged

Fetutsi, beside him, in low-voiced conversation in Sungao.

Salazar thought: That Lothario will try to make time with anything female, regardless of race, age, or even species. He whispered to the Ritters:

"What'll this do to the zuta watching?"

"Can't tell," murmured Hilbert Ritter. "Depends on whom Yaamo blames for his scare—assuming he made it back to Sungecho."

As in late afternoon the wagon rumbled into Sungecho, Fetutsi dropped off the tail. She said: "I go report. Good-bye, honoraber George."

Off she went at a run, with her rifle slung across her back. Cantemir squirmed around to say: "Hey, Igor!"

"Yes?"

"Why didn't anybody take a shot at the makutos when they started for us? Neither Miss Fetutsi nor the chief's guards fired a shot. What was it, buck fever?"

"Shooting them with rifles would merely annoy them," said Tchitchagov. "They're too big for anything but a real cannon. And how is it that Fetutsi said goodbye to you and ignored the rest of us?"

Cantemir grinned. "Guess I just can't help bein' nice to the ladies. I was explaining how our little mix-up occurred."

The wagon creaked to a stop in front of Levontin's Paradise Palace. Guided by Tchitchagov, Cantemir limped away toward Doctor Deyssel's to have his ankle strapped, followed by a gaggle of Patelians who had sustained minor injuries in the flight or thought they should have their hearts medically checked after their extreme exertions. As the passengers dispersed, Salazar heard a mutter from the sultry-looking Miss Dikranian beside him. Glaring at Cantemir's receding back, she said:

"Somebody ought to shoot that man!"

"Somebody probably will, sooner or later," said Salazar.

"Wouldn't do any good," said Hilbert Ritter. "He has a foreman or second in command, Dhan Gopal Mahasingh, every bit as hard-nosed as he. The Adriana Company has lots of tentacles. Besides, if you said that where people could hear you and then George was found shot, whom do you think they'd suspect?"

Shakeh Dikranian gave a sound between a sniff and a snort. "You're one of those cold north European types, always calculating results a year in advance. Like a Kook!"

"Thanks for the compliment," said Ritter. "I try to use what brain I have."

As Salazar neared the entrance, a Kook stepped forward. "Prease, which of you is honoraber Sarasara?"

"I think you mean me," said Kirk Salazar in Sungao. "Are you that cousin of the student Hakka?"

"Aye. I am clept Choku. My cousin wrote me, telling me I could perhaps get a post as assistant to you. Spake he the truth?"

"Aye, if we can come to terms."

Half an hour later Salazar was in his room explaining to Choku the purpose of each piece of equipment in his duffel bag. He held up an empty plastic case with a closure having a combination-number lock.

"This will be used for keeping all records, notes, exposed film, and the like. When the job is finished, it will be our most important—"

A knock interrupted. When he opened the door, Ilya Levontin, the stout innkeeper, said: "Mr. Salazar! High Chief Yaamo is calling a conference with the leading Terrans of your group in half an hour. He commands you to attend."

"Huh? Where?"

"In the conference room—that room on the left at the end of the corridor."

"Why me? I'm not a leader of anything."

Levontin shrugged. "He has not told me. He also demands the presence of Mr. Cantemir, the Doctors Ritter, the Reverend Dumfries, and Mr. Tchitchagov."

"All right, I shall be down as soon as I have cleaned up." Knowing the Kooks' formality, Salazar thought it inexpedient to go directly to the conference in dirty khakis. To Choku he said: "I suspect that this has to do with our being chased by makutos today."

"Indeed, sir? Methinks that a tale well worth hearing."

"Tell you later," said Salazar, washing his face.

Leaving Choku, Salazar sought the conference room, which doubled as a game room. The card tables and roulette wheel had been put away, and six of Levontin's better-upholstered chairs were set in a row.

Tchitchagov and the Ritters were already seated; Dumfries and Cantemir came in after Salazar. Across the room, standing, were Chief Yaamo, one Terran, and four Kooks. Salazar recognized one Kook as their erstwhile guide, the female Fetutsi. Two of the others he assumed, from the rifles slung across their backs, to be the chief's bodyguards.

When Salazar sat down beside Hilbert Ritter, the latter leaned over and whispered: "Yaamo's in a bad mood. That's why he brought interpreters instead of struggling with English."

Chief Yaamo spoke to his human interpreter. Although Salazar was fairly familiar with Sungao, a dialect of Feënzuo, the chief spoke so fast and with such a pronounced local accent that Salazar caught only an occasional word. Then the interpreter said:

"His Highness commands that this meeting come to order."

The six Terrans sat in silence. Yaamo spoke some more, in bursts of a sentence or two each, to give the interpreter time to translate. The interpreter said:

"This morning, his Highness was chased for three or

four *itikron* by a herd of makutos . . . Thanks to his ancestral spirits, his car stood the test, and the makutos at last gave up the pursuit . . .

"His Highness has ordered investigation of this unto-ward event . . . His faithful retainer, the onnifa Fetutsi, informed him that the zuta watchers became unruly at the sight of makutos . . . Several, against orders, insisted on going closer than the permitted distance, thus arous-ing the creatures' hostility . . .

"His Highness says this is an example of the erratic, irresponsible conduct that, he believes, characterizes Terrans. Their mere presence on Sunga poses a threat to public order . . . Since his Highness is not a physician skilled in treating the human brain, he is inclined to solve the problem by removing the cause, namely, the mem-bers of the Patel Society, who from Fetutsi's account ap-pear the most irresponsible of your lawless species."

"His Highness is misinformed," said Tchitchagov. "I do not know what Fetutsi has told you, but our dif-ficulties were caused by one Terran only, who is not a society member. I mean Mr. George Cantemir. You may ask the Doctors Ritter or Mr. Salazar, who saw the whole thing."

Tchitchagov plunged into an account of the arousal of the makutos, pausing for Yaamo's Sungarin interpreter to render his speech into Sungao. When he had finished, there was fast, low-voiced talk between the chief and the onnifa. Then Yaamo, fingering his disk of office, spoke through the interpreter again:

"Then let the Doctors Ritter and Mr. Salazar give their stories."

The Ritters told their tale, and Salazar told his, essen-tially the same as Tchitchagov's. Yaamo's human inter-preter announced:

"His Highness says that unlike you aliens, real human beings lack your ability to utter lies with straight faces. He suspects that you four Terrans got together before this meeting and cooked this story up."

"Let him ask other Terrans who were there," said Salazar.

Yaamo spoke to his Terran interpreter, who went out and soon returned with six zuta watchers whom he had rounded up. In turn, they told their stories, differing only in trivial details from Tchitchagov's. When all tales had been told, the interpreter said:

"His Highness says he has heard that Terrans can transfer thoughts from brain to brain by mental power alone. I think he means what is called telepathy. If you had it, he says, your leader, Mr. Tchitchagov, could easily give you all the stories to tell."

Tchitchagov replied: "Terrans have speculated for centuries about telepathy but have not found conclusive evidence that it exists."

"His Highness says, ah, but that is just what you would claim, is it not? He knows you have those devices for communicating by electricity, which most human authorities forbid as dangerous to their ancestral spirits. It seems plain to his Highness either that you are carrying electrical devices concealed or that you do in fact have the rumored telepathic powers."

Tchitchagov said: "Mr. Cantemir has said nothing yet. If I may question him, perhaps we can clear up this matter."

Receiving permission, Tchitchagov asked for Cantemir's version of the event. It proved the same as Fetutsi's, fleshed out with more colorful details: ". . . and every time I got ready to shoot with my little old camera, one of the others would crowd up in front of me, gettin' in the field of my picture. Well, I didn't come out for shots of the backs of these other folks' heads. So at last I stepped a couple of paces out in front of the rest, took my shot, and came right back."

Attempts by Tchitchagov to cross-question Cantemir failed to dent his story. *"Kroklyatiye!"* exclaimed Tchitchagov. "How can one prove that he is *not* telepathic?"

"What about crocodiles?" asked the interpreter.

"Nothing; just a Russian swear word."

"His Highness," said the interpreter, "says that is your problem, not his . . . The mere possibility of such powers is enough reason to take the action he deems important to safeguard his people. In this case, that means the removal of the disorderly aliens."

"Excuse me," said Salazar. "I think I know how to prove that Mr. Cantemir went closer to the makutos than he admits."

"His Highness would be glad to know."

"Mr. Cantemir took photographs. We know the approximate size of the largest makutos. If his Highness will take that camera into custody and have the film developed and printed, we can estimate how far away the makutos were from the size of their images."

"That don't prove a thing!" said Cantemir loudly. "With a zoom lens I can make the critters look as close or as far as I like."

"But you weren't using a camera with a zoom lens today. It's a pocket model, the Hayashi Z-706, which has a simple setting for three distances: face, group, and distant. I know because I owned one a few years ago."

"I'll fetch my camera and show you—" began Cantemir, rising.

"Stop him before he gets his hands on his cameras and switches things!" said Salazar.

When this had been translated, the interpreter said: "His Highness says come back and sit down! He will send someone else to fetch your camera."

Cantemir was already out the door, but one of the chief's bodyguards bounded after him and soon returned, gripping Cantemir's arm. Cantemir kept muttering in Sungao: "Take your hands off me!" But he came nevertheless.

"Is there a camera shop in Sungecho?" asked Salazar.

The interpreter, walking towards the door, turned to say: "Yes, McGloin's. He sells knickknacks and also does photographic work.'' The interpreter closed the door behind him; Cantemir, fuming, resumed his seat.

Half an hour later the camera had been brought, examined, and found to be as Salazar had said. The chief ordered it taken to McGloin's shop for processing.

''Until that is done,'' said the interpreter, ''His Highness will suspend judgment. Until this matter is settled, Mr. Cantemir must suspend his timber-cutting operation.''

''Now wait just a minute!'' rumbled Dumfries, who had not yet spoken. ''The Adriana Company cannot afford to pay our lumberjacks to sit around waiting for His Highness to make up his mind.''

''His Highness,'' replied the interpreter, ''says that, as in the case of proving telepathy, that is your company's problem, not his. He asks: Were you on this animal-watching expedition?''

''No, I was not. My business is with human souls, not the lower beasts. If his Highness expects the usufruct of our operations—''

''Excuse me, expects the *what*?''

''The gain, the profit.''

''His Highness says he will not be dictated to by an alien monster; so his order stands.''

''But—''

''His Highness says the subject is closed.''

Tchitchagov said: ''Meanwhile, may the Patel Society proceed with our travel plans? We have a car reserved on the Unriu Express for the day after tomorrow, to Amoen.''

Chief Yaamo took his time. At last the interpreter said: ''His Highness does not see how you can do much harm up on the mountain . . . He wishes you to understand that you do so at your own risk . . . That is wild country. If you perish as a result of your foolishness or other forms of Terranism, that is no concern of his.''

''We thank the honorable chief,'' said Tchitchagov.

Going back to the private rooms with the Ritters, Salazar said: "Sounds to me as if Dumfries and Cantemir want to flood the area with Terran settlers and kick out the Kooks, the way our ancestors did with the Native Americans."

"Sure," said Hilbert Ritter. "There's a party in the Settlements, small but growing, that wants to do that to the whole planet. But on Kukulcan, Terrans don't have the advantage that Europeans did in the Americas."

"What's that? Iron metallurgy?"

"That, too, but I had in mind that they brought in smallpox, measles, and other Old World diseases that the Native Americans had no resistance to; so they died off by millions. Nobody has yet found a disease that a Kook can catch from a Terran."

"Will this incident derail Dumfries's project? I could see from his neck spines that Dumfries and Cantemir made Yaamo pretty angry."

"For a while, maybe. But Dumfries makes huge amounts from his Holy Gnostic Church. He knows how to use it to dissolve away opposition, as acid eats metal. The worst is, he's probably sincere. Thinks he's doing the will of God—or those Demiurges he talks about. So we'd better make the most of our time."

"Wouldn't the IC step in? They talk a fine line against planetary imperialism."

"If the reverend can get enough of his people on Kukulcan—and I hear he hopes to bring in thousands—he can shrug off the Interplanetary Council on the ground that it's an internal planetary matter."

III.

The Unriu Express

Two days later, Epsilon Eridani had not yet risen when Kirk Salazar reached the railway station. Carrying Salazar's duffel bag, Choku followed. Salazar had stored some of his gear at Levontin's.

Other members of the Patel Society's field trip stood on the platform, stamping and waving their arms against the pre-dawn chill. Terran passengers clustered beside the last car of the Unriu Express. This was the only car showing an attempt to meet Terran standards of comfort, having a roof over its red-painted body. A passenger car for Kooks was merely a flatcar with a railing around its deck. Kooks thought nothing of standing for hours, clutching the rail, or squatting on the deck, swaying with the motion.

The car before the Terran or "soft-fare" unit was an unrailed flatcar whereon four Kook station workers were piling passengers' baggage. Having given Salazar's bag to the workers, Choku said:

"Honorable boss, I understand not why you Terrans need to travel with such mountainous masses of luggage. I have gone all over Sunga and the mainland with no more gear than I now have in my pouches."

"Just a point of Kukulcanian superiority," said Salazar. "In my case, however, the fact that I have to lug some scientific instruments and recording devices gives me an excuse." He approached the Ritters, asking: "Will Cantemir be with us today? It might make things a bit sticky."

"Don't worry," said Hilbert Ritter. "George has more brass than a samovar, but this time he won't be around. Yesterday he bought four jutens, for himself and his three Kooks, and took off early for Sungara. He'd have used the express except that it runs only on alternate days. Jack Ravitch heard him say he could make his base camp by hard riding, sore foot and all, faster than if he took the local to Amoen and rode a local animal from there."

Salazar thought. "Maybe he figured he'd better get all his lumbering preparations done before the chief makes up his mind on whether to order him off the island. With the speed things move among the Kooks, he could get a lot done before the word got to him up on the mountain."

"You're an astute little fellow," said Ritter, making Salazar wince. "If George remained here, he'd never know when a pair of Kook cops would grab him and hustle him aboard an outbound ship."

"Poor Miss Axelson is heartbroken," said Suzette Ritter. "He visited her room the night before last, and whatever he gave her, I guess she was looking forward to more of it."

Up forward, two railed flatcars preceded the baggage car. Beyond them the little locomotive was slowly backing. Salazar said:

"Excuse me a minute!"

He hurried forward, because the details of railroading had long beguiled him. Kook railroads ran on tracks that in Terran terms had a gauge of 141.8 centimeters, just a shade narrower than that of most Terran railroads. This worked out to a handier figure in Kukulcanian units. The Sunga railroad was converting from a coupling of the chain-and-buffer type to an automatic coupling like Terra's Janning coupler. All the newer rolling stock therefore had two couplings on each end, one of the chain type and, above it, one of the Janning kind. When automatic couplings were in use, the chains were allowed to dangle.

The locomotive had a vertical boiler with a lofty stack, puffing coal smoke. Forward rose a mass of driving machinery. Four vertical pistons in a line whirled a crankshaft, joined to the axles by gearing. There seemed to be a gear-shift mechanism. Behind the boiler rose a small cab, and abaft the cab was the coal bin in place of a separate tender.

In low gear, the locomotive backed up to the leading flatcar. The couplings met with a clank. On the locomotive, the firekook shoveled coal through a trapdoor.

From aft came the sound of a gong. Salazar threaded his way through the crowd of fishy-smelling Kooks, who were scrambling up on the railed flatcars. He passed the Kook conductor, holding his copper gong at arm's length with one clawed hand and whaling it with a mallet in the other.

On the baggage car, loading had been completed and the load secured by lashing down a tarpaulin of coarse gray Kukulcanian canvas. As Salazar passed that car, Choku spoke in Sungao:

"Is all correct for you, honorable Sarasara?"

"All is fine. Come on back with me."

"Are you sure, good sir? Terrans like it not to have us human beings in the same enclosures with them. They say we stink. When they come amongst us, we are too polite to compain of their smell."

"Oh, come on, Choku! With that car so open, they will have naught to complain of."

"Very well, sir, if you say so." Choku followed Salazar back to the scarlet soft-class car.

Tchitchagov was herding the last of his flock aboard. He called out: "Hey, Salazar! Hurry up!"

Suzette Ritter leaned out of the car and called: "Kirk! Come sit with us!"

"Is it okay if I bring my assistant?" He gestured at Choku.

"Sure; there's plenty of room."

Salazar climbed the step. The interior was lined with benches, alternately parallel and perpendicular to the sides, forming a series of alcoves without partitions. The crimson sides of the car arose from the floor about a meter and stopped, save for rows of posts supporting the roof. From the undersides of the wall plates—the longitudinal members joining the tops of the posts—hung a series of rolled-up curtains to lower in bad weather. Otherwise the car was open to the ambient air. A compartment at one end contained a toilet and a washbasin; another at the other end served for storage.

Two-thirds of the seating space was filled by members of the Patel Society and a few other Terrans. There were no Kooks. Salazar took the seat the Ritters were saving in one of the alcoves and motioned Choku to another seat. Following Salazar, Tchitchagov entered the car and stood at the end, counting heads on his fingers. He said:

"Hokay, all present. Doctors Ritter, may I sit with you?"

Receiving assent, he lowered his lank form into the remaining seat in the alcove. Presently he said: "I wonder what George Cantemir is up to that he returned to Amoen in such a hurry?"

"Besides wanting to get away from Yaamo's cops," said Ritter, "do you think he'll try some devilry?"

Tchitchagov shrugged. "How should I know? From all I hear, he and Dumfries are very determined men. Be prepared for anything."

"Where is the Reverend now?" asked Salazar.

The tall Suvarovian shrugged again. "As far as I know, he is staying in Sungecho. I do not think you are likely to encounter him on Sungara; he is too fat for mountaineering."

"From what I heard," said Salazar, "those two plan to wipe out the local wildlife to make room for Terran settlement. I can't imagine that Yaamo would sit quietly while a horde of Terrans took over his island."

Hilbert Ritter said: "Yaamo's in kind of a cleft stick. He wants to modernize his Kooks just as fervently as Dumfries wants to turn Kukulcan into a second Terra, ruled by his own species. But Yaamo needs money. Dumfries has it, in incredible amounts, which he will pay out to Yaamo to keep him quiet while he infiltrates Sunga with his followers."

Salazar said: "Perhaps Yaamo and Dumfries each figures he can double-cross the other in time to save his own program. Like those dictators from the Massacre Era—what were their names?"

"Hitler and Stalin?" said Suzette Ritter.

"I guess so; my Terran history isn't—"

"Tickets, prease!" said a Kookish voice. The conductor appeared at the end of the car. The Terrans brought out little red rectangles of stiff Kukulcanian paper, while Choku produced a yellow rectangle from one of his pouches.

"What is this?" said the conductor in loud Sungao. "This is no ticket for soft class! Get you back where you belong!"

"Honorable Zuiha!" protested Choku. "I did but enter the car at the command of this Terran, whom I have contracted to serve."

"It is nonetheless wrong, and well you know it!" shouted the conductor. "Now get you hence."

"Pardon, honorable conductor," said Salazar. "I will pay the extra fare my assistant requires."

"Very well, very well," grumbled the conductor. "You Terrans are never satisfied to do things in an orderly way. It is irregular, and I must needs write a note in the log to account for it. Does none of you other Terrans object to this human being's presence? Very well, then."

Salazar brought out his small change—a set of copper polygons with holes for stringing—and peeled off the requisite number. Conductor Zuiha, still grumbling, passed on through the car. Choku said:

"Zuiha is in a bad humor because his application for a change of caste status has been rejected."

The locomotive blew a shrill whistle and shuddered into motion. It swerved right and left as the train passed clicking over switches, then rumbled out the yard and along a street.

The train slowed and screeched to a halt. Looking around, Salazar saw the conductor straining at a hand brake at the end of the car. The breathing sounds of the idling steam locomotive wafted back, along with sounds of altercation in hissing, guttural Sungao.

"See what it is, please," said Salazar to Choku.

Choku went to the end of the car and with effortless ease swung himself up onto the roof. When he returned, he said in his version of English:

"Some person tie kyuumei to ray. Rook for owner. If not find, conductor cut rope."

At length the train moved on, though Salazar never learned whether the owner of the rail-tethered buffalo-lizard was found. They puffed and pounded on past dwindling houses, through the remains of the obsolete defensive wall, past more houses that shrank to mere shacks, and out into farmland.

"Ow!" said Miss Kingsby. "I've got a cinder in my eye!"

"Let me get it out," said Mr. Antonelli.

As speed increased, so did the rocking and shaking. The train became so noisy that passengers had to raise their voices to converse. Among the Patelians, Mrs. Eagleton became carsick. Miss Axelson, on her way to the toilet, was thrown by a lurch of the car into Salazar's lap.

"Oh, Kirk!" she cooed. "I'm so-o-o sorry!"

"That's all right," muttered Salazar. Too embarrassed to exploit the incident to further his acquaintance with Miss Axelson, he set her back on her feet.

They clanked and rattled on. A shift of wind filled the

car with smoke. Passengers coughed, grumbled, and wiped off soot. Choku said in Sungao:

"Honorable Sarasara, are there railroads on Terra?"

"So I am told. My father rode upon them ere he came to Kukulcan. He says they are much bigger than these. For a century or two most travelers drove automobiles or rode in flying machines instead of traveling on trains. But then the Terran mineral oil called petroleum, which furnished fuel for these machines, became scarce, and people perforce went back to trains. Most, however, get their power from electricity, which does not smoke but which your folk would forbid."

"It is no wonder," said Choku, "that Terrans know naught about their ancestral spirits. With all those electrical machines whereof I hear, your spirits have probably all been destroyed."

"You may be right," said Salazar, who had been taught to avoid arguments. A passenger complained:

"If this is the express, I'd sure hate to have to ride the local! We can't be doing over thirty kph."

"With their bumpy track and rickety rolling stock," said another, "you'd better be glad they don't try to go faster."

"Locals stop on signal at every crossing," said still another. "The express stops only at towns."

After a while the train slowed and screeched to a halt, as Conductor Zuiha and his trainkooks heaved on the brakes. They were at a small town or large village announced as Torimas. Houses were simple gray cubical blocks of wood, stone, and concrete, unadorned save for the symbols, painted in a kaleidoscope of colors, indicating the clan, caste, occupational, and familial identities of the owners.

"Antics! Buy antics!" cried a young Kook, holding a tray of glittery merchandise up from the station platform.

A couple of Patelians paid for bits of glitter. Tchitchagov grumbled: "I warned them they would get only what

you call junk, not real antiques. But some people simply
must buy; some sort of neurotic compulsion.''

The whistle blew, the gong bonged, the train started
with a jangle of couplings and chains. Passengers opened
their luncheon packages.

In the early afternoon, some zuta watchers were doz-
ing as best they could on the cushionless seats. The train
climbed a long incline, weaving through a country of
rolling, rocky hills. In low gear it moved no faster than
a brisk jog. Salazar watched the broken country wind
past. The vegetation was sparser than along the coast,
with bare earth showing among the shrubs, boulders, and
occasional trees. Hilbert Ritter said:

"I think the sun is low enough to break out some personal lubricant. Will you get it out, darling?"

Suzette dug into her bag and produced a bottle and a
stack of paper cups. She poured a slug of Kukulcanian
"whiskey" into each and asked: "Water, anybody?"

Choku declined a drink, but the other four were served.
Ritter raised his cup. "Here's to—"

The train screeched to a halt so abruptly that half the
drinks went flying. From the rest of the car rose cries of
pain and outrage, especially from dozers spilled from
their seats.

"*Tchyort!*" said Tchitchagov. "Choku, will you see
what it is?"

Choku went out and soon returned, saying: "Iss pi' of
rocks on track."

"Natural or artificial?" asked Salazar.

"Some individuar put zere, sir."

Tchitchagov said: "I think this is an ambush. If I had
my gun . . . Choku, do you know where my bag is on
the baggage car?"

"Iss in midder, on right side."

"You will show me where, and I will get the gun—"

A gunshot cut through the babble. Then came a fusil-
lade, with the rattle of small arms and the impact of

bullets against the sides of the car. Shrieks arose from the passengers.

"Get down!" shouted Tchitchagov, rising. "Everybody down! Is anyone hit?"

None claimed that distinction, but every passenger shouted a question at once. Tchitchagov kept shouting "Down! Down! *Vniz! Xía dĭ!*" until all save him were sitting or kneeling on the floor.

Salazar, crouching with the rest, heard more shots. He was thankful that Kukulcanian technology had not yet come up with plywood; hence, the sides of the car were of good stout timber, which stopped small-arms projectiles. But the car's bright red color made it an obvious target.

"Pomogitye!" shouted Tchitchagov, clutching his right arm with his left hand. "Now I am hit!"

"Get down yourself!" said Salazar.

"Get the first aid out of the carryall, Suzette," said Hilbert Ritter.

A bullet had drilled a hole in the director's bicep, missing the bone. While Suzette busied herself with disinfecting and bandaging, Tchitchagov said: "Kirk, did you bring a gun in your baggage?"

"Yep, two of 'em. But I saw them load my bag. It's in the middle of the car, on the bottom of the pile."

"Then perhaps you can get mine out." He spoke in Sungao to Choku. "Know you where my bag is in the pile?"

"Mean you the big blue one with the yellow tag?"

"Aye."

"Then methinks I do: on the right side as you face forward, against the covering."

Tchitchagov said: "Thank the gods for these eidetic memories! Kirk, you will have to get my gun out of the bag and use it. Can you assemble a K-94?"

"I think so; mine works much the same way. Come, Choku."

At the end of the car Salazar looked cautiously out.

The firing seemed to have come from a ridge to the left of the train. The crest of that ridge was about two hundred meters away. Up ahead, all the Kooks on the flatcar had leapt off and crouched in the dirt on the descending slope to the right, where cars and embankment offered cover. From the ridge the guns still banged. Bullets cracked overhead, thudded into woodwork, or ricocheted, screeching off metal.

"Show me where Tchitchagov's gun is," said Salazar.

Choku led him half the length of the baggage car. "About here, sir."

Salazar fumbled with the lashing of the tarpaulin, then drew a knife and sawed through a couple of ropes. Choku pushed and pulled the bags and suitcases until he said:

"Methinks this be it."

Salazar winced as a bullet struck nearby. He slashed open the canvas bag and hauled out a massive leather case. This proved to be locked. Remembering the strength of Kooks, he said:

"Can you pry this open, Choku?"

The Kook sank his claws into the leather and heaved. The case came apart with a rending sound. With qualms, Salazar beheld the parts of a K-94 rifle; but he set to work, attached the stock, and screwed in and locked the barrel.

The firing died down. "Make haste, honorable boss," said Choku. "The attackers advance upon us."

"I'm working as fast as I can," snapped Salazar, fumbling with a thirty-round magazine. He finally got it inserted, worked the bolt once to arm the weapon, and ran crouching to the aft end of the baggage car. There, he thought, he would get a better view of the attackers, between the piled baggage and the crimson soft-class car.

Meaning to fix his gaze afar on the ridge, shooting from which had ceased, Salazar was taken by surprise when he found another Terran between the cars. The man was on the farther side, whence the attack was coming, in rough work clothes with his visage hidden by a bandanna. He was straining at the handle on the side of the car, whereby the pin could be withdrawn from the coupling, allowing the paired couplings to part when the locomotive started forward.

For silent seconds wherein the only sound in Salazar's ears was the pant of the idling locomotive, Salazar and the man stared at each other. The man let go of the locking-pin handle and reached for a rifle, which he had leaned against the step of the passenger car on his side. As the stranger straightened up with the gun, Salazar, holding the butt of Tchitchagov's rifle beneath his arm, fired a burst of three rounds from a distance of two meters.

The man pitched over backward to sprawl supine on the ballast. After another second's hesitation, Salazar remembered his original intent and bent his regard to the ridge.

Several human figures were coming down the hillside, bounding down the slope in long leaps. As they neared, Salazar saw that they, too, were armed and masked.

Salazar aimed at the nearest bounding figure. Although the man was in the plainest of plain sight, as soon as one tried to draw a bead on him, he shrank to a flyspeck.

"It were well for you to shoot, honorable employer," said Choku.

"What think you I am doing?" snarled Salazar. He made an extra effort to line up the nearest attacker in his sights and squeezed off another burst.

The man disappeared from Salazar's view until the biologist lowered the rifle and saw the body rolling doll-like down the slope. Then it stopped and lay sprawled. Salazar traversed the field with his eyes until he picked up another bounding assailant. Another burst felled that one, too.

"The others flee," said Choku's emotionless voice.

Salazar chose one of the half dozen fleeing men and sent a burst after him. As far as he could see, he missed.

Before he could find another target, the attackers were all out of sight. Shooting from the ridge began again, but more deliberately.

Their leader, Salazar thought, must be telling them to slow down before they shot away all their ammunition. To Choku he said: "Could you go forward and see what is being done to clear the track?"

Choku ran off crouching. Soon he came back, neck spines twitching mirthfully. "Zuiha was lying in the dirt with the others. I bade him organize a party to clear the track whilst you furnish covering fire. If he did not, when the story came out, his chances of promotion were nil. He unhappily agreed to try."

"Good!" said Salazar. "Can you go back to our car to borrow a pair of binoculars? Mine are packed, but many Patelians keep theirs with them."

Presently Choku returned with the glasses. "Chief Tchitchagov's."

Keeping covered, Salazar scanned the ridge. When he looked at the place where his third victim had fallen, there was no sign of the man. Salazar located him crawling up the slopes on hands and knees. The biologist aimed but hesitated; shooting a wounded man somehow did not seem right. By the time he had overcome this qualm, the man had reached the top of the ridge and disappeared.

He resumed his search and soon thought he had picked out movement to the left of a scrubby olive-green tree. Putting away the glasses, he aimed for the spot and fired a burst. When he applied the binoculars again, he could not see movement there. He continued to scan, pausing to wipe his watering eyes, until he found another spot that might be a man's distant head. A burst caused the spot to disappear.

Several shots struck the cars near Salazar. He moved to the other end of the baggage car and resumed searching and firing. When his magazine gave out, he got another out of Tchitchagov's eviscerated case and inserted it. After the first three attackers whom he had felled, he never could tell whether any of his shots had hit home.

Choku approached. "Conductor Zuiha led a group to the rock pile and rolled the rocks away. Soon he will start the train."

"How many were hit up forward?"

"None, sir. All shots seem to have been aimed at these last cars."

The whistle shrieked. Salazar fired a final burst and scrambled up the steps into the soft-fare car. The train resumed its way with jerks and clanks.

Salazar handed the binoculars to Tchitchagov, who sat glumly with his bandaged arm in an improvised sling. "Thanks, Igor. I guess people can get up now. Oh, oh! Look what's coming!"

As the train gathered speed, several Terrans on jutens came out on the right-of-way behind it. The juten riders overhauled the train and started to ride past it on either side, firing pistols. Salazar aimed over the sill of the car side and gave the nearest one a burst. The juten pitched forward, throwing its rider in a heap ahead of it. The other riders halted, clustering around the fallen one. A curve soon hid them from sight.

When the passengers retook their seats, Salazar turned to Tchitchagov. Blood had begun to soak through the bandage on his arm. "Are you all right, Igor?"

"As well as could be expected," growled the director. "You can thank Metasu the attackers were amateurs at this sort of thing, or we should all be dead."

"What should they have done?"

"The first was to mine the track. If they did not have explosives, they could have pried up a rail. These rails are light compared to those I saw on Terra as a boy.

"Then they should have posted themselves closer to the train, so they could pick targets. As it was, they fired at random, sprinkling bullets over the landscape the way half-trained Terran soldiers do. A few through the locomotive boiler would have stopped it. If they had charged as soon as the train halted or if those bandits on jutens had arrived sooner, they would have reached us before you could get my gun into action.''

"They weren't the only stupid ones," said Salazar. "Knowing we were dealing with fellow Terrans and not just the orderly, peaceable Kooks, we ought to have kept our guns with us.''

"You amaze me, Kirk," said Suzette. "You always seemed such a quiet, harmless little fellow. And here you turn into a fearless warrior, saving us all!" Salazar winced.

"It's the same with his father," said Ritter.

Salazar looked at his feet. "Well—ah—it all happened so suddenly that I didn't have time to get scared. Now that it's over, don't be surprised if I faint.''

In fact, Kirk Salazar was as surprised by his own performance as the Doctors Ritter. A shy, gauche young man of average height and slender build, he had thought of himself as a weak-kneed wimp who would probably panic under stress and be too frightened or confused to do anything right. He had also supposed that if ever forced to kill a fellow human being, he would be so filled with guilt and revulsion that he would either puke or go into a hopeless funk.

Here he had shot a couple of fellow Terrans with resolution and dispatch, with no more reaction than if they had been mere biological specimens! Perhaps he had hopes of attaining his father's calm competence in tight situations.

"But who," asked Suzette Ritter, "would have wanted to attack us? As far as I know, we have no enemies on Sunga.''

Tchitchagov grunted. "I thought Cantemir might be up to something when he rushed away from Sungecho. Knowing the Patel Society to be ardent conservationists, he might think they would make trouble for Dumfries's project. So he tried to wipe us out with one blow.''

Ritter said: "Sounds fantastic, but people try all sorts of strange things away from the Settlements, where Terran laws don't apply and the Kooks won't bother. Kirk, were any Kooks on the flatcars hit?"

"Apparently not; were they, Choku?" Then Salazar struck his forehead with his palm. "I'm stupid again! That first man I shot was trying to uncouple this car. I suppose they wanted to catch us alive while letting the Kooks and the rest of the train go on."

"Cantemir is clever," said Tchitchagov. "He knows that Yaamo would not stand for shooting up his people, but if Terrans want to kill one another, who cares?"

Salazar said: "I don't think they really meant to kill us, or we should have dead and wounded all over. They stop the train, shoot a lot to immobilize us, detach the car, let the rest go on, and order us to leave the car with our hands up. What they'd do then, I have no idea. Too bad we couldn't have collected that first Terran I shot for evidence."

"*If* we could prove he acted under Cantemir's orders," said Ritter. "George would deny it, of course."

Conductor Zuiha scrambled down from the pile of luggage forward and entered the soft-fare car, calling: "Iss anyone hurt here?"

Tchitchagov raised his wounded arm. "I think I am the only one."

"You are rucky," said Zuiha. "I wirr ask superiors not to ret monsters from ozzer pranets ride on trains. If you ay-yens wish to kirr each ozzer, prease do it where it wi' not endanger human rife or disrupp rayroad." Neck bristles rippling with indignation, the conductor departed.

Two hours late, the Unriu Express pulled into Amoen. The station platform was lit by the smoky light of vegetable-oil lanterns, giving off a sour-sweet smell.

On the platform, Patelians clustered around Tchitchagov, asking about his wound. Salazar expected an explosion of complaints, but the only fuss was from Mrs. Eagleton, whose suitcase had been missing when the baggage car had been unloaded. A harassed Tchitchagov explained:

"But madam, it undoubtedly fell out through the gap that Mr. Salazar made in the tarpaulin to get my gun."

"Well, then, commandeer a special car to go back to look for it!"

"I fear that is impossible."

"But you can't expect me to go on without my things!"

"You will have to borrow from the other ladies."

The argument continued until Tchitchagov said: "Excuse me, but I must sit down. I feel a little faint."

"Here," said Hilbert Ritter, pushing his own massive suitcase forward. "Sit here, Igor. Think you can manage the field trip?"

"I do not know. I should get to a Terran doctor, but the nearest is at Sungecho." Tchitchagov looked up. "Hilbert, could you take over for me? I will give you my maps and everything."

Ritter looked doubtful. "Why not ask young Salazar here? As a biology student, he's at least as well qualified. How about it, Kirk?"

"Well, ah—" began Salazar, but Tchitchagov spoke:

"No, Hilbert. He is a brave young man, but you have had much more experience with handling groups."

The argument limped along until Salazar, looking along the platform, cried: "Alexis!"

She strode toward them, followed by a small procession of Kooks bearing gear of poles and canvas lashed into large, elongated bundles.

"Good heavens!" said Suzette Ritter. "The last I heard, she never wanted to set eyes on us again."

Ritter shrugged. "You've known her as long as I have, darling."

"Hey there!" Alexis called. "How are my dear old fuds? And Kirk Salazar! Just the people I wanted!"

"Good evening, Miss Ritter!" said Choku, standing at Salazar's elbow.

Alexis paused. "You are—oh, I see! You're that Choku who worked for Kashani and then for me. Is that right?"

"Iss right," said Choku. "Iss aw wey wiss you?"

"All is well with me. Is all well with you?"

"Sanks to pranetary spirit Metasu, aw iss wey wiss me."

Alexis cut short the endless formulas required by Kukulcanian etiquette and turned to her parents. Ritter asked:

"What brings you here, Alexis?"

"I'm going to take you back with me, to our community, to show you what a happy, harmonious life we've achieved."

"I fear not. Igor is hurt, and I've agreed to take his place while he goes down the line to get patched up."

Alexis's face fell. "Oh. No, really; I insist on your coming up the mountain with me, as we originally planned. I'll prove I'm right."

"Sorry, but I'm needed here."

"Oh, damn! At least you'll come, won't you, Mother?"

Suzette said: "I'd love to, but—ah—I'd better stay with your father. He'll need me."

"Oh, go to hell, both of you! Kirk, you'll come! The community is near the edge of the venom-tree forest, so it'll give you a base for research."

"When are you starting out?" asked Salazar cautiously. "I don't suppose you'd set forth at night."

"Don't be silly! Kooks can't see worth a damn in the dark. We'll light out before dawn. It's about twenty-seven kilometers, which we could never do in a day on foot, so I brought my Kooks along with litters. They trot ahead on those long legs at a dead run all day."

"Sounds interesting," said Salazar, "but now I'd better help get everybody settled. Igor's rented the town hall as barracks, since there are no hotels."

"You don't want to bunk with all those old lizard-bat chasers! I'm camping, and you'll be at least as comfortable as on a pallet in the town hall. Inflatable mattresses and everything. Come on!"

Feeling inadequate in the face of this masterful female, Salazar let himself be cajoled and bullied into following her off the platform. Choku trailed after him with Salazar's bag. The Kook said:

"Honorable boss!"

"Aye?"

"There is something that I fain would tell you, but it is also something whereof I promised to say naught." In the dim light Salazar saw Choku's neck spines rippling in an unusual manner. "That makes a painful choice."

"On Terra they call it a dilemma, from words meaning 'two horns,' as when one is charged by a wild kyuumei and is likely to be caught on one horn or the other."

"But sir, how can I resolve this 'diremma'?"

"Forget it for now. If you let the matter rest, it may solve itself."

Looking back at Salazar, Alexis said: "Hurry up, lazybones! How did Igor get hurt? I heard something about an attempt to hold up the train."

"Well, this afternoon we were coming up a long grade in low gear . . ."

When Salazar had finished his tale, in which he modestly minimized his own part, she said: "It's that fuckomaniac Cantemir! I'd better get out one of our big-game rifles and clean it. If I ever get George in my sights, he'd better have his insurance paid up."

"You'd kill him on mere suspicion?"

"Damn right! Here in the outback it's often kill or be killed, like on the old American frontier. He wouldn't be the first."

As dangerous in her way as Dumfries was in his, thought Salazar; she was as addicted to power as Cantemir was to sex—or as he, Kirk Salazar, was to making his mark in science. He had better keep his guard up with Alexis at all times.

Alexis's campsite was not far. On command, the Kooks opened a bundle containing a tent. In short order they set up the poles, attached tent ropes, hammered in stakes, and spread canvas.

"There!" said Alexis. "See? You've even got a portable washstand."

"You certainly manage these things efficiently."

"Thanks to the Kooks' literal-mindedness and eidetic memories. If you once explain something clearly and correctly, they've got it for good."

"But—ah—where will you sleep?"

"You'll learn. Go to bed; we get up before sunrise."

A quarter hour later saw Salazar, naked in the sultry air, stretching out on a large inflatable mattress. Distant thunder growled.

Salazar was about to turn out the little oil lamp, when the flap gaped and Alexis slipped in. He goggled as she whipped off shirt, trousers, and underwear. Staring down at him, she said:

"Get over on your side! You didn't expect to have this tent all to yourself, did you?"

"Well—ah—do you mean—are we going to—ah—"

"Going to fuck, you mean? Let me explain. What I do in Sungecho is my business. But from Amoen to Kashania I'm a holy high priestess, as virginal as a newborn Kook, and don't ever let me hear you say anything different around my people!"

She frowned at Salazar's midsection. "Another thing. In the community we wear clothes only to keep warm, any more being regarded as an affectation. But when we're naked, it's a terrible breach of manners for a man to show an erection. Down, Towser, down! That's better. It's that silly Judeo-Christian tabu which makes mundanes equate nudity with sex. They have nothing to do with each other; you can screw dressed or undressed, just as you can standing, sitting, or lying. But give a male mundane a glimpse of a tit, and he gets the hots. We're beyond that medieval nonsense. Are you all washed and toothbrushed?''

"Uh huh," said Salazar. Thunder sounded closer, and rain began to patter on the canvas.

"I'll put out the light," she said, turning off the lamp. In the darkness Salazar felt the motion of the mattress as she lay down on her side.

A blinding flash, visible even through the canvas, was instantly followed by a terrific crash of thunder. Rain roared. Salazar was seized by female limbs as Alexis, slithering across, wrapped herself around him like an amorous octopus.

"I'm frightened," she murmured.

Feeling virile, Salazar held her while rain drummed and celestial fireworks continued, diminishing. At length—perhaps a quarter hour later, Salazar thought— she stopped trembling. Then he felt a hand exploring his person. She said:

"Oh—oh, it's up again!''

"Well, what do you ex—''

She murmured: "Guess I'm not so holy-virginal to-night after all. Put your hand here . . . All right; ready when you are . . . Ouch! Watch where you put those bony knees.''

Soon she cried: "Oh, damn! Why did you have to go off when I was just getting warmed up?''

"Sorry; I couldn't help it.''

"Don't worry; we'll try again in an hour or two. But you seemed pretty amateurish. How much have you done?''

"Well—ah—perhaps I shouldn't admit it, but this is my first.''

"Great Shiiko, d'you mean I've deflowered a male virgin?''

"If you want to put it that way.''

She burst into a sputter of laughter. Salazar asked in a hurt voice: "What's so funny about that?"

"Nothing, nothing. You must be a neo-Puritan."

"It's in the family background."

"Poor fellow!"

"Why? There's no law against *not* fornicating."

"But what a dismal life!"

"As my father says, celibacy may not be the most fun in the world, but nobody ever died of it. Anyway, I've been too preoccupied; a doctorate comes hard. By the way, are you safe?"

"Of course! Had myself tubed years ago so I can take my fun when I want it."

"What about love? Do you ever think of it?"

"Me fall for that sentimental nonsense? Ha! The main thing is power. Get that, and it'll get you whatever else you want. Now go to sleep!" She adjusted the poignet on her wrist. "This'll wake me up about the time you'll be ready for another."

IV.

Mount Sungara

The Kooks who bore Salazar's litter, one before and one behind, trotted tirelessly along the trail. The litter bounced in time with their jog, one-two, one-two, until Salazar felt as if he were trapped in a chemical agitator. He would have preferred to walk; but although a good hiker, he knew he could never keep up with that distance-eating lope.

Alexis's litter bounced in front, flanked by her two reptilian bodyguards. Just behind Salazar came two others full of baggage. Choku's brought up the rear.

Kirk Salazar tried to watch the landscape as it jiggled past, to connect the fauna and flora he saw with what he had read. But his mind kept slipping back to his night with Alexis. Her lush curves blanked the occasional glimpses of animals, bipedal or quadrupedal but always semireptilian, watching the train from the edge of the timber or breaking into flight.

Mixed feelings troubled him. On one hand he felt older, stronger, and readier for contingencies than ever before. He had read about the ethology of the large Terran mammal called the elephant, now reduced to a few thousand in semidomestication. It was said that while elephants of both sexes and both species could be tamed and trained to do useful work, a male once allowed to breed was likely to become unmanageable, as if it told it-

72

self it was now a *bull elephant* whom nobody could order around. He thought he felt a little as a bred bull elephant must have felt.

It was time he put his mind upon his profession, but that proved hard. Damn it to hell! he thought. Can't I think of anything but sex? He had not come to Sunga for that. He did not even much like Alexis, whom he judged to be an aggressive, domineering egomaniac.

Nor did this intimacy with her leave him comfortable. While he was not restrained by religious tabus, his family's neo-Puritan background left him uneasy after violating them. Perhaps he should have saved it for Calpurnia Fisker, whom it seemed inevitable that he should marry, unless she got tired of merely dating and waiting and decided to cast her hook elsewhere. He and she had a tacit understanding that neither would screw around until they made their relationship formal.

Now he was angry at himself for not taking his courage in his hands and marrying the girl; if he had, he might have enjoyed this ecstasy for years. They suited each other very well, a fact he had not appreciated until becoming involved with a really difficult female. He had been too careful, like the man whom the fyunga ate while he was trying to remember the polite imperative in Feënzuo for "Help!"

Still the picture of Alexis, lush and pink in the yellow lamplight, kept crowding into his mind, and blood kept crowding into his loins. He thought: Ah, sweet mystery of lust! paraphrasing an old song from the Massacre Era.

Towards noon the procession halted. Salazar slid out of his litter, thankful for a chance to stretch his legs and relieve the tender backside that constant bounce was giving him. He found Alexis talking intensely with one of her Kook bodyguards. As he approached, the Kook departed, running up the trail.

"What's this?" asked Salazar.

Alexis said: "This trail passes close to Cantemir's

lumber camp. I want to scout it before I try to run past. We'll eat while waiting for Hagii.''

At her command, the other Kooks produced a pair of folding chairs and a folding table. They set out the luncheon in a formal, well-rehearsed way as if serving for royalty. Alexis poured two generous glasses of bumbleberry wine, first for herself and then for Salazar.

The biologist attacked his food. For a few minutes he was able to keep his mind off Alexis's maddening body. He said:

"Think George might try to ambush us again?"

"Can't tell. Whatever he does, I want to be ready. Where are your guns?"

"They're both in my baggage."

"Well, get one out, silly! What good would it do us buried in that duffel bag?"

Salazar strolled back to the litter containing his bag. When he opened the bag, he was startled by Alexis's voice close behind him. She had a way of silently stealing up on one.

"What's that funny smell, Kirk?"

"Oh, that. I bought a supply of mitta nuts to tempt the kusis."

"So they'll eat out of your hand?"

"Not quite, but close enough so I can watch and take pictures." He was fitting his rifle together.

"But if they become half-tame, they won't behave the same as they would in the wild alone."

Salazar shrugged. "That's the dilemma of the field biologist, observing without being observed by the observee. It's a chance I have to take, since I can't hover invisibly over them like one of the spirits these island Kooks believe in." He finished assembling the piece and rose.

In her dictatorial manner Alexis said: "Don't you dare make skeptical remarks about spirits around my followers! Shiiko is a Kukulcanian spirit, and our faith in her holds the community together.''

"I'll try to be careful."

He slung the gun across his back. Then a need for privacy compelled him to walk off into the forest. His visions of the previous night's adventure crowded back into his mind, so that he nearly stepped on a boshiya, a venomous black-and-white wriggler sometimes called a snake-lizard by Terrans. He saw it in time and jumped back.

When he returned to the trail, Hagii had come back from his errand. The Kook was talking with Alexis, who turned, laughing.

"Kirk, you'll never guess! Hagii talked to the head Kook in the camp, an oldster named Juugats, without showing himself to the lumberjacks. They're on strike against Cantemir for exposing them to gunfire. They had two killed and several hurt, after they'd been promised there would be no danger. So before they do anything like that again, they want combat pay, at least twice what he's paying them now.

"So we can keep on up the trail. But now your litter shall go first, and you're to have your gun ready. Understand?"

"Okay," muttered Salazar.

He did not relish being point man; his newfound virility would have liked to find an excuse for contradicting her dogmata and defying her commands. But those orders had so far seemed reasonable, and he could not think of an excuse that would not make him sound craven. Alexis was an able if exacting boss.

The party passed the lumber camp closely enough for Salazar to smell the smoke of a cook fire and hear sounds of Terran talk and movement. The sounds faded away as the Kooks with the litters trotted along the trail, the slope of which became steep enough to slow even Kukulcanians' iron muscles and leathern lungs.

Hours later, at a word from Alexis, the cortege again halted. Salazar got out and watched as she walked briskly aft to fumble in her baggage. She pulled out a white, gauzy garment. Stripping off her dirty khakis, she flipped the white robe over her head, pulled it into place, and tightened its straps. She came forward, saying:

"Kirk, from here on I go first."

"You mean we're near your community?"

"Of course! When I come in, the Kashanites will make a big production of my return. Play along with them, understand?"

"I'll do my best," said Salazar. "What's expected of me?"

"Nothing much; just be polite and do as I ask."

A ray from the low sun caught Alexis slantwise, turning her coppery hair to a flaming halo. Half-seen through the gauze, Alexis was even more exciting than Alexis naked. But either the bull elephant had gone away or Salazar rationally thought Alexis too difficult and dangerous for a love object. He said:

"What—ah—arrangements will be made for tonight?"

"If you're thinking of a repeat," she snapped, "I'm now the Supreme Choraga, a pure and holy ascetic. Anyway, you've had it three times in twenty-four hours, which must set a record for a beginner. And by the way, if you tell anyone about our little—ah—exercises, I will kill you, and I don't mean that as a figure of speech."

"All I wanted," rasped Salazar, "was to know where I'm to sleep. I have my own tent, if someone will show me where to put it."

"You'll be shown, never fear. What's your plan for your professional work?"

"First I must hike around the neighborhood until I know it well enough not to get lost in the woods. Then I buckle down to serious study of the local biota, and the kusis in particular."

"Okay. Tomorrow I'll take you up the mountain. If we start early, we can make the crater Shikawa by midday."

* * *

A space around the community of Kashania was given to plowed fields and vegetable patches. Salazar saw no one at work in the fields, but the sun was setting and the workers must have gone back to the village. The Kooks trotted past the fields and halted at the edge of a village-sized clearing encircled by huts. Young trees, apparently planted by the designer of the settlement, stood between the cabins. Another circle of tables ran around inside the circle of the huts and concentric with them.

The space within the circle swarmed with Terrans of both sexes and all ages. All were naked but for sandals and but for the sweaters and shawls that a few had put over their upper bodies against the cool of evening. Some were building a fire in the center; others were setting tablewear on the circle of tables.

Salazar's litter approached the village behind that of Alexis. Her conveyance halted where the trail ran through a gap in the circle of huts. She slid out of her litter, her gauzy draperies floating, and motioned Salazar's litter forward to a position beside hers.

Salazar got his first good look at the Kashanites. He had once seen a flier promoting a naturist colony. In its photographs of jolly naked crowds playing vigorous outdoor games, all the men had flat, hard-looking bellies and the women firm, outstanding breasts. That could not be said of most of the Kashanites.

As Alexis advanced, the Kashanites began pointing and jabbering. When she raised a hand, they cried in unison:

"Hail, Supreme Choraga! Hail, mouthpiece of the great spirit Shiiko!"

All but the youngest children dropped to their knees and bent to touch their foreheads to the ground. Alexis raised her arms, lifting her gauzes with an effect like spreading wings. In a strong, penetrating voice she called:

"Arise, ye faithful!"

As the Kashanites rose, she waved her arms and led the crowd in a song in a language that Salazar did not know. It seemed to have a wailing, Oriental-sounding tune, but most of the singers were so far off key that the melody would have been hard for a musician to recognize.

The song was mercifully short. At its close, Alexis beckoned Salazar. As he climbed from his litter, she cried:

"My faithful ones, I present Doctor Salazar, who comes among us as a visitor, studying our mountain with the methods of Terran science. While here, he shall be treated with kindness and hospitality, thus illuminating the path to virtue and salvation before him, that he may be persuaded to tread it in his turn."

Salazar suppressed an urge to blurt out: "Hey, but I'm not a doctor yet!" Common sense asserted itself, and he merely bowed to the throng. One of Alexis's bodyguards touched his arm, saying in Sungao:

"Pray step hither, sir, and I will show you where to put up your tent."

As he followed the Kook, with the laden Choku trailing, Salazar saw Alexis march with regal dignity through the parting mass of Kashanites to the largest cabin, on the farther side of the circle.

Salazar dined at one of the tables in the circle with a squad of Kashanites. He wryly noted that the sight of a lot of naked women all at once ceased to stimulate him sexually after the first quarter hour. Alexis, he thought, was on the right track in blaming the Judeo-Christian nudity tabu for the sexual excitability of males of those persuasions at a glimpse of those parts of the female body normally kept covered.

He uneasily observed that whereas the diners at the other tables chattered and gossiped, those at his were relatively quiet, as if his presence inhibited them. One was a small boy, who said loudly to a fat woman beside him:

"Mama, who is the man with those funny clothes on?"

"Shh, Nelson! He is our distinguished visitor."

"Well, I don't like our stinkish visitor. Why does he wear those funny things all over?"

Salazar was not long on repartee, but embarrassment forced it upon him. He spoke emphatically: "To give little boys like you something to talk about!"

The boy subsided for a minute but then asked his mother in a stage whisper: "Is he Shiiko's next husband?"

"Shh! We don't talk about things like that in front of strangers."

Salazar quickly finished and excused himself. Back at his tent he found Choku arranging his belongings inside. Kooks were neat to a degree that drove some of the more disorderly Terrans crazy.

"Honorable Sarasara," said Choku, "I have a message from the Supreme Choraga. If you will be at the door of her temple—"

"What temple?"

"The big house where she lives; that is what her servants call it. If you will be there at six o'clock by your Terran system, she will escort you up the mountain."

The news gave Salazar a moment of puzzlement; such an expedition would take a good part of a day, and why should she, unasked, offer to spend it thus with him? Perhaps she wanted more sex and figured that she could get it unbeknown to her followers up on the mountain.

"Fine," he said. "Please see that I am up in time."

"I will rouse you in ample time, honorable boss."

Salazar's mind, which he had kept off topic A for a whole hour, rushed back to the contemplation of Alexis's curves. Although he told himself that he should not be foolish, that such fancies were but tickets to trouble, he still did not sleep well.

At a quarter to six Salazar marched up to the front door of Alexis's house, a canvas pack on his back. He munched a snack from his emergency food supplies.

Choku had stepped out to boil water for acha. Salazar thought that Choku meant to accompany the safari to the crater. But if a chance for lovemaking arose along the way, Salazar did not wish his assistant present. Without awaiting his acha, he slipped out and strode briskly towards the circle of cabins.

The door of the larger cabin swung open; there stood Alexis in a gauzy gown like that of the night before.

"On time, I see," she said. "Good! This way, Kirk!"

She led him down the hall. As she went, she picked up a little bundle with a strap to retain it. Out the back door, she set a brisk pace along the trail leading up the long slope from Kashania.

"I can carry that bundle as well as my pack," said Salazar.

"Nonsense! I'm strong, too, never fear!"

"You—certainly—are," said Salazar, beginning to pant a little. He wondered that one so efficient and matter-of-fact as Alexis should set out in a costume so ludicrously unsuited to mountaineering.

The community fell away behind them, shrinking as they climbed until the intervening trees obscured it. When the trail leveled off for a stretch, so that Salazar had breath left for speech, he said:

"What was that song you led the congregation in last night? I know several Terran languages, but I couldn't get a word."

She snickered. "That was the *'Færda be-Shiko khahim ræft.'* The language is Farsi."

"The language is *what*?"

"Farsi; Persian to you. The title means 'We go to Shiiko tomorrow.' "

"Does your community speak Farsi? Those I heard all used English, except for a couple who spoke Russian."

"Not at all; they just learn the sounds by rote. I know a little but don't really speak it. You see, Rostam Kashani was an Iranian. He composed the song as the official hymn of the movement, and I haven't dared to try to change it—yet.''

"What happened to him?''

"He named me his successor and a little later decided to 'go to Shiiko'—in other words, to dive into the crater. I begged him not to, but he was determined. So I've struggled along with my position as best I could.''

"Do you, a Terran, really believe Shiiko is the volcano spirit, to be propitiated?''

She smiled grimly, and her reply showed a flash of steel. "If I didn't, do you think I'd be fool enough to admit it? If some scoffer made a scornful remark in the community, I'd need only to give my zealots a sign, and they would tear the unbeliever to pieces, never fear.''

"I'd better keep my mouth shut around there,'' said Salazar.

The trail became steep again, so for a while they hiked in silence. When it leveled off, Salazar said:

"My maps show the zone of nanshin trees solidly encircling the mountain between certain altitudes. How can we get through without being stung?''

"The growth is not so solid as that. The trees grow in clumps, or forests I guess you'd call them. We're going through one of the gaps. There are some nanshins now.'' She pointed.

Salazar looked. The nearest nanshins looked somewhat like Terran longleaf pines. He knew the nearest tree for a female from its crimson berries. The fruits and berries that Kukulcanian plants had evolved as a way of spreading their seeds around widely provided a striking example of evolution parallel to that on Terra.

"I saw a few in the woods lower down,'' said Salazar, "but I wasn't sure of the species.'' He glanced at Alexis, who had opened her bundle and was taking out a work shirt and trousers. She shed the gauzy gown with Kashanite indifference to nudity.

"The trail gets rougher,'' she said, carefully folding the sacerdotal garment. She glanced at Salazar, whose vision was fixed upon her. "From the gleam in your eye, I think you're hoping for a quick one, right here. Forget it, boy! I know better than to fish off the company pier."

At the word "boy," the bull elephant gave an unexpected trumpet. "Damn it, Alexis!" roared Salazar. "If you don't want to be screwed, don't waggle your pretty personal parts at me!"

"You're just a damned Judeo-Christian mundane with those barbarian tabus, so you get horny at a glimpse of a tit—"

"Just a normal male. You make it hard for me to stand up with my pants on." Salazar's hormones raged like a forest fire. His blood pounded, his breath came short, and there was a haze before his eyes. His tongue clung to his palate.

"You idiots," she said, "think the sight of a woman without clothes is an automatic invitation to a free fuck. I've told you what's what, and if you're too dumb to get the message . . ." She fumbled in her bundle and brought out a huge knife with a thirty-centimeter blade of the sort once popularized by the adventurer and slave smuggler Colonel James Bowie. "One step towards me . . ."

"Honorable sir!" said Choku's voice in Sungao. "Wherefore did you go off without me?" The knife disappeared as the Kook came forward. "Pardon me, Madam Supreme Choraga! I promised to help and protect Mr. Salazar, as by carrying the pack he bears."

Without sign of embarrassment, Alexis donned her shirt and pants and belted on the sheath knife. She said to Choku: "I was merely changing from my sacred garment."

"I understand, madam."

Salazar, waiting for Alexis to finish her preparations, caught a flash of brown in the nanshins, which whisked out of sight. My first stump-tailed kusi! he thought. Alexis's body vanished from his mind. Examining the contents of his pack, he suddenly cursed his own stupidity, saying: "Choku, I seem to have forgotten a camera. Will you please run back to our tent and get me one? The smaller Hayashi will do, with extra film.'' *Serves you right,* he added to himself, *for letting this hypocritical floozy come between you and your scientific task.*

''As you say, honorable boss.'' Choku trotted back down the trail.

She was on her feet with her bundle slung over her shoulder. ''Come along! We can't spend the morning fooling around or we'll never get to the crater for lunch.''

She set off with a resolute stride, as if daring Salazar to follow. He felt a twinge of resentment at having his abortive suggestion of lovemaking scorned as ''fooling around,'' but that was Alexis. He deserved it, for he was like a moth circling too close to a flame.

They hiked between somber, looming groves of nanshin trees to the right and left, interspersed with thickets of jade-green, canelike plants reminding Salazar of the smaller kinds of Terran bamboos. Now and then he saw kusis, but they scampered away with piercing whistles before he had more than a glimpse. Occasional zutas flitted on rainbow wings, like bizarre combinations of butterfly, lizard, and bat.

Larger beasts were few compared to the fauna below the nanshin belt. Once they met a wild kudzai, an old tusker somewhat like a reptilian wild boar. While Salazar unslung his pack and got out his smaller gun, a pistol with a detachable stock, kudzai and Terrans eyed one another. Before Salazar got his weapon assembled and aimed, the kudzai snorted, trotted back up the trail, and vanished into a gap among the nanshins.

When the trail was comparatively easy, Salazar asked: ''Alexis, what's the attitude of the community toward the Adriana lumbering project? Really, it's the Reverend Dumfries's enterprise.''

With audible irritation, she snapped, ''We went all over that in Sungecho. We'll just take things as they come. If

Shiiko takes a dim view of Adriana's plans, she'll take care of them, never fear!"

"How would a spirit do that? Haunt the lumber camp?"

She smiled grimly. "Shiiko lords it over storms, eruptions, lightning, and earthquakes."

"Would you pray to her for those things?"

"No; we merely call her attention to Adriana's intentions. The rest is up to her."

"Seems to me you take a pretty laissez-faire attitude towards an ecological disaster."

She halted and faced him with an expression that showed her hair-trigger temper unleashed. "Oh, shut up, Kirk! I've run Kashania well so far, and I won't let any skinny little rabbit-faced priss dictate to me!"

"I merely pointed out—"

"Shut up!" she screamed. Then in a normal tone: "Come on! If we're to make the crater, we've got to move."

For an hour they tramped in silence. The footpath carried them up the slope to the upper edge of the nanshin belt. Above that zone, the air was cooler and the plant life sparser: stunted shrubs, discouraged-looking patches of gray-green grassoid, and the corpse of an occasional young nanshin that had given up the attempt to sprout and grow above the climatic zone to which evolution had adapted it. Ahead rose the final cone of Sungara's summit with its plume of vapor.

As they climbed, Salazar noted increasing signs of former lava flows. They clambered over ridges of glassy black lava rock, snaking down the mountainside like the roots of a giant tree. When they reached the final slope, the vegetation almost ceased, and they walked on the tormented surface of solidified lava.

Salazar was glad of his heavy, thick-soled boots; the lava's glassy fractures, where its millions of gas bubbles intersected its surface, would soon cut common shoes to pieces. They scrambled over irregularities. Alexis

bounded ahead, leaping pits and trenches with a reck-
lessness that frightened Salazar. If she fell and injured
herself, he wondered how he could get her back to the
community. He was no weakling; but she was a big girl,
probably weighing more than he.

The terrain leveled off as they neared the crater. To
right and left, little plumes of vapor rose from holes and
chinks in the rock, merging into an all-pervading, heaven-
veiling mist. A breeze whistled about the hikers' heads.

Alexis said: "Here we are!"

At the rim of the crater, Salazar moved cautiously forward, testing every step. The level surface of the summit
fell away abruptly into a circular pit almost a kilometer
across, with vertical walls descending over fifty meters
to the lake of lava. On most of the lake, the lava had
cooled to a scum of silver-gray rock traversed by zigzag
fissures. Through these cracks, the liquid lava below the
surface shone red even in the misty sunlight. Here and
there across the surface rose fountains of bright red liquid lava, rising and falling in short, thick columns. From
the crater came a continuous *swish-swish, swish-swish*
like the sound of a surf.

As Salazar watched, some fountains died down while
others broke through the crust and spouted in their turn,
throwing up dark fragments of scum with the molten lava.
Alexis said:

"There's your crater, Kirk. The Kooks call it 'Shikawa,' from the volcano spirit Shiiko. Let's walk along
the rim." She started off to their left.

Salazar followed cautiously over the twisted surface.
Presently they reached a place where the rim bent sharply
to the left and back again, forming an embayment en-
closed by a nearly circular wall about four meters across,
with a point on either side. She said:

"You get a fine view out there on the point, if you're
not afraid."

"Me, afraid?" With a snort, he stepped out on the
tapering point, saying: "Looks like the old Christian pic-

ture of hell, doesn't it? Those fountains could be sinners tossing their arms in the flames.''

He moved still further out on the point. He suffered a mild acrophobia, so that looking down almost vertically into the lava made his testicles crawl. You damned fool, he berated himself, letting this masterful bitch taunt you into risking your life to show you're not afraid!

A shout in Sungao made him start. Choku called: ''Mr. Sarasara! Honorable boss, I have your camera.''

Salazar stepped abruptly back to the base of the point, colliding with Alexis close behind him. With a yelp of dismay, she fell back and ended sitting on a bulbous mass of lava rock, crying:

''Ouch! That hurt, you clumsy bastard!''

''I—I'm sorry!'' said a flustered Salazar. ''I didn't know you were so close.''

''Oh, shut up! I'll have a sore rump for a week, with a bruise the size of a saucer. Now where in hell's lunch?''

She rummaged in her bag while Salazar did the same in his. Choku asked:

''Is all well with you, sir?''

''All is well. And with you likewise?''

''Likewise. I had a certain worry about you, but I see that I arrived in time.''

''Good of you,'' grunted Salazar, munching a sandwich. He pulled out a bottle of bumbleberry, filled a paper cup, and handed it to Alexis, who muttered an ungracious thanks. He poured his own in silence. He sneezed; he had worked up a sweat during the climb, and now the cool wind made him shiver.

His lunch consumed, Salazar took his camera from Choku, rose, and scouted around the crater, shooting. He said: ''Alexis, will you stand up so I can get a shot at you?''

''No, I won't!'' she snapped.

He thought: Jeepers, what a termagant! And to think I once found her attractive—even irresistible! Then she said:

"I didn't mean that the way it sounded, Kirk. It's just that I don't like pictures of me floating around where my enemies, like the Reverend Dumfries, might get hold of them and use them against me."

He took more pictures, wondering to what extent these enemies were real and to what extent paranoid delusions. At last he said:

"Alexis, you called Dumfries an enemy. But I thought you had reached a modus vivendi with the Adriana people."

"I have, but they'll double-cross me the minute they think it's to their advantage. Dumfries has gotten so filthy rich from his church that most big shots, Terran or Kook, sit up and beg or roll over when he tells them to."

"Doesn't say much for the integrity of either species," mused Salazar. "I wouldn't sit up and beg, or roll over either."

"Maybe not, but you're an unworldly scientist. In the struggle for power you don't count. Actually, I think Kooks have more of what you call 'integrity' than we do. People like Dumfries call it 'blind obstinacy' when they resist Terrans' attempts to diddle them out of their ancestral lands. In this regard, Yaamo is more like a Terran than most of his—what do you call somebody of the same species?"

"A conspecific."

"Than most of his conspecifics."

He asked: "How has Dumfries worked up such a huge, fanatical following on Terra in a few years? He's not much to look at."

"They tell me he's a marvelous speaker, potbelly and all, practically hypnotic. And his Holy Gnostic Church is the first major religion to face up to the fact that there are other civilized planets."

"But the Neognostics were just a small sect."

"Were, but their growth has put them right up there with the biggies. The others—Christianity, Judaism, Islam—all assume Terra to be the center of the universe and the only inhabited world. Dumfries gets away from that with his multiple Demiurges, one for each planet.''

"How about the Hindus and Buddhists?''

"The Neognostics haven't made much progress in countries like India and Sri Lanka, because they are not so firmly tied to Terra. Their mythology, like that of the Theosophists, is full of other worlds already.''

Salazar sneezed again. "Shouldn't we start back now?''

"You go on; Choku can guide you. I'll follow later. I'm going to commune with Shiiko.''

"Are you sure? I don't like to leave you alone.''

"Of course I'm sure! Run along; I know the way as well as I know my own house.''

"But—''

"Go!'' she shouted, pointing.

"Very well, your Holiness,'' grated Salazar. "Don't blame me if you break a leg or meet a hungry *porondu*. Come, Choku.''

Salazar turned away with a shrug. One so willful as Alexis could probably not be persuaded once she had made up her mind. Anyway, he wanted to question Choku out of her hearing.

Salazar and the Kook marched off. When they got beyond the mountaintop area of tumbled lava rock and did not have to watch their steps so vigilantly, Salazar asked:

"Choku, what did you save me from?''

"Honorable Sarasara,'' said the Kook, "I know that you Terrans have powers, from your science, beyond those of us human beings. But can you walk on molten lava?''

Salazar looked narrowly at his assistant. "I have never tried but am sure I cannot. Do you mean that she . . . .''

"Aye, sir; I mean that I arrived in time to save you from being pushed off the cliff. Miss Ritter was bracing herself to shove you into the crater when I called.''

"Tell me more!'' said Salazar.

"Sir, pray understand that this has been difficult. I worked for her after Mr. Kashani met his death, and a condition of my employment was that I must never tell what I saw her do or heard her say. We human beings take such promises more seriously than, I fear, do you aliens.

"I also promised you, as a condition of employment, to succor you and ward you from peril. Now, I foresaw that these promises would conflict. I could not adhere to one without violating the other."

Salazar had a flash of insight. "You mean you had seen her shove Kashani into the crater and thought she might try the same thing on me?"

"Precisely, sir. After long thought I concluded that whereas revealing her secrets would have only a suppositious effect on the Supreme Choraga, failure to warn you would likely give you a fatal bath in lava. So the latter promise, meseemed, took precedence over the former."

It was like a Kukulcanian, thought Salazar, to work such a dilemma out by laborious logicization and then to give a blow-by-blow account of the process. Still, Salazar realized that he owed his life to it.

"I most gratefully thank you," he said.

"And I thank my ancestral spirits that I was able to carry out my agreement with you, sir. I trust that I have done so to your satisfaction."

"Eminently so. Had you not, I should not be here to complain. But why in the name of Metasu should she want to kill me? I have not wronged her; in fact, she once seemed to like me well, at least in bed. I can understand her killing Kashani to seize his place as head of Kashania, but why me?"

"Are you familiar with the history of Sunga, sir?"

"In a general way. I understand the Sungarin used to practice the sacrifice of some of their own folk but gave that up on the urging of Terran missionaries."

"That is not quite my understanding, sir."

"What, then?"

"I believe that the Sungarin sacrificed to Shiiko chosen ones from their own number by casting them into Shi-kawa. They sought to choose the wickedest criminals for the purpose, thus, as you would put it, slaying two zutas with one projectile.

"But sir, crime amongst us human beings is but a tiny fraction of that which, I am told, obtains amongst you aliens. So when no egregiously wicked criminals could be found, the high chief had to devote to the spirit some person who had committed only a trivial offense. It was feared that soon some wholly innocent being, chosen by lot, must needs be sacrificed.

"Mr. Kashani proposed to the Sungarin that in return for a lease on the land now occupied by the community, he should sacrifice one alien of his own species each year to Shiiko by the traditional method. The then high chief doubted whether Shiiko would accept the sacrifice of aliens, but he gave Mr. Kashani's scheme a trial. When, after the first such sacrifice, the land enjoyed beneficent weather and bountiful crops, this was taken to signify Shiiko's assent. You can perceive why mainlanders like me tend to look down upon the Sungarin as a backward, superstitious folk, only partly civilized."

"How does the leader of the community get his—or her—victims?" asked Salazar.

"This may be a visitor like yourself, or perhaps a Ter-ran can be lured from Sungecho by curiosity or prom-ises."

"It figures. At dinner last night a child asked if I was Shiiko's next husband; that must be what he meant. I was stupid not to catch on sooner. I guess it is premature to say that *Homo sapiens* has altogether given up the sacri-fice of its conspecifics. Is that what happened to my old classmate Latour?"

"I believe so, sir, albeit I did not witness the actual immolation. This occurred last year, after Miss Ritter had devoted Mr. Kashani to the volcano spirit. I believe that she beguiled Mr. Ratoo to her village by a promise of sexual pleasure, and her followers did the rest.''

''Know you if she upheld her end of the bargain?''

''Sir? Oh, I see; you mean did she permit him sexual access? I cannot say that she did from direct knowledge, since you aliens have a cultural tabu on performing sexual congress in the presence of others. A professor in Machuro once explained to me that this tabu went back to you aliens' primitive times, because your practice of copulating lying down rendered you vulnerable to a spear thrust in the back.

''Miss Ritter, however, passed a night with Mr. Ratoo in her tent on the way from Amoen to the village of Kashania. I did not witness the actual intromission but, from what I know of Terran sexual customs, infer that it probably took place.''

Salazar shivered, but not from the cold. ''I think the sooner we move our tent and baggage away from the Kashanite community, the better for us.''

''The logic of the situation compels me to agree, sir.''

For a while Salazar walked in silence, making better time on the downward slopes than he had coming up. At last he said:

''I was sorry for Kashani when I heard he was pushed into Shikawa. But he only got what he asked for. And Chief Yaamo must have lied when he told me he knew naught of Latour's fate.''

''If he lied, the movement of his cervical bristles would betray the fact, sir.''

''But I wasn't looking at them, and I am not expert at interpreting those wiggles, anyway. Another thing, Choku. The Kashanites' indulgent attitude toward Adriana's lumbering puzzles me. I should expect Miss Ritter to oppose it, since it would cause her people much trouble. I can imagine what some of those roughnecks would do if they saw young women running around naked. What is behind it all?''

''Sir, I do not wish to accuse without due evidence.

But the chief human being of the community, Juugats, has passed on a rumor that Mr. Cantemir promised Miss Ritter a generous bribe to keep her followers from interfering.''

Choku's neck bristles rippled in a way that betokened mirth. ''You aliens are strange. You seem so clever, yet when you hire us human beings as servants, you forget that many comprehend some Terran tongues. You talk amongst yourselves about intimate matters, ignoring the fact that a human being overhears, as if we did not exist.''

So much for the Kashanite quest for spiritual perfection, thought Salazar. ''Well, let us display some of our vaunted Terran cleverness. First, I think our present location is unhealthy. We should move to another site on the edge of the nanshin belt and get on with our work.''

''I think, sir, that you have made a wise decision,'' said Choku.

Ever since Alexis had proposed a picnic hike to Shikawa, a thought had buzzed at the back of Salazar's mind that there was something phony about that proposal. Why should she take the time and trouble to lead him to the crater when she was apparently not interested in his science and, as it proved, did not wish to fornicate again, at least not on the mountain?

With Choku's explanations, the parts of the puzzle fell into place. She would rely on her proven sexual appeal to lead him by the nose and push him into the lava, thus paying her rent for the year to Yaamo. She would also get rid of a former bedmate who, if he turned out a blabbermouth, might compromise her standing with the Kashanites.

If Salazar had been thinking with his brain instead of with his gonads, he would have caught on sooner. He thought: When Keats wrote ''La Belle Dame sans Merci,'' he didn't know the half of it!

V.

The Stump-Tailed Kusi

Salazar and Choku pitched their tent in a bay or recess on the outer or lower edge of the nanshin forest, a kilometer west of the Kashanite community. At mealtime Salazar invited Choku to eat with him. The Kook politely declined, saying that his rules of caste forbade that. He also preferred his native Kukulcanian porridge, which Terrans found as appetizing as library paste.

Salazar, now usually wearing his pistol, went about his scientific work in an orderly, systematic way, a contrast with the shyness and gaucherie that he often showed in his relations with people. First, he had to get the local kusis used to his presence. When he and Choku had arrived, the animals in the neighboring trees had scampered away with barks and whistles.

Salazar settled down and for a while ignored the local fauna, save for the constant battle against biting arthropods, analogues of Terran mosquitos and biting flies. He swatted and sprayed and coated his exposed skin with oily repellents.

Some species of Kukulcanian arthropods, hunting by smell, left Terrans alone; but many others, hunting by heat radiation, attacked them as energetically as did their Terran analogues. Salazar had learned from xenobiology that these small biters, after a meal, usually curled up and died of acute indigestion, since their systems were not adapted to Terran blood. But this was small comfort to the suffering Terran.

He assisted Choku with the chores, collected firewood, and read his books: O'Sullivan's *The Trees of Sunga*, Kaufmann's *Fauna of the Eastern Littoral*, and Yorimoto's *The Pithecoidea of Kukulcan*. All, he knew, were mere preliminary surveys. Enormous amounts of work had to be done before the cataloging of Kukulcanian species began to approach that prevailing on Terra. There, the known number of species ran to over two million, including tens of thousands driven to extinction by human expansion. In addition, Terran biologists estimated that there were perhaps another million not yet identified and classified.

For three days Salazar saw no sign of kusis. On the fourth, while he sat on his folding chair, his eye caught a flash of brown amid the green of the nanshins. He continued reading, pretending not to notice, but the kusi scout did not reappear.

The next day he sighted glimpses of brown among the branches. Still Salazar sat over his books as if unaware.

The day after that a couple of kusis came into plain sight in the nearest female nanshin. They moved about deliberately, plucking and eating the scarlet berries. The noisy creatures uttered barks, howls, grunts, growls, hoots, screams, and whistles.

From Terran analogies, Salazar suspected that the nanshin and the stump-tailed kusi were symbiotic. The trees furnished the kusis with food. The kusis cultivated the trees by eating the berries and defecating the undigested seeds far and wide so that the seedlings would not be overshadowed by the parent tree. Once a zuta fluttered close to the tree as if to snatch a berry; the two kusis leapt at it, barking, and it flew away.

Moving slowly, Salazar picked up his binoculars and focused. Gripping the glasses in one hand, he held his recorder close to his mouth in the other and spoke into it in a bated voice, telling the time and describing the kusis' movements.

The animals seemed monkeylike in a reptilian way. They had grasping feet on all four limbs, little round external ears, and, as the name implied, stumpy tails between one centimeter and two centimeters long. They used their handlike forefeet, each with three fingers and an opposable thumb, in quite a human way for plucking berries.

Salazar knew of other species of the Pithecoidea. Some had long tails, in some cases prehensile. Taxonomists were not yet agreed on dividing those species into families and genera. Progress was slow because Terran scientific resources on Kukulcan were minuscule compared to those back on Terra.

Then Salazar sat up and reached for his camera. A smaller kusi approached one of the two larger ones that he had been watching. Coming close, it extended a forelimb and pulled it back in what looked like a beckoning gesture.

At first the adult ignored the gestures, but at last it took a berry, bit it in half, swallowed one half, and handed the other to the juvenile mendicant. With subdued but rising excitement, Salazar described the scene. He dropped the recorder on its lanyard and put the camera to his eye.

Like some Terran anthropoid apes, the kusis had evolved food-sharing behavior! Some xenanthropologists deemed this instinct a necessary precondition for the evolution of an intelligent, civilized species.

Just as Salazar was getting his long-distance lens adjusted, the kusis burst into barks. Instantly all three, with a chorus of hoots and whistles, leapt into other trees and disappeared.

Damn! thought Salazar. He knew that, to many Terran wild animals, a staring eye was viewed as a threat or a challenge. To such a beast, the lenses of cameras and other optical instruments presented an especially menacing threat. Salazar had hoped that he was far enough from the trees for the animals not to notice the camera, but their eyesight must have been keener than he thought.

It must have been pure luck that they had not noticed his binoculars aimed toward them; when he had dropped the glasses and picked up the camera, the motion had attracted their attention.

The next day there was no sign of kusis, but Salazar had other troubles to occupy him. He awoke to find the tent swarming with a Kukulcanian arthropod somewhat like a Terran cricket, but non-jumping. They were attacking the bag in which the food supply was tied up, purposefully gnawing at the rope securing it.

Salazar yelled for Choku, who had been standing watch outside. They hunted frantically through their baggage, swatting insectoids that crawled up their legs. Choku found the spray can. Salazar sprayed until the tent was littered with dead and dying arthropods, some feebly kicking on their backs.

"Did you pack not a broom with your supplies, honorable boss?" asked Choku.

"Nay; meseemed one would not be needed." Salazar squatted and began picking up insectoid corpses, which in death emitted a horrible smell. There were hundreds.

"Permit me to expedite matters, sir," said Choku. "Take your ease whilst I obtain the needed instrument."

The Kook left the tent and soon returned with a tree branch trimmed to a broomlike shape. He began sweeping corpses out. In a few minutes the tent was clear save for a few in odd corners. Salazar collected those by hand.

On the second day after the camera incident, Salazar caught sight of more kusis in the nanshin trees. Soon the animals became bolder, showing themselves openly and ignoring Salazar's camera and binoculars. Sometimes a couple of young would come down and chase each other round and round the grassoid between Salazar's camp and the nanshins.

Between swats at biting arthropods, Salazar continued dictating notes on the beasts' behavior. He observed the begging of the young and the pair-bonding of the older kusis. One day the nearest pair appeared with the female in heat, betokened by a conspicuous genital swelling. After the pair had for some time nuzzled each other and squeaked, the female climbed down to the ground and crouched with her rump raised.

The male of the pair, whom Salazar identified by a patch of darker scales on his neck, climbed down after her. So did three other males, who appeared out of nowhere. One moved towards the female, but the male—Salazar though of him as her mate, though he knew that assessment was premature—bared his teeth and chattered at the interloper. The strange male retreated to a prudent distance. Another of the trio made a similar approach and was likewise driven back.

The "mate" then went up to the female from behind, grasped her hips, and mounted. After a dozen thrusts he gave a shriek and withdrew. The female remained in her crouch.

One of three other males approached not the female but the dominant male. The newcomer made the same begging gesture that Salazar had seen the young do for food. The mate gave a chirp, and the newcomer hopped over to the female and copulated as the mate had done.

Another of the trio then repeated the whole performance. But when the third, who up to then had not even approached the female, tried the same begging gesture, the mate barked and rushed at him with bared teeth. The lorn lover fled away into the trees.

Poor little bastard, thought Salazar. I know just how he feels, always odd man out with the other sex. When I get back to Henderson, I must make up my mind about Calpurnia. Maybe we should get engaged.

The kusis' pair-bonding, he thought, must have been less exclusive than that which he had read about among Terran gibbons, though developed beyond that of the Terran gorilla and chimpanzee. The relationship he had witnessed had parallels in some primitive Terran tribes—at least, it had before all the erstwhile primitives had donned pants and shirts and taken up computers and golf. With some, monogamy had been the rule, but a husband might grant a highly esteemed friend or kinsman the privilege of copulation with his wife. What the wives thought of it was not reported by any of the anthropologists whose works Salazar had read.

Salazar dug a mitta nut out of its bag. He laid the nut on the grassoid, halfway from his tent to the nearest nanshin trees, and waited.

An hour after Salazar had set out his bait, a young male kusi appeared at the base of the nearest nanshin. Attracted by the smell, it made little tentative rushes this way and that. Then it zeroed in on the nut. It hopped across the grassoid for several meters but halted short of its goal, looking warily at Salazar on his camp chair. Its courage failed, and it ran back to the tree and climbed out of sight.

Several more kusis made similar approaches during the day. Toward dusk, as Salazar was helping Choku prepare dinner and not watching the kusis, one bold fellow raced out, grabbed the nut, and ran back into the trees. Salazar looked around in time to see the animal disappear.

After two more days the kusis, drawn by the smell of mitta nuts, became tame enough for Salazar to walk within a couple of meters of them before they fled. Now he could attack the serious question: How did the kusis neutralize the poison of the venom trees? He had heard that the best antidote, if one got a drop on one's skin, was sodium acid carbonate, but the kusis certainly had no baking soda.

The animals' growing tolerance of Salazar allowed him to approach their trees within two or three meters to watch. When they moved about, barking, hooting, and whistling, the needles of the nanshins curled away from them. Salazar suspected that the whistling, one of the kusis' wide repertory of sounds, caused this reaction.

But the true explanation might still be a chemical one. To make sure of his doctorate, he ought to eliminate possibilities other than the correct one.

He did not take seriously Alexis's belief that the kusis were in telepathic communication with the trees. If all other explanations failed, he might have to investigate that one. It would be a daunting task.

Salazar's apparatus included a phonometer and an odorometer. The phonometer measured and recorded the pitch and intensity of sounds all the way from the subaudible frequencies used by elephants in communicating, to the ultrasound frequencies used in surgery and dentistry, and to even higher than the clicks and squeaks employed by bats for echolocation. Thus it recorded sounds both above and below the frequencies audible to the human ear. The odorometer analyzed the smellable compounds in the air and recorded them.

Salazar waited until nightfall, when the kusis huddled in clumps on branches and slept. Then he carried the phonometer to a nearby tree and set it down at the base. He likewise set the odorometer at the base of another. He had to crawl to reach the base without touching the venom-spraying needles. Remembering what he had read of the destructiveness of Terran monkeys, he laid a couple of dead branches over each instrument.

The next day, as the kusis began to move about, one uttered a shriek, staring down at the base of the tree where Salazar had laid the odorometer. In a flash, all the kusis in sight, a dozen or so, bounded away. No more appeared for the rest of the day or for two days following. Salazar knew that he had not sufficiently hidden the instrument.

Then, as before, the kusis began returning to the site— first a bold young male as point man, jittering about and scuttling out of sight at Salazar's slightest movement, only to reappear an hour later.

In three more days, the kusis were as thick as ever in the neighboring trees. Salazar noted that they kept away

from the tree at the base of which he had laid the odorometer. But the next day a couple gingerly returned to
that tree, keeping well up from the ground.

Salazar determined to collect his instruments and read
their records the next day. But when, the following morning, he neared the tree of the odorometer, he was appalled to see a glitter of little metal and plastic parts
spread over several square meters. He dashed forward to
find the casing broken open and the contents—gears,
spools, levers, filmstrips, and all the rest—spread around.

He bitterly reproached himself for letting the kusis make
free with this costly piece of machinery. They were made
on Terra, and it would take a couple of dozen years to get
another from mankind's distant home planet. Nobody on
Kukulcan could produce so complex an instrument.

If the answer was chemical, like the pheromones produced by moths and many other Terran organisms to lure
the opposite sex, he would have no way to prove it. If
the answer was phonic, his phonometer might settle the
question if he could get enough significant recordings
with it, though this would not be enough if the correct
answer was a combination of sound and chemicals. If the
answer were something other than either of those, he
would have to cross that bridge when he came to it.

He bore the phonometer back to his tent, since there
was no sense in letting the little devils ruin that one, too.
Apprised of the catastrophe, Choku said:

"Honorable boss, surely you will wish to salvage the
parts of that machine. If nobody on this world can create
one, it might still be possible to reassemble it from the
separated parts and to repair or replace any parts broken
or missing."

"You are right," said Salazar. "Back in Henderson I
have an instruction book on the machine, showing where
every little widget goes. Where is a bag to collect the
pieces? We shall also need your broom to sweep the parts
beneath the tree out to where we can reach them."

An hour later, with Choku's help, Salazar had gathered

and bagged every piece of the odorometer that either could find. Salazar spent the morning studying records on the phonometer. He thought he could identify the seismographic wriggles on the filmstrips with some of the kusis' repertory of sounds. In particular, the piercing whistles registered at about twenty thousand hertz, or cycles per second. This, Salazar thought, would put them up in the ninth octave of the diatonic scale, close to the upper limits of audibility to the normal human ear.

What he needed to do was to make a sound film of kusis going about their business and synchronize that film with the phonometer. But for a good phonometric record he needed to put the apparatus near them. When they saw it, they would flee in terror. When they got used to it, they would tear it to pieces. Their claws and efficient Kukulcanian muscles would make short work of even a strong metal casing.

"Choku," he grumped, "if I could only make the kind of squeals that the kusis do, I should soon discover whether their sounds stop the nanshins from giving them a bath in venom. On Terra, people make high-pitched whistles to control their pets." He paused. "Why could I not make a whistle right here? Know you of a patch of canes nearby?"

"Aye, honorable boss. The last time I went out for firewood, I saw a large growth of them west of here, around the curve of the mountain. I estimate that you could walk the distance in one of your hours, sir."

"Good! If you will put me up a bite to eat, I will set out forthwith."

Salazar was on his way back from the patch with a bundle of canes when he saw the sky, which had been fair in the morning, now fast clouding over. As he quickened his pace, the skies darkened further. Thunder rumbled. Then lightning flashed, followed at shorter and shorter intervals by thunder.

As the flashes came closer, Salazar noted that the initial

pitch of the thunder rose in frequency. In theory one could make a fair guess at the distance of a flash not only by measuring the interval between flash and thunder but also from the frequency of the sound at the beginning of the thunder roll. If he only had the phonometer along . . .

A vivid flash lit up the landscape as it came to earth somewhere in the nanshin forest on his left. Less than a second later there came a sharp, high-pitched crack, then a deafening crash of slightly lower frequency and a long roll, running down the scale to a bass rumble. Then came a drop of rain, followed by a downpour.

Salazar had become so interested in natural phenomena and in planning a possible scientific paper on thunder frequencies that he had forgotten to haul his yellow slicker out of his pack. Dropping the canes, he repaired the omission, though not without getting fairly wet.

He looked around. The nanshin forest on his left offered shelter, but of a dangerous sort. To the right the slope was fairly open, with stretches of grassoid, herbs, and scattered trees. Salazar knew better than to stand near an isolated tree in a thunderstorm. Farther down the mountain, the trees merged into the solid forest of the lower altitudes, but distance made it impractical to seek shelter thither.

There was nothing to do but to slog ahead through the rain. After a quarter hour the downpour subsided to a light rain. In half an hour the rain let up, and patches of sky appeared through the breaking clouds. When Salazar stopped to shed and fold his slicker, he heard a human yell.

The sound was repeated from ahead. He thought he heard: "Help! *Au secours! Pomogitye!* Help!" There seemed also to be an animal noise.

Dropping the slicker, Salazar pulled out the skeleton stock for his pistol and broke into a jog. Soon, around the curve of the mountain, he discerned a knot of figures. As he came closer, he saw that two Terrans were ringed by three poöshos, the continent's principal pack-hunting predators. They could be called reptilian wolves: quadrupeds of about wolf size with ears and fangs somewhat like those of a Terran canid. But their hides were hairless and scaly, and their bodies tapered smoothly aft into serpentine tails. They galloped round and round the people, snarling and wailing, now and then darting in to snap.

As he ran, Salazar unfolded the skeleton stock and fitted the butt of the pistol into it. If he tried to shoot at this range, he would as likely hit one of the Terrans as their attackers. As for shooting without the stock, forget it!

Another score of paces, and he thought he would have a chance. He recognized the two attacked as members of Ritter's zuta-watching party, Jomo Mpanza and Shakeh Dikranian. Mpanza, a stout, black-skinned man with a head of close-cut gray wool, was holding them off with his knobby walking stick, while Miss Dikranian, the sultry-looking, black-haired beauty, threw stones.

Salazar halted and put the stock to his shoulder. It would not be so accurate as the rifle, but it was all he had. He sighted on a poösho and squeezed. *Bang!* No change; he must have missed.

Salazar ran forward a few paces more, knelt, and tried again. *Bang!* A poösho leapt into the air, fell on its side, and lay writhing. The other two ran off down slope and disappeared. Salazar came forward and fired another round into the wounded animal, whose writhings ceased.

"Oh, Kirk!" cried Shakeh Dikranian, dropping her stone. She dashed forward and seized Salazar in a crushing embrace, pressing her full breasts against his damp bush jacket and making him even wetter. She kissed him rapturously. "I thought we were done for!"

She sneezed. Both rescuees' wet clothes clung to their skins.

"What are you two doing out here by yourselves?" asked Salazar.

"We got lost," said Shakeh.

Mpanza, speaking educated British English, said: "We thought we saw a *Nicterophis melas*, a rare species. We took a few steps towards it to confirm our identification, and when we turned around, the rest of them had vanished. We hurried after them, or at least in the direction we thought they had gone; but we must have got turned about.

"After an hour of wandering and yelling, we came out on this grassy place. Then the poöshos came after us. They remind me of the wild hunting dogs of my native continent." He held up the blackthorn stick and kissed it. "Souvenir of Ireland. God bless the Irish!"

"I'd better get you to my camp," said Salazar, "where you can dry out. I dropped some pieces of gear; please wait while I go back for them."

Soon Salazar returned with his pack, properly filled again. He had just rejoined the Patelians when he realized that he had absentmindedly forgotten to retrieve the bundle of canes, which lay scattered where he had dropped the pack. Nevertheless he set out for his camp.

They had been walking only briefly when more Terrans issued from the trees and came towards them. Hilbert Ritter, in the lead, called: "What in Metasu's name are you doing here? We've been hunting all over for you!"

Shakeh Dikranian repeated the explanation. Ritter burst out: "Damn it, I've warned you and warned you not to straggle! The next one who does will be sent back to Sungecho on the next train."

"We're all going back tomorrow, anyway," said Shakeh.

Ritter grumped. On the way to Salazar's camp, Mpanza and Miss Dikranian apologized for the trouble they had caused. Salazar asked:

"How are you making out otherwise, Hilbert?"

Ritter shrugged. "It goes. One piece of good news: A trainkook on the way freight saw Mrs. Eagleton's suitcase on the embankment and picked it up. She got it back."

"Where on Terra would a workman turn in lost property like that?"

"That's Kooks for you. Of course it hasn't stopped her bitching."

"What about?" Glancing about, Salazar saw that Mrs. Eagleton was not with the party that day.

"The case arrived somewhat beat up, which is hardly surprising." Ritter sighed. "Most of the zuta watchers are good people, but in a group like this there's always one pain in the podex." He paused. "Kirk, today's field trip is our last. We have a car reserved back to Sungecho tomorrow on the express. Coming with us?"

Salazar scowled. "Damn it, I think I know the answer to my problem; but I need more days to nail down my proof. I figure that the next ship to Oöi after yours will take me back to Henderson in time to get my next term's class lessons ready. On the other hand, by the time I pay off Choku, I shall be just about broke."

"So you'd better come with us, or you'll lose the low rates on the trains and the ship. Oh, I almost forgot. Here's a letter I picked up at the Amoen post office."

Salazar took the letter. "How much do I owe you for postage due?"

"Fourteen and a half of the local unit. If you're pressed, you can pay me back in Henderson."

Salazar saw the tiny logo of the university museum. As he opened the letter, a grin overspread his features. The letter read:

Dear Kirk:

You know that old bore, the financier Maximus Flamand? The other day he practically hauled me into a bar by force to have a drink. Soon he was weeping into his liquor and telling me what a wonderful thing the museum was and what a great director I was and so on.

Then he said he had long wanted to do something nice for us, and without warning hauled out a check for fifteen hundred that you will—if the Kooks haven't burned down the Sungecho bank as a plot to steal their property—find deposited in your name in that bank. Only a few Kooks here understand commercial paper, and I doubt if any on Sunga do. As some Terran writer once said, the strongest human emotion is fear, and the strongest kind of fear is fear of the unknown.

Flamand said he was giving it to me as director of the museum with no strings attached. I could use it in any way I liked. So I thought, How better to use it than in support of a small biological research expedition in the hands of a conscientious young scientist?

Kara sends love. Affectionately,
Keith Adams Salazar

PS: I am doing what I can about the other matter mentioned in your last letter.

Kirk Salazar said: "It's okay, Hilbert. My old man has deposited money for me in the Sungecho bank, so I shall stay on until the job is done."

Shakeh Dikranian asked: "Kirk, what's the latest on George Cantemir's lumbering project? Is he going to scalp the mountain like he said?"

"I suppose so," said Salazar.

"Can't you get the Kashanites to help? If George's project goes through, it'll spoil their little paradise."

"They won't do a thing. For one thing, their pacifistic cult doesn't approve of violence, and nothing short of violence is going to stop the Adriana Company. For another, there's a rumor that Cantemir has promised the Supreme Choraga—"

"My daughter," growled Ritter.

"—a whopping bribe not to oppose him. And the cult members will do whatever she says."

"Couldn't you lurk around the lumber camp with your rifle, knocking off lumberjacks one by one? They'd either go out on strike again or quit the job."

"No. For one thing, I'm not a murderer. These lumberjacks aren't scoundrels, just workmen doing what they're hired to do. For another, they're a tough lot, probably better at bushwhacking than I. They'd be more likely to pick me off.''

After a pause Shakeh said: ''Well, then, all I can think of is for you to start a rival cult. You could do it; I saw your performance on the *Ijumo*.''

Half an hour later Choku had welcomed his employer back to the camp and rigged a frame of branches near the camp fire on which to dry Shakeh's and Mpanza's clothes. The other Patelians had been under a clump of broad-leaved trees when the storm passed and so got only slightly wet.

Salazar was taken aback when Shakeh Dikranian emerged from the tent, naked but for a towel around her middle and holding her clothes in a bundle. Catching Salazar's eye, she said:

''What are you goggling at, Kirk? Haven't you ever seen a woman before?''

While Salazar mentally compared Shakeh's form with that of Alexis, she hung her clothes on the frame. Jomo Mpanza entered the tent and presently thrust out an arm bearing sodden garments, calling:

''I say, will someone kindly hang these up for me?''

''Aren't you coming out?'' asked Salazar, taking the clothes.

''I can't. I am not decent.''

Salazar chuckled at the relativity of human customs.

Hilbert Ritter's reunited zuta watchers had vanished along the trail to Amoen. The sun was low in a western sky barred by intermittent clouds. Then Choku, preparing dinner, said:

''Sir! Look around! I do believe we have more company!''

Along the trail from the east came George Cantemir with a big-game rifle slung across his back. His beard shone gold in the setting sun. After him came a Kook, a female from its lack of crest, bearing a couple of bulky bundles. Cantemir called:

"Hey, Kirk!"

"Hello, George," said Salazar. "Isn't your helper the one who acted as guide when we saw the makutos?"

"The same one. When I told Tootsie how good she was, she switched her allegiance from Chief Yaamo's government to me."

"Flattery will get you everywhere, even among Kooks," said Salazar. "But what brings you here?"

"You do, kid."

"What do you mean?"

"I got word from Henderson that you've put your old man up to interfering in my business. I won't stand for that, get me?"

"I merely told my father what had happened. How's your strike going?"

"Settled, though it cost us a bag of frick and put us a sixtnight behind schedule. The boys are ready to start cutting, and I won't let any loony idealist like you interfere! By God, I mean that! You academics are all alike. Never having had to meet a payroll, you think you're somehow above such shitty considerations as money. You'd let this useless wilderness—" He made a sweeping gesture, "—go to waste just so you can sit around admiring it and writing books about it that nobody reads. Well, we practical businessmen will have something to say about *that*!"

Keeping a hand near his pistol, Salazar shrugged. "Don't see how I could interfere with anybody out here in the boonies with nobody but Choku yonder."

"Well, I'm not underestimating you. You're too damned smart under that wimpy manner. So I'm giving you an order."

"Who the hell are you to order me—"

"Shut up! I'm talking. You're to fold up your tent and get the fuck out of here inside of twenty-four hours or face the consequences. Understand?"

Choku quietly emerged from the tent, carrying Salazar's rifle. The Kook did not raise the gun, and Cantemir ignored him.

"I hear you," said Salazar. "I shall have to think about it. I need at least a few days to finish my work here."

"I said twenty-four hours, and that's what I mean. Consider yourself lucky I don't order you out right this minute. I'm doing you a favor by giving you a day's notice, because you helped me through that fence when the makutos chased us. But after that you're on your own. You dreamers think you've got a right to step in and ruin a man's lawful, legitimate business just because it don't fit some woolly-minded theory, like you was a bunch of those spirits the Kooks here believe in." He paused for breath. "Okay, then, you'll be out of here and off the goddamn mountain tomorrow, or else. That's what I came to say, and I've said it. Winnow me?"

"I understand," said Salazar. "Is there anything else?"

"Hell, no." Cantemir looked around. "Haven't you killed anything yet?"

"I'm not here to hunt but to solve a scientific problem."

Cantemir snorted. "A real man would rather hunt any day. You ought to see the heads of game on the walls of my house. Don't forget, now!"

Cantemir turned and walked back down the trail. The Kook Fetutsi followed him out of sight.

Salazar gazed after the departing lumberman. "Choku, what would you do in my situation?"

"Sir, I could never be in your situation. Our institutions, at least in the civilized human nations, have arrangements for resolving such conflicts before they threaten the peace."

"I know, I know. Your governments are all bureaucratic dictatorships, under an overgrown civil service promoted by competitive examination. We tried that on Terra several times, but the system always broke down."

"Perhaps, sir, human beings are more inherently suited to our forms of government than you aliens."

"Maybe so." After a silence Salazar said: "I certainly am not fain to let that bravo chase me out with my work half-done. I suppose a 'real man,' as he is always saying, would have shot him in the back as he turned away to go down the trail, buried the body, and said nothing about the visit. I fear I am not up to that sort of—well, there is an English word, 'swashbuckling,' that fits.

"I must remember to wear this pistol; I keep forgetting. I have heard of a retired Kukulcanian philosopher who lives up on the mountain. Maybe he could make useful suggestions. He was called—damn, the name slips my mind."

"Doctor Seisen, sir?"

"That is it. Know you where on the mountain he is? Sungara is virtually a range in itself."

"Nay, sir. But if you will wait a few hours, methinks I can learn from some of Miss Ritter's human attendants."

After dark, Choku returned with a crude map. "Luckily I found Juugats, who keeps up with everything. You see, sir, if we go west another itikron and a half, we shall come upon another passage through the nanshins. Then, if we go up slope for another half itikron, Doctor Seisen's abode should be in sight."

"Fine! I shall set out the first thing tomorrow morning. That will still give us time to pack up if we decide to cut and run. Please pack supplies for a one-day, one-man hike, with enough to eat for lunch, and supper, too, in case I am delayed in returning."

"But sir! Surely you do not wish to go to this philosopher alone! I should be with you."

"No, I shall go alone. Someone must guard the camp; if we left it vacant, the kusis would rip it to shreds and the insectoids would clean up anything left."

Choku's neck spines rippled in the equivalent of a sigh.

"If you are determined, sir. If you carry the rifle, pray leave the pistol with me."

"I will make do with the pistol."

Remembering that Seisen demanded a book as a consultation fee, Salazar looked over his library. He chose O'Sullivan's *The Trees of Sunga* as the volume he would miss least and sat up rereading it to get the most he could from it before giving it up.

VI.

The Hermit Seisen

Beneath a brilliant morning sun, the retired philosopher's hut of fieldstone and bamboolike canes stood on the barren slope above the nanshin belt. Adjacent rose another building, from the look of which Salazar took to be a barn. Around the buildings grew a scanty cover of herbs, patches of grassoid, and a few stunted trees. The mountain breeze whistled; Kirk Salazar pulled his bush jacket out of his pack.

One of the big, predatory zutas of the heights, two meters in wingspan, swooped over the hut, veered away, and flapped off around the curve of the mountain. Noting the pattern of black spots on the pale yellow wings, Salazar automatically thought: *Nycteraetus romeroi*.

To one side of the hut a pair of neat, precise rectangles of cultivated ground stood out from the waste. One showed bare, turned earth; the other bore a crop of some edible Kukulcanian vegetable.

Salazar saw no signs of life outside the hut. He warily circled the structure with a hand on his pistol. He felt a little foolish, as if he were acting the part of a hero in a Terran entertainment strip dealing with one of Terra's wilder historical periods, such as the western United States in the nineteenth century. But, he told himself, he would feel even sillier if he walked into an ambush unaware.

* * *

Still finding no sign of life, Salazar stopped before the door, a rough but solid piece of homemade carpentry. When he pushed, the door creaked open. Within, a voice spoke in Feënzuo:

"Do you aliens invade each other's houses uninvited?"

"I b-beg your pardon," said Salazar, mortified and flustered.

"I am not a judge about to sentence you for an offense and so have no authority to pardon you," said the voice. "If you wish to enter, simply say so."

"May I please come in?"

"You may."

Entering, Salazar took in the scanty furnishings. The walls were lined with sagging shelves on which stood rows and rows of books. One wall bore books of the Terran codex type. On the other stood rows of Kukulcanian books: boxed, glass-fronted scrolls on a pair of spindles, with little cranks for reeling the scroll past the window. The Terran book of the codex type had only begun to be accepted by the Kooks.

More books rose in piles like stalagmites from the floor. On the far side stood an aged male Kook holding a book in his claws so that the daylight through the window illuminated it.

This Kook differed from most in that he wore eyeglasses strapped over his reptilian, turtle-beaked muzzle. Kukulcanians did not suffer the progressive presbyopia that afflicted middle-aged and elderly Terrans, but extreme age nevertheless reduced their visual acuity. Kooks were wearing spectacles when Terrans first landed on the planet, but only a handful out of a thousand used them. Salazar said:

"Are you the philosopher Doctor Seisen?"

"Seisen is the name whereby I am known. As to whether I merit the term 'philosopher,' that depends on which of my colleagues you ask. And you, alien sir?"

Salazar noted that Seisen used the grammatical forms proper for addressing a person of lower social status.

Salazar identified himself and explained his reason for being on Mount Sungara. "But I understand that you require a book as a consulting fee. May I give you this?"

He held out the paperback copy of O'Sullivan. Seisen took it, turned it over, and handed it back, saying:

"I already have a copy hereof. If, however, you will promise to send me a copy of your doctoral thesis when completed, I will essay to answer your questions. I guarantee naught."

"I promise."

"Let us hope that your promise is more valid than those of most of your conspecifics. What is your problem?"

Salazar had been on his feet for two hours, but when he looked around, he saw no chair. Remembering the Kooks' indifference to what a Terran would deem comfort, he asked:

"May I sit on the floor?"

"By all means," said Seisen, squatting with his back against the wall.

Salazar then gave an account of his difficulties with George Cantemir and the Adriana Company. "And so," he concluded, "Cantemir has given me—" He glanced at his poignet "—until six hours hence, or four jakin by your system. If I am still there at the end of that time, he will shoot me dead unless I am lucky enough to shoot him first."

"And what would you of me, alien?" grated Seisen.

"I wish to know: Should I flee or fight?" Salazar felt as if he were taking the orals for his doctorate before a peculiarly hostile faculty committee.

Seisen spoke in the rhythmic, rhyming speech that Kooks used for oratory, their most advanced art. "How can I answer that? If you flee, you will run a minor risk, at the cost of completion of your thesis. If you remain, you will run a much larger risk for the sake of making sure of your thesis. I cannot evaluate those risks from the scanty information I have.

"Were I a meteorologist, belike I could tell you that there was a chance, let us say one in nine, that it will rain here tomorrow. But such a statement would be based upon data gathered on this site over years or, better yet, on the reports of a network of weather observers scattered over southern Sunga. I am told that you Terrans have such networks on your home planet, but we do not. For one thing, the metaphysical beliefs of us human beings forbid the use of electrical communications."

Salazar: "No offense intended, Doctor, but do you really believe that such technology destroys ancestral spirits?"

"I lack many beliefs that to my fellow human beings are self-evident. Whereas we human beings are far less given to imposing our beliefs on others under threat of torture and death than your peculiar species, I often deem it inexpedient to disclose my incredulity." Seisen's neck spines signaled amusement. He continued:

"As to your particular problem, all I can say is that your chances of major disaster were greater if you stayed; how much greater I have no grounds for estimating. The question of whether the added risk be worth the goal of completing your work, you alone can answer. Are you willing to retreat and write your thesis on the basis of what you have already learned?"

"Nay," said Salazar. "I have what we Terrans call a phobia against leaving a task only partly done. Those who admire this quality call it 'determination'; those who dislike it term it 'obstinacy.' Moreover, I suspect that the committee that reviews my thesis will be especially tough to avoid the appearance of letting the son of an eminent scientist get away with sloppy work.

"Can you not think of any other course to avoid both horns of this—this . . ." Salazar fumbled for the Kukulcanian equivalent of "dilemma."

"Of this diremma, you mean to say," Seisen interpolated. "That is a Terran term which civilized human tongues have adopted because it fills a semantic need hitherto unmet. But as to your last question, unfortunately nay. If it be any consolation, know that in the long run it makes little difference. Whichever course you choose, you and Mr. Cantemir will somehow manage to ruin your respective prospects. I believe your English tongue has a colloquialism that translates as 'to copulate up' or 'to fertilize up' the situation."

"Why take you so pessimistic a view of Terran activities?" asked Salazar.

"I do so because you are Terrans, and I have some knowledge of Terran history." Seisen waved a claw at the shelves of books. "For example, are you familiar with a work beginning—" He dropped into English. "—thus: 'In ze second century of ze Christian Era, ze Empire of Rome comprehended ze fairest part of ze eart', and ze most civirized portion of mankind'?"

"Nay, sir. But the literature of Terran history is so vast that no one Terran, even with our extended life span, could master it even if he spent all his waking hours reading. What is the answer, pray?"

Seisen returned to Feënzuo. "The quotation is from a work entitled *Ze Decrine and Fawr of ze Roman Empire* by one Edward Gibbon. It teems with examples of the amazing Terran aptitude for 'copulating up' even the most rational and beneficent plans out of personal egotism and lust for immediate gratification."

"Do you Kukulcanians do better?"

"Indeed we do. When you know our history as well as I know yours, you will be able to compare them. Our wars are trivial affairs compared to yours, which on several occasions embroiled half the planet. The first, in fact, occurred during the lifetime of this Edward Gibbon; it was called the Seven Years' War."

"From all I have read," said Salazar, "you Kukulcanians are not so peaceful as all that. My own father fought against the Chosha nomads when they tried to conquer the Feënzuo Empire.''

''Ah, but Chief Kampai had not bothered anybody, save perhaps some of his rival nomad chiefs, until one of those Terran busybodies called 'missionaries' converted him to a set of widespread Terran supernatural beliefs, a creed about as factually based as our idea that electricity destroys ancestral spirits. Kampai forthwith adapted this dogma to a justification for his own self-aggrandizement.

''One of our advantages resides in the fact that when one group of us human beings venerates a particular spirit, either local or ancestral, that group feels no compulsion to force others to revere the same entity. The same applies to theories of politics or economics. Our view is: If our neighbors wish not to embrace our superior beliefs, so much the worse for them! Belief in spirits other than the ancestral ones, like the planetary spirit Metasu, has largely disappeared from the mainland. Whether this will in the long run prove favorable or otherwise to social order remains to be seen.''

''You make your kind sound wholly rational, like thinking machines,'' said Salazar.

''That was an exaggeration. Amongst us, also, individuals display less socially useful traits, such as caprice, mischief, egomania, and *sahides*—''

''Excuse me, sir, but what was that last word?''

''I said *sahides*, for which I believe the English equivalent would be something like 'cratomania'—an obsessive passion for ruling others. The female Terran who leads the Kashanite community is an example.

''The frequency and extent of these deviations are far less than amongst Terrans, as far as I can judge from your records. In fact, I have heard Terrans refer to us human beings as 'all alike' and 'an insufferably dull, stodgy lot.' If that be the price of being a reasoning being, it is one that I am glad to pay.''

''Well,'' said Salazar, ''our flightiness, as you call it, has put us far ahead of you technologically in only a fraction of the time it took you to reach your present level from hunting-gathering primitivism. That is how we Terrans took to space and discovered you long before you were ready to discover us.''

''And what practical good has that done you on your native planet?''

''We have learned much, which the more enlightened amongst us think a worthy end in itself. We have eliminated many diseases and lengthened the life span.''

''And have thus,'' said Seisen, ''painfully overcrowded your planet. We are more realistic, preferring slower but surer and less destructive progress.''

''What, think you, accounts for these differences between our respective species?'' asked Salazar.

''For one thing,'' said Seisen, ''until recent advances in your medical science lengthened your lives, your natural life spans were much shorter than ours. Since your primitive ancestors—those which survived the perils of infancy, that is—had lifetimes of a mere thirty or forty of your years to look forward to, they were under no evolutionary pressure to develop longer outlooks. Hence the troubles caused by unchecked population growth, beyond the carrying capacity of the planet, and the consequent degradation of the environment. If a Terran was warned of the catastrophic consequences of some policy an octoquadrate of years later, his response was: 'What of it? I shall be dead then, anyway!'

''Another difference arises from the very quality that has put you so far ahead technologically: your fondness for tinkering and experimenting. The result was that having mastered fire and simple toolmaking and learned to survive in inhospitable climates, you went on and on, from one technological triumph to another, since each invention opened the way to others. So invention became a self-propelled social engine, ever accelerating.

''Hence your species crossed the border into civilization whilst most of you were still ruled by the same primitive instincts and drives that propelled you when you first came down from the trees and became terrestrial, pack-hunting omnivores. I refer to your persistent tribalism, feuding, rapacity, competitiveness, and vindictiveness. One might say that you reached civilization millions of years before you had evolved to the point of making good use thereof. Imagine a crew of kusis of one of the larger species in charge of one of our railroads and you will grasp the idea!

"In fact, even the allegedly civilized members of your species retain many traits and habits that we deem barbaric. Such, for instance, is the hunting of wild animals to eat their flesh, like that group of hunters who came through lately, killing some animals to collect their heads as trophies and others to devour. We human beings confine our meat eating to the flesh of domesticated species. Only the barbarous, nomadic Choshas gather heads to demonstrate their virility.

"I understand that Terrans were outraged some years ago when the Choshas' high chief, Kampai, hung heads of Terrans as well as those of human beings from the trophy pole before his tent. But I learn from my reading that this was once a common practice amongst some Terran tribes, such as the Celts.

"Finally, having through your science eliminated most of the natural checks on population growth, you failed to control your increase until recently, when the population of your world became so packed as to be insupportable, even by the most advanced methods of food production. This failure aggravated all your other difficulties and made some insoluble; hence millions died of starvation. You seem never to have grasped the fact that a system that works well for a hundred individuals will probably work badly for a thousand and break down completely for a million.

"Your philosophers long ago warned of this threat, but one of them said something like 'We learn from history that people do not learn from history.' Most of you still obeyed the ancient drive to increase the group at all costs to enable you to defeat any hostile neighboring tribe.''

Salazar said: ''I gather that you do not much like Terrans.''

Seisen gave a reptilian hiss, and his forked tongue flicked pinkly out and back. ''What has 'liking' to do with it? We human beings like what is good for us and dislike the reverse. You aliens, contrariwise, form a multitude of likes and dislikes on what appear to us frivolous bases, such as another's clothes, expression, or general appearance.

''Methinks I understand how this came about. In the course of evolution you Terrans developed highly mobile facial features, capable of expressing emotions, as the movement of our neck spines functions with us. To assist the integration of primitive Terrans into bands and tribes, you developed amongst yourselves an acute sensitivity to nonverbal signals, especially facial expressions, gestures, and tones of voice. Whereas the movement of our cervical spines is largely independent of conscious control, a Terran can learn to send deceptive signals to a conspecific, as by smiling when really angry or hostile. Hence, you are much abler deceivers than we.''

It occurred to Salazar that he had suffered all his life from inability to read other Terrans' nonverbal signals. He had once been told that he was ''blind to body language.'' Now all he said was: ''Pray continue.''

''This facility,'' said Seisen as if he were addressing a class at a Kookish institution of higher learning, ''while it speeds intraspecies communication, also makes you vulnerable to deception. I know something of your religious or occult fads and crazes, like that which your conspecific Ritter is now managing in place of the defunct Rostam Kashani. From our point of view you are an incredibly credulous lot. I have read accounts of Terran leaders who led their peoples in attempts to conquer the entire planet. The result was the death of millions and the downfall of the leader and his faction, but they never seem to learn. They have not matured mentally since the days when a primitive chief sent his tribesmen against a foe by assuring them that by a magical spell he had made them invulnerable to the enemy's arrows or bullets.

"The would-be leader need only master the complexities of Terran voice tone, expression, gesture, and so on, and he can persuade your masses that their planet is flat, or hollow with them on the inside. When the masses are free to choose a leader by an honest secret vote, they may pick a murderous maniac, provided that he can control their emotions by these artifices of voice and gesture. Or they may elect a blockhead of a public entertainer with no qualifications but a superficial charm.

"But to return to your remark about liking Terrans, to me you are all merely exotic organisms, like intelligent jutens or kudzais. I daresay that if one of you served me for years as a faithful servant or an affectionate pet, I might develop a certain fondness therefor. For the species as a whole, however, I entertain adverse feelings because of the threat that it poses to our civilization. If you would keep to other planets, I could contemplate your existence with equanimity."

"There may be truth in what you say," Salazar admitted. "What would you suggest to ameliorate this situation?"

Seisen's neck spines signaled a shrug. "From my human point of view, the only effective cure is for all you aliens to board your spaceships and return to Terra—or at least to other planets with a viable atmosphere and no intelligent other species. I am quite sure that you will not do that. In fact, I shall be pleasantly surprised if those of your United Settlements, in consequence of your growth in numbers, do not soon begin to seize lands outside those granted to you by the Empress Datsimuju. This happened repeatedly on Terra when a society with better weapons encountered another less advanced in the destructive arts. The latest manifestation of the Terran compulsion to conquer and subdue is unfolding right now near the Kashanite community.''

"You mean Cantemir's lumbering project?''

"Cantemir is but a servant of the Terran Dumfries, who remains in Sungecho but governs the enterprise through subordinates. Know you this alien?''

"I have met him,'' said Salazar. "I came from Oöi on the same ship with him.''

"What can you tell me of him?''

"He is very fat—''

"Nay, nay, not his physical characteristics but his plans and motivations.''

"As to that, I can only tell you what I have guessed from many small bits of information and rumor. He is what we Terrans used to call a 'natalist,' convinced that Terrans should multiply as fast as nature allows. Since Terra has no space for any more people, Terrans should conquer and exploit other planets to give the species room for indefinite expansion.''

"He will not find the conquest of our world easy,'' said Seisen with a flick of his forked tongue.

"Do you foresee an interspecies war?'' asked Salazar with a sinking feeling. "On Terra, international relations have been brought under fair control. We have not had a real war for a century. How do you Kukulcanians propose to ward off the attacks of Dumfries's followers and others of that kind?''

"Our governments—at least, all the more civilized ones in this hemisphere—worry about this. For centuries we have discouraged inventive progress in weapons. Now, as you see, our governments reward the human being who can design a gun to shoot faster. We do not yet have your zappers, but if superstitious objections to electrical machinery can be overcome, we shall doubtless attain ray weapons, too. If the situation demands, we shall eventually get to atomic explosives, of which Terrans have told us.''

"Many Terrans would be glad to leave well enough

alone," said Salazar, "even if it meant curbing their drive to reproduce."

"Some, perhaps, but with a species as variable as yours, 'some' never means 'all.' The rest, by and large, are still motivated by the instincts and urges that drove you millions of years ago, when your forebears, then on a level with the larger members of our kusi order, began to tame fire and chip stones for tools. So I look forward with foreboding. Ask any of the peoples conquered during the great European expansion, from years fifteen hundred to nineteen hundred of your common era, such as the natives of the American continents.

"Another matter. Besides Terrans' obvious motivations for wishing to snatch our world from us—tribal loyalty, personal gain, and lust for power—there is another, which I understand not. To many Terrans the mere sight of a human being provokes revulsion and horror. They call us by the term 'repti',' as if a repti' were a peculiarly loathsome creature. I am told that they use it to one another as a term of opprobrium. Why is this? What is a repti'?"

Salazar said: "The word is 'reptile.' The Terran animal kingdom includes a class called Reptilia. Some reptiles, called 'snakes,' resemble your boshiya but without legs, and some of these snakes are venomous. Hence, the species evolved a susceptibility as infants to a phobia against snakes. They likewise easily develop phobias against other things that in primitive times were sources of danger: high places, dark enclosures, torrents, thunderstorms, and strangers.

"Not all reptiles are dangerous; in fact, only a small fraction of the kinds of snakes are venomous. But our primitive ancestors made no fine distinctions amongst them, and fear of snakes is often extended to other reptiles. Since your species resembles Terran reptiles, they inherit some of that irrational fear."

"Thank you," said Seisen. "You have clarified a mystery. I need not belabor my point about Terrans' primitive minds.''

Salazar rose stiffly. "And I thank you, honorable sir. I must return to my base to prepare defenses.''

Seisen also rose. "I regret that I could not advise you more precisely.'' Salazar noted that the philosopher now used the forms due a social equal. "That is the fault not of my failing mental powers but of the amorphous nature of the problem. May your health remain good, and forget not to send me a copy of your thesis!''

Back at camp, as the sun sank in golden and crimson glory, Salazar returned. He had picked up the armful of canes he had dropped the day before. Choku asked:

"Honorable boss, what was the upshot? Stay we or flee we?''

"I could not get a firm answer. Seisen would like all Terrans off the planet. Since he cannot bring that about, he is not unhappy to see us shooting each other. It means that our army will be weaker if war breaks about between your species and mine.''

"That is a most unwelcome thought, sir. I enjoy Terrans, ever up to something new and interesting. One never knows what crazy thing they will do next.''

"Perhaps, but that solves our problem not. Has there been any sign of Cantemir? Our time was up an hour ago.''

"Nay, sir; no sign.''

"Perhaps he was bluffing, though I should not care to wager my life on the chance. Anyway, it is too late to set out for Amoen tonight. We must go wait and watch. With two guns, we should be a match for him. How good are you with the rifle?''

"Terran guns are awkward for us human beings, being designed to fit your arms and shoulders. But I can hit an alien-sized target with one nine times out of ten at fifty rokuu.''

Not having completely mastered Kukulcanian measures, Salazar was not sure what degree of accuracy those words implied, but they sounded impressive. "Very well, you shall take the first watch. There is no cover nearby for him to sneak up on us—except the nanshins, and they have their own security system."

The next morning there was still no sign of Cantemir. Salazar's confidence mounted; it must have been a bluff, after all. He should, of course, keep his guard up.

Midmorning saw Salazar sitting before his tent, holding a large clasp knife and carving whistles out of lengths of cane. On his lap lay a copy of Vladovich's *Elements of Physics*, open to the section on sound. He carved whistles of various lengths. As he finished each, he blew it at the phonometer and noted the frequency recorded by the instrument. He wrote the figure on a tag, attached the tag to the whistle, and compared the length of the whistle with that given on the table in Vladovich for a vibrating air column of that frequency, corrected for barometric pressure.

At last he blew a faint, shrill toot on whistle number 23, which sounded rather like the sounds made by the kusis.

"Mr. Sarasara!" said Choku. "Look about you!"

Salazar was startled to discover that he was sitting in a semicircle of nine kusis, staring up. As he looked up, they thrust out their forelimbs in begging gestures.

"They want mittas," said Choku. "Shall I give?"

"Get one and throw it as far as you can."

Choku ducked into the tent, came out with a mitta nut, and threw. But missile throwing was not a native Kukulcanian skill—perhaps, Terran biologists speculated, because their fingers ended in claws. The nut flew up and landed in Salazar's lap.

At once a rush of kusis swarmed up Salazar's trouser legs in a scramble for the nut. Their talons pierced the fabric and the skin beneath it. The two who reached his lap first both tried to grab the nut and ended by clawing and biting each other.

With thirty-odd kilos of kusi clinging to him and more contesting for a hold, Salazar struggled to his feet, knocking off one scaly tormentor after another and yelling:

"Get out, you little sons of bitches!"

Choku dashed forward, shouting *"Katai! Katai!"* With one clawed reptilian foot doubled into a fist, he kicked a kusi aside. Another he picked up and threw a dozen meters away.

As Salazar rose, the mitta nut fell to the ground. A kusi snatched it and ran. All the others abandoned Salazar to run after it; the whole troop vanished into the nanshins.

"Whew!" said Salazar. "You are better at throwing kusis, Choku, than at throwing nuts. Did they get aught else?"

"I think not, sir. But you bleed! You must needs care for your wounds."

"You bleed, also."

"The animal I kicked snapped at me. It is naught. But you aliens are such delicate creatures that you had better nurse your injuries at once."

"Mere scratches, but you are right."

The next day Salazar set out with a pocketful of whistles in his bush jacket. The nearby kusis, noting his purposeful approach, fled with barks and whistles. Choku followed with the rifle.

Salazar stopped close to the nearest nanshin and fumbled for a whistle. Its tag read "19,800 Hz," meaning 19,800 hertz, or cycles per second. He blew a thin, high note. The nanshin did not respond.

He tried another at 18,700, another at 21,500, and another at 22,100. The last of those he could not hear at all, but in any case none affected the nanshin.

When he came to whistle number 23, rated at 20,200,

which was 20.2 kilohertz, the tree seemed to shiver. All the nearer needles bent away from him as if the whistle, instead of sending out a shrill sound, was blowing a mighty blast of air at the tree.

"O Choku!" he called. "Methinks we have it!"

"That is good," said the Kook. "What now?"

"I will see if the sound really protects me as I move through these trees. Have you the baking soda where we can quickly get at it in case this fails to work?"

"Aye, honorable sir. It is with the salt and the cleaning powder. But perhaps you were well advised to don your goggles lest you get the venom in your eyes."

Goggled and blowing whistle number 23, Salazar plunged in between the nearest nanshin and its neighbors. As he brushed through the interlacing branches, each tree's needles bent away and none sprayed any liquid. When he emerged triumphant, Choku said to him:

"Sir, permit me to point out that you got a drop of venom on your right trouser leg."

"Careless tree," growled Salazar.

"You had better give me those trousers to wash at once, ere the venom eat a hole in them."

"They will hold until we reach the tent." Salazar strode out feeling, for almost the first time in his life, something of a hero.

"Sir!" cried Choku. "Behold yonder!"

Before the tent a pair of kusis appeared, dragging the bag of mitta nuts. Each grasped a corner of the bag with one forelimb and hopped along on the remaining three limbs.

"Get out of here!" yelled Salazar, breaking into a run. Behind him he heard the snick of the bolt as Choku armed the rifle. He shouted back: "Shoot not! If you do, we shall never see them again!"

Choku did not shoot. The sight of the rifle raised and pointed sent the two kusis on a mad dash for shelter. They made wide sweeps about Salazar and his assistant and took off in grand parabolic leaps to the lower branches of the nanshins.

"Damn it!" said Salazar. "That venom begins to hurt! Where is the baking soda?"

He ran to the tent. Choku snatched up the half-empty bag of nuts and followed.

"Hell's bells!" shouted Salazar in English; then in Sungao: "How shall we find anything?"

The interior of the tent looked as if a tornado had passed through it. All the smaller equipment was scattered about. Choku said:

"I am sure, sir, that the kusis threw things around in seeking the bag of mittas. I do not believe that much is broken. If you will permit me to return the objects to their previous order—"

"Metasu, damn it, get the baking soda! This is painful!"

A frantic search turned up the can of baking soda. Salazar shed his pants, in the right leg of which a hole the diameter of a finger now appeared.

An hour later Salazar, now wearing shorts, sat before his tent with a baking-soda poultice strapped to his leg. He examined the bag of mittas, now less than half-full.

"The little bastards," he grumbled, "ate all they could. When they were stuffed full, they started to haul the bag away for future use.

"The bright side is that if you Kukulcanians were to disappear, the kusis might evolve into a civilized species in a few million years. They are clever enough."

"That is a comforting thought, sir, in case we human beings commit the same errors as, I am told, Terrans have done. I hear that they once came close to blowing themselves clean off their planet. Whither go you, sir?"

Salazar had risen. "This damned leg hurts too much for me to keep my mind on studies. I think I will stroll over to the nanshins to see if our kusi friends are about. Could you get me some mittas?"

Choku produced a fistful of nuts, which Salazar pocketed. He sauntered toward the nanshin forest, looking sharply into the shadowy branches.

A kusi appeared, clutching a branch with three prehensile limbs while making begging gestures with the fourth. It chirped at Salazar, who tossed it a mitta. The kusi caught the nut in flight and devoured it.

"Good!" mused Salazar. "You could evolve into a ball player. But if you evolve along the lines of the Kooks, you won't want to play games, save as infants. They look upon Terran golf and tennis as childish. An admirable species in many ways, but not much fun—a deadly dull lot when you get to know them."

The afternoon calm was shattered by the thunderous boom of a fourteen-millimeter big-game rifle. A severed branch over Salazar's head fell past him. The kusi fled with a shriek.

Salazar spun. In front of his tent stood George Cantemir with the rifle at his shoulder. Behind him Choku was locked in a struggle with Cantemir's Kook retainer, Fetutsi. Salazar realized that with all the events of the past two days, he had forgotten to go armed at all times. Rifle and pistol were both in the tent.

Panic seized him. He could not shoot back at Cantemir; he had nothing to throw but mittas. To charge Cantemir would be suicide. He was furious with himself for letting his guard down; that was just the sort of unworldly behavior for which "practical businessmen" like Cantemir scorned intellectuals like Kirk Salazar.

Cantemir had not given up; he was merely late. If Salazar plunged into the nanshin forest, he would be sprayed unless he used his neutralizing whistle, which hung on a string around his neck. It took him but seconds to snatch it out, blow, and plunge into the long-needled foliage.

"Hey!" yelled Cantemir; then came another gunshot. Salazar did not know where the bullet went; he was too busy whistling the deadly needles away from himself. Cantemir shouted:

"That won't do you no good!"

Salazar plunged on. The heavy rifle boomed again. At least, thought Salazar, the gun was not one of those military firearms, with a clip holding scores of rounds, that sprayed bullets as a hose does water.

As he plunged on, sounds implied that Cantemir was pursuing him into the nanshins. He must, thought Salazar, believe that because I can do it, he can, too. Again the gun banged. When Salazar looked back, he could not discern a human form. In full daylight, he thought, he might be able to see Cantemir outlined against the open area between the forest and the tent, but now the sun was low and obscured by clouds.

He pushed on away from the camp, then halted to listen, still blowing his whistle. He could faintly hear Cantemir's thrashing progress through the vegetation. He heard a distant cry: "Where the hell are you, Kirk? Come out where I can see you!"

He must think me even stupider than I am, thought Salazar. Then came another cry:

"Hey, Tootsie! The goddamn trees are pissing on me! Ouch! That hurts! Yeow! Help! I'm burning up! Help!"

Still more faintly came the voice of Fetutsi: "Close eyes! Close eyes! I get you!" There were crashings, with Fetutsi crying: "No worry! Hold hand! Forrow me!"

The sounds diminished to silence. Salazar, still playing his whistle, cautiously felt his way back towards the camp. The sun was just setting.

At length he saw light through the trees. Step by step he approached, determined not to give Cantemir another free shot at him. A metallic gleam caught his eye; it was Cantemir's rifle. Salazar stooped to pick it up, then reflected that it must be smeared with venom. He wiped the barrel near the muzzle with paper handkerchiefs, wrapped more around the barrel, and picked up the gun where he had wrapped it.

When he could discern the terrain between the forest and the tent, he saw no sign of his visitors. Choku had resumed his preparation of dinner as if nothing had happened. At the edge of the wood Salazar called:

"O Choku!"

The Kook looked up. "Yea, honorable boss?"

"Have they gone?"

"Aye, sir. When Mr. Cantemir called for help, Fetutsi let go of me and ran to the woods. As soon as she released me, I got your rifle from the tent. Then she came out of the woods leading Mr. Cantemir. His clothes were spotted with drops of venom, and he was shouting in pain."

"Were there any more words between you and them?"

"The onnifa asked if I had any baking soda. I told her no, I did not. She knew from the movement of my spines that I lied to her, but I had the gun and they did not. Mr. Cantemir had lost his, which I see you have recovered.

"Meseemed we should reserve our baking soda for ourselves. She appealed to me as a fellow human being, so at last I gave her a worn-out towel to wipe the venom from her scales. It was beginning to pain her, even though we human beings have tougher hides than you fragile aliens.

"All the time Mr. Cantemir kept shouting for her to get him back to the lumber camp. The last I saw, she was trotting back towards the Amoen trail with Mr. Cantemir bouncing on her shoulder and screaming curses."

"You didn't think to shoot them?"

Choku's spines registered amazement. "Nay indeed, sir. Why, that would have been *illegal*!"

"You mean it is legal for Cantemir to shoot me but not for you to shoot him?"

"You are entirely correct, sir. The Chiefly Council enacts the laws that govern the actions of us human beings toward one another. High Chief Yaamo's covenants with you aliens have the force of law. These laws forbid us to slay an alien save to prevent a crime against oneself or another human being. It dictates not the acts of Terrans with one another, any more than your Terran laws, upon your native planet, regulate the number of kills that one of your beasts of prey may take in a given time.

"That is doubtless why Fetutsi was given the task of preventing me from interfering while Mr. Cantemir undertook to shoot you. He could not hand her the gun and command her to slay you while he essayed to stop me from interfering. She would have refused to perform an illegal act, since you were not threatening her with any crime. On the other hand, it would have been lawful for me to slay him to stop his destroying my source of income—namely you, sir. Of course, I could bring a charge of assault against Fetutsi, albeit I doubt that such litigation were worthwhile."

Salazar grumbled. "You Kukulcanians are all born lawyers. How about dinner?"

VII.

The Sungecho Library

Two days later Salazar was testing his whistles and tap-ing the sounds and actions of the kusis. The animals now ignored him save occasionally to beg for mittas. He was working at the edge of the nanshin forest, dictating into his recorder, when a new sound brought him about. From around the curve of the mountain came the chug of a Kukulcanian steam engine. Salazar called:

"O Choku!"

"Aye, sir?"

"Will you please go see what is making that noise?" Salazar pointed.

"Aye, aye, sir!" Choku took off at a trot.

A half hour later Choku reported: "It is Mr. Cante-mir's people, sir. They have widened the trail and brought up a big machine, preparing to cut the nanshins."

"Is Cantemir bossing them? I should expect him to be still laid up from the nanshin venom."

"I did not see Mr. Cantemir, sir. Mr. Mahasingh seems to have taken command."

"I had better look into this. Choku, get the rifle—mine, not Cantemir's cannon."

They set out eastward. Less than a kilometer away, Salazar sighted a huge, smoke-belching tractor combine with a power saw mounted on a boom in front. A cou-ple of the Adriana Company's lumberjacks ran the ma-

133

chine, while others, in long hooded slickers and goggles, prepared to haul away logs with the help of several kyuumeis.

The saw shrieked, and a nanshin crashed down. Lumberjacks with hoods fastened close waded into the brush and began to trim the limbs from the trunk with axes. Salazar thought that with Terran power saws and other tree-harvesting machinery he had read about, they could have done the whole job in a fraction of the time; but such devices were impractical on a technologically backward planet.

Salazar sighted a man who stood out from the rest, mounted on a juten. This man directed operations. He seemed very tall, not wearing a slicker, and had a lavender scarf wound around his head. As Salazar approached, he saw that the man was very dark of skin, with a curly black beard reaching halfway down his chest. Salazar tilted back his head to say:

"Mr. Mahasingh?"

"I am he," rumbled the man in a deep bass, looking down with large, liquid brown eyes. "And you, I think, are that Mr. Salazar, the young scientist who gave Mr. Cantemir grief."

"Served him right for trying to kill me. How is he?"

"He was recovering well from the nanshin stings under the care of his Kook helper and was expected to suffer nothing worse than pockmarks. But then something went wrong, and he sustained a most unfortunate injury."

"What happened? Break a leg?"

"Please, Mr. Salazar, the nature of the injury is one I should be embarrassed to discuss. In any case, I shall send him down the line to Doctor Deyssel."

"And you're going ahead with clear-cutting?"

"As you see."

Salazar thought that possibly this man might be more open to an appeal to principles than would a tough opportunist like Cantemir. "Are you aware of the damage your project will do to the whole environmental area, destroying the local biota?''

"I know what opponents of our project say. But the decision is for the directors of the Adriana Company, not for me.''

"Doesn't your conscience bother you?''

"It might, save that when one works among Europeans—''

"Hold it!'' Salazar broke in. "I'm no European. I was born on Kukulcan, as was my mother; my father was a native of the United States of America, on Terra.''

Mahasingh waved the objection away with a smile. "With persons of my ethnic background, 'European' means anyone of the pale-skinned branch of the Caucasoid race. I belong to the dark-skinned branch, as do Iranians and Arabs. To continue, when one works among Europeans, one must to some extent follow their ways.

"The question did bother me for a time. But I prayed to Shiv, and the god instructed me to take Arjuna's advice. Arjuna advised Krishna, when Krishna found himself playing the rôle of a warrior, to be the best warrior he could. Likewise, since the cosmic wheel has placed me in the rôle of lumber-camp foreman, I should try to be the best lumber-camp foreman I could. So I shall strive to obey that counsel.'' Mahasingh turned his head. "Ah, our talented neighbor, Miss Ritter, has come to investigate the noise. Good morning, Supreme Choraga!''

"Hello. Hello, Kirk,'' said Alexis Ritter. She wore rough work clothes, as she had in the climb to the crater. "I see what you're up to. Kirk, go away! I have something private to discuss with Dhan.''

"Okay, your ineffable Highness,'' growled Salazar. He walked to where Choku stood waiting and whispered: "Lag behind and hear what you can.'' Then Salazar strolled away toward his own camp.

He had nearly reached the tent when Choku caught up with him. "Honorable boss! As you suspected, they talked freely within my hearing, as if I could not understand English. Miss Ritter asked whether Mr. Mahasingh would carry out Mr. Cantemir's offer to pay her money at the end of the operation if she kept her people from interfering. Mr. Mahasingh replied that he knew naught of any such agreement and would certainly not pay on his own initiative out of company funds. If she had a complaint against the company, she should take it up with their higher officers.

"As you know, sir, Miss Ritter is a Terran of what you aliens term a fiery temper. She eloquently cursed Mr. Mahasingh and might have physically assaulted him, despite his great size, had not Mr. Mahasingh been out of reach up on his juten. As it was, she threatened him with dire consequences ere walking off."

Salazar could not help a sly grin. "Lunchtime!"

In the afternoon the sky clouded over. The shriek of the saw from the Adriana Company's timber harvester seemed to disturb the kusis, for they all disappeared from Salazar's neighborhood. After watching for an hour in vain, Salazar gave up and decided to write up his notes.

He was sitting in his camp chair, swatting arthropods and working on a sheaf of papers, when sounds from the lumbering operation drew his attention. The shriek of the saw fell silent, and there were human mob sounds, with yells and curses.

"O Choku!" he called. "I must see this! Come on and fetch the rifle!"

He set out at a jog towards the sounds. Soon they came in sight of the timber harvester. A mob of men, naked but for sandals, and a few women similarly clad were attacking Mahasingh's lumberjacks with crude clubs and cudgels cut from saplings and branches. The lumberjacks fought back with axes and brush knives. One lumberjack lay on the ground, moving slightly, while a couple of wounded cultists hobbled away from the battlefield.

Each lumberjack was assailed by one or more naked

cultists, threatening him with their clubs but not daring to get within reach of his steel. Although the cultists outnumbered the lumberjacks, the disparity in weapons resulted in a standoff, neither party yet doing much more than superficial harm to the other.

Then came Mahasingh's deep voice, bellowing orders. The foreman appeared on the trail from the lumber camp, mounted on his juten and waving a pistol. Behind him came the rest of the lumber crew, brandishing tools from axes and shovels down to wrenches.

The pistol banged twice, and a Kashanite screamed and fell. As the lumberjacks charged, the other Kashanites fled with howls of terror. They bolted into the nearest woods, crashing through the brush, and soon all had vanished save the one shot. Salazar heard a lumberjack say:

"He's dead, all right."

Mahasingh commanded: "Carry him back to the camp. I shall send a message to Miss Ritter asking if she wishes us to bury him or to send someone to take him back to their village."

"I think not that we should be welcome here," said Salazar. "Let us return to our own camp."

When Choku was rustling up dinner, the Kook asked: "What propose you to do now, sir?"

"I think I must go back to Sungecho. I want to try out an idea that Miss Dikranian suggested."

Choku's neck spines wriggled in a pleased way. "I shall be glad to see civilization—of a sort—again."

"I am sorry, but you cannot come. Someone must stay to guard the tent and my materials. You know what the kusis might do if given a chance."

Choku's bristles signaled a sigh. "Very well, sir. I believe the next express runs the day after tomorrow."

The rising sun was thrusting golden lances through the surrounding trees when Salazar, patting a yawn, walked along the platform of the Amoen station. Up ahead, the locomotive gave rhythmic sighs and the firekook shoveled. On the southbound trip of the Unriu Express, the soft-fare car, tolerable by Terrans, was directly behind the locomotive. The railroadkooks had reversed the locomotive on the Y track north of the station but saw no reason to reverse the entire train.

Salazar flashed his ticket at Conductor Zuiha and climbed into the car with the roof. He had just made himself comfortable when sounds of altercation led him to look out. On the platform stood two Kooks bearing a stretcher with folding legs. On the stretcher lay a bulky form.

Apart from this trio, the female Kook was arguing with Zuiha. Salazar could not make out the symbols painted on the female's scales with naked eyes, but his binoculars identified her as Cantemir's attendant, Fetutsi. He guessed that the swaddled figure on the stretcher was George Cantemir.

At last the conductor gave in and waved the group aboard. The two Kooks set down the stretcher in the aisle at the forward end of the car. Then they left the soft-fare car and climbed on the next flatcar, where other Kooks had gathered. Fetutsi said in Sungao:

"Good morning, Mr. Sarasara. May you enjoy robust health!"

"Hail, Fetutsi," said Salazar. "May you stay healthy also. I hear that your boss has had some sort of accident."

A growl from beneath the blankets answered: "You're goddamn right I came down with an accident! If Doc Deyssel can't fix it, I may have to go back to the mainland. They've got a couple of decent plastic surgeons in Harrison. You okay, Kirk?"

"I guess so. What happened to you, George?"

Cantemir peeled back the blanket from his face, which had lost its beard. His round, ruddy visage now bore a host of large red spots like carbuncles. "Goddamned if

I'll tell you! Nothing personal, understand, but it's the kind of thing you don't care to talk about.''

"Okay," said Salazar, pulling out a book.

No more Terrans appeared. Zuiha blew his whistle and beat his gong, and the engineer tooted. The locomotive sent up a cumulus of smoke and vapor, and the wheels began to turn. The Unriu Express clanked and rattled out of the station. On the first of the flatcars after the soft-fare car, the Kook passengers stood clutching the rail or sat on the bare planks. The remaining flatcar was piled with boxes and bundles beneath a tarpaulin.

Salazar found that the noise of the train made it hard to concentrate on the difference between *Ulmoides syngata* and *Ulmoides styrax* in O'Sullivan's *Trees of Sunga*. When the grade ascended, the roar of the nearby locomotive drowned out the other sounds. When it ran downhill, the conductor and his trainkooks wound the wheels controlling the hand brakes, with a rattle of chains and a screech of brake shoes. Now and then coal smoke billowed into the car, making Salazar cough and wipe his eyes. Up forward, Fetutsi tenderly succored Cantemir.

When a section of straight track with a slight downgrade allowed the noise to quiet, Salazar was surprised to hear a human sniffle. He glanced forward. Sure enough, tears were rolling down Cantemir's spotted face. Forgetting for a moment that Cantemir had tried to murder him, Salazar called:

"Are you all right, George?"

"Oh, sure," groaned Cantemir. "Kirk, tell me just one goddamn thing. How did you frog around in the nanshins without getting holes in you the way I did?"

Salazar grinned and moved to Cantemir's end of the car. He pulled his reed whistle out from beneath his shirt and blew a shrill blast.

"Huh?" said Cantemir. "What'd you do?"

"Didn't you hear?"

"Naw, not a goddamn thing."

"You see, this is a whistle with an extremely high pitch. I can barely hear it. You're older, and as a man gets older, he loses hearing in the highest registers."

Too late, Salazar realized that his knowledge of how to disarm the trees was a secret he should certainly not have shared with a man like Cantemir. To cover his blunder he asked:

"What did the venom do to you, George?"

"Not so much as it might have. I was wearing a good thick outfit, and the venom ate it full of holes like a sieve. Some got through to my skin and ate holes in it, too. Luckily, Tootsie got me back to the camp and dumped me in a tub of water with a whole boxful of baking soda. They tell me it'll leave a lot of pockmarks."

"Then what's the other injury?"

"Yeah. You got to understand that Tootsie has been awful good to me, better than any of my wives and girlfriends ever was. So when she got the last of the goo scrubbed off and I was feeling pretty good, she sat me down for a serious talk.

"She explained the customs as regard an onnifa and the master she's sworn allegiance to, kind of like some medieval knighthood thing. One requirement is that the master, whenever he isn't with his legal wife, is supposed to screw the onnifa instead. The Kook wives don't mind, since this is an ancient custom, and you know how set the Kooks are in their ways. So now she wanted to know when we were going to do our thing.

"Well, Tootsie may not be exactly the kind of gal you'd lay in Erika's place in Suvarov. She's not even human. I've heard of screwing sheep but never a lizard or a crocodile. On the other hand, I hadn't had any for a month, and my poor neglected whang was driving me crazy. And what real man would pass up a chance for a free fuck? So I thought, let's try it!

"What I didn't know was that she-Kooks have scales inside as well as out, and what happened to my poor joystick was what happens to a pencil in a pencil sharpener. Damn near skinned the poor thing.''

"How is it now?''

"Hurts like hell every time the train jerks. If you had a shot of whiskey in your baggage . . .''

"Okay,'' said Salazar, digging out his flask. Cantemir drank, coughed, and drank some more. When he handed back the flask, a shake told Salazar that the flask was empty. He had brought it to ameliorate boresome stretches of the trip, but he would have to find another anodyne.

The liquor abated Cantemir's reticence, and the lumberman began to blubber again. "My God, just think of it! Never to be able to fuck again!''

"Won't you?'' asked Salazar.

"Dunno. Have to see if the docs back in Henderson can patch me up enough to function. But oh, just think of it!'' The voice rose to a wail, and the tears came in a stream. "Never—to—fuck—again!''

"You'd be all through some day, anyway,'' said Salazar. "If you can still do it at a hundred and fifty, you're remarkable.''

"But goddamn it, I'm not yet fifty!'' screamed Cantemir. "It's not fair!''

"Who said life was fair? If it were, you'd have dissolved in nanshin juice for trying to kill me.''

"And if it was, I wouldn't have missed the one good shot I had. Serve you right for interfering with a man's legitimate living, all for the sake of some seven-legged bug or slimy reptile that shouldn't have been let live in the first place!''

"All you businessmen think of is a quick profit and getting out. You'd turn the whole planet into a lifeless desert if you thought there was frick to be made.''

"Oh, go stick your head in a bucket of water and forget to take it out!''

Fetutsi intervened in Sungao: "Mr. Sarasara, you must not disturb my patient!''

"I shall be glad not to," said Salazar stiffly, returning to his seat and O'Sullivan's book.

Although the trip downward was faster than the ascent from Sungecho, Salazar found time heavy on his hands. It occurred to him that if Cantemir ordered Fetutsi to do him violence, as by throwing him off the train or tearing him limb from limb, she just might obey despite any Kook regulations. He wished he had the faithful Choku along, but he could not have done that and also secured his camp.

In Choku's absence, Salazar got the pistol out of his baggage and clipped the holster to his belt. Watching from his stretcher, Cantemir called:

"Hey, Kirk! Was you thinking of bumping me off? I warn you: If you get me, Tootsie'll get you!"

"Relax, George," said Salazar. "It was along here that you set up an ambush. Just dumb luck your lumberjacks didn't kill half the zuta watchers."

"Wrong, as usual! In the first place, nobody was supposed to kill nobody, just take prisoners. In the second, it wasn't my doing, but a cockamamy idea by Mahasingh. I raised hell with him when I found out. So you don't need the gun now."

"Says you! I'll keep it handy, thanks."

"If the stupid mounted gang on jutens hadn't gotten lost and arrived late, they'd have scooped up the lot of you before you could organize resistance."

Salazar wondered which one, Cantemir or Mahasingh, had truly ordered the ambush, but that was probably another insoluble mystery with which he would have to live.

The locomotive whistled; brakes squealed. Conductor Zuiha put his head in the door to announce: "Station Torimas!"

The train pulled up alongside another, a way freight waiting on a siding. A vendor walked along the platform, crying:

"Moriin! Moriin!"

Salazar leaned out and bought a bladder of bumble-berry wine. It proved neither very good nor very bad. Cantemir called:

"Hey, Kirk! Let's not stay mad at each other all the time just because we don't agree on everything. I admit I shot at you, but it wasn't anything personal."

Salazar grinned. "Seems to me that shooting a man is about as personal as you can get. What you're hinting at, with all the subtlety of a charging tseturen, is that you'd like a drink of this, wouldn't you?"

"Well—ah—now that you mention it, that would be nice."

"Okay." Salazar dug a pair of cups out of his bag. "You are without doubt the crassest son of a bitch I've ever met."

"Huh? What's that mean?"

"Nothing personal." Salazar poured. "And this isn't exactly what Omar had in mind when he wondered what the vintners bought one-half so precious as the stuff they sold. But here you are."

"Who's Omar?"

"Never mind. Drink up!"

As Salazar munched his luncheon sandwich, Cantemir continued: "That guy who sold us the moriin wine reminds me I once had a girlfriend named Maureen, between my third and fourth wives. Her face was nothing much, but she had the prettiest tits."

Between the bites that Fetutsi fed him, Cantemir rambled on about the women with whom he had been intimate. The supply seemed endless. While Salazar had a normal, healthy young man's interest in such matters, he found that even sex could become a bore. Under the endless concatenation of copulations, he found his eyelids growing heavy.

"Excuse me, George," he said. "I'm taking a nap." While he worked his bag into position as a pillow, Cantemir droned on. The last Salazar heard before dropping off was:

". . . and then there was Yasmini, who had the longest orgasms I ever knew . . ."

The train pulled into Sungecho at sunset, only an hour late. Fetutsi rounded up her Kook stretcher bearers to carry Cantemir off to Doctor Deyssel. Watching the procession march away, Salazar remembered Seisen's comment on the incorrigible Terran talent for "copulating up" their enterprises. He took a room at Levontin's Paradise Palace.

The next morning Salazar was waiting at the door of the library when it opened at ten hours by Terran clocks. The librarian said:

"Good morning. Aren't you Kirk Salazar, Professor Salazar's son?"

"Why, yes. How did you know?"

"I heard you had come to Sunga and was watching for you. Your father's a big name around here since his work on Fort Yayoi."

Salazar asked for tapes of religious and occult movements and cults. She handed him a stack, and he said: "Thanks. Now, where's your viewing room?"

He spent the day running tapes of noted Terran religious and occult leaders. He was particularly struck by the histrionics of the Reverend Alma Schindler Ferguson, who for a quarter century had moved multitudes of fanatical followers in North America. Her downfall had begun when she was caught in a love nest on Sea Island, Georgia, by the wife of her love of the moment, a media liaison officer for her Church of the Holy Pentagram.

The tape showed her standing on a plinth upon a stage. Black velvet covered all, while a spotlight picked out the priestess, in a white, gauzy, glittery gown like that worn by Alexis Ritter for her rituals. When Mrs. Ferguson raised her arms, the gown spread like the wings of a zuta. The costume, the voice, and the mannerisms were so much like those of Alexis that Salazar had an uneasy feeling that Alexis was a second coming of Mrs. Ferguson, dead for a century. More likely, he decided, Alexis had studied this same tape.

By the end of Mrs. Ferguson's sermon, in spite of himself, Salazar had the feeling of being revealed the inmost secrets of the cosmos, although he could not recall anything definite that she had said. It was all gauzy figures of speech interlarded with snatches of pseudoscience and commonplace truisms such as "Is it not true, my children, that people whom you like are likely to like you in return?" But she spoke with such verve and conviction as to give the impression that nobody had ever thought that thought before.

Perhaps, Salazar thought, Yaamo had by now heard that he, Salazar, was opposing the Adriana Company's project, even if not very effectively so far. Since the plan promised Yaamo revenue for developing the island, he would want to get Salazar out of the way. Possibilities ran from murder to a modest bribe. He wondered how big a bribe it would take to subvert his own rectitude. More likely he ought to worry about being arrested, tried, and sentenced to a flogging that, while merely painful to a Kook, was fatal to a Terran.

Salazar, however, had all his father's stubbornness in carrying through, despite hell or high water, a task he had started. Since Yaamo's police might be looking for him, they would probably try the railroad. When they learned that he had come down on the express the day before, they would next go to Levontin's to see if he had taken quarters there. Before he left the library, Salazar asked:

"Have you any books on the religions and philosophies of India?"

"You mean full-sized printed books, not cards or reels?"

"Yes."

The librarian consulted her file and came up with Panikkar's *Creeds and Cults of the S.A.F.* The initials stood for "South Asian Federation."

"May I borrow it?" he asked.

"Have you a card?"

"No. I haven't been here long enough to get one."

The librarian produced a form, which Salazar filled out. As she handed over the book, she said:

"I wouldn't let anyone else have one of our real books if he didn't have a local address. We don't have many, and they're hard to get from Henderson. But since you're a Salazar, I can make an exception."

Salazar thanked her and walked out with the book. In his rectilinear mind he would never have thought of using family connections to bend the rules, which made him angry when someone else did it. But, he supposed, as the human species was addicted to the practice, he might as well take advantage of it. A microfiche card would have been more convenient than this half-kilo tome, but he had no viewer on Mount Sungara to read it by.

Salazar walked past Mao Dai's retsuraan to Levontin's, swiveling his eyes for signs of being followed. On the waterfront street he passed Terrans and an occasional Kook. One of the latter was a policeman with rifle and painted-on badges. Salazar said: *"Wangabon!"* meaning "Good afternoon."

"Wangabon!" the Kook replied with a nod, while his neck bristles rippled in a pleased way. Doubtless, thought Salazar, he was pleased at being treated with ordinary courtesy by an alien. The cop otherwise showed no interest in stopping or questioning Salazar, who inferred that no order had yet gone out to watch or detain him.

When Salazar entered Levontin's, he found the lobby full of tourists, Suvarovians from the rumble of Russian consonants. Levontin came up saying:

"Mr. Salazar! I did not expect you or I would have saved you a room."

"Mean you're full?"

"Ah, yes! Today the *Ijumo* dumped all these Russkies on me, twice as many as I was prepared for! So Olga and I sleep on pads in my office, having given up our own room.''

''Has anyone been asking after me?''

''No, sir, no one.''

''Well, can you find another pallet for me? I can sleep on the lobby floor if I must.''

''I don't think . . .''

''What's this?'' said Hilbert Ritter, who had materialized out of the crowd with Suzette on his arm. ''Hello, Kirk; what are you doing here?''

''Library research. What are *you* doing here? I thought you'd gone back to Oöi with the other Patelians.''

Ritter replied, ''We thought we'd make one more try at talking sense into Alexis. So we turned the Patelians over to Igor, who was out of the clinic with his arm in a sling, and saw them off. We figured we'd make a quick trip to Amoen and get back in time for the *Ijumo*'s next sailing.

''We got to Amoen and Kashania all right, but as for Alexis, we might as well have argued with a tornado. Then the down train had a breakdown, so we missed the sailing. The *Ijumo* was supposed to go out again tomorrow, but Captain Oyodo says that's canceled. She'll be laid up a few days while he fixes some engine trouble. Anyway, you needn't sleep on the floor just anywhere. We have an inflatable mattress you can use in our room.''

''Thanks; glad to,'' said Salazar.

''Had dinner yet?'' asked Ritter. ''No? We were setting out for Mao Dai's; figured we'd beat the crowd.''

''Let me stow my gear and wash up,'' said Salazar, ''and I shall be with you.''

At Mao Dai's, the kyuumeis plodded in their eternal circle, giving the outer ring of the restaurant floor its slow, creaking rotation. Salazar turned in his holstered pistol at the check room in obedience to a sign in Reformed English:

PEITRƎNZ WIL PLIIZ CEK WEPƎNZ IN KLOUK RUUM

They crossed the inner, stationary ring of flooring to
the outer, rotating ring as Mao ceremoniously ushered
Salazar and the Ritters to a table for four on the rotating
ring. Salazar looked around, memorizing the decor lest,
if he had to visit the gents', he have trouble finding his
place coming back because that place would have moved.

Things loosened up after two rounds of drinks. Hilbert
Ritter talked of his research into the caste system of
Sunga. Suzette talked of notes she was making for a book
on the dialects of Feënzuo. Salazar told of the ethology
of the stump-tailed kusis.

While they talked, the annular dining room filled with
Slavic tourists. Then Mao Dai appeared with the vast,
globular form of the Reverend Valentine Dumfries. Mao
said:

"I hope you will not mind letting Mr. Dumfries have
your vacant seat. All others are taken."

"No-o, of course not," said Hilbert Ritter. "Sit down,
Reverend."

"Thank you," said Dumfries, carefully lowering his
bulk. Salazar had visions of the chair's collapsing or of
Dumfries's getting wedged between the chair arms and
requiring carpentry to release him.

"Well, now," said Dumfries, "isn't it nice to be all
together peacefully? Mr. Salazar, I understand you have
just come down from Mount Sungara. What is going on
there? I have just come from Doctor Deyssel's clinic,
where I visited poor Cantemir. He tells an extraordinary
story of which I cannot make sense."

"He ordered me off the mountain," said Salazar, "and
when I refused to go, he tried to murder me."

"Oh, not really! I cannot believe that George—"

"If shooting at someone with a big-game rifle isn't
attempted murder, I don't know what is."

"That's not what he says at all. Furthermore, he claims

that you tied him up and mutilated his private parts in a most indecent manner.''

''Not true,'' said Salazar. ''He tried to scr—excuse me, to have carnal intercourse with his female Kook helper and got his *membrum virile* skinned.''

''Incredible! I know that George is a bit wild at times, but I must use such instruments as the Demiurge puts into my hand. I fear things at the Adriana camp have gotten into a mess, and I shall have to go north to take personal command. As you see, I am hardly built for roughing it in the outback.'' He gave a little self-deprecating laugh.

''Still,'' continued Dumfries, ''I cannot believe that George would so flagrantly violate the strictures of the Terran Bible. In eighteenth Leviticus congress with beasts is forbidden, and in twentieth death is prescribed for the offense.''

''Didn't know you were a Judeo-Christian fundamentalist,'' said Salazar.

''I am not, young man! But we take the Bible as our point of departure, interpreting its messages in the light of modern knowledge, just as we do with the Holy Qur'ān. The passages I cited were put there for sound, scientific, modern reasons.''

''What's that?''

''Why, any sexual act in which there is no possibility of conception is a waste of precious seed. This applies equally to contraception, masturbation, sodomy, and bestiality. He who indulges in any of these fails in his duty to increase the tribe—nowadays, the whole human species—to enable it to rule the universe.''

''Why should anyone want to rule the universe? My fellow primates have enough trouble ruling much smaller units, like a city or a nation.''

''It is the destiny laid upon us by the Supreme God!'' roared Dumfries, causing diners at other tables to look around. He glowered at Salazar from under his bushy brows. ''Cantemir tells me that you and the other Patelians are environmentalist fanatics who want to preserve this planet just as it is, in the possession of a race of revolting reptiles. You—''

"Who's revolting?" Salazar interrupted. "The Kooks are sentient beings like us, and their moral standards are at least as high as ours. They have nothing like the local underworld for which Sungecho is notorious.''

"A reptile is a reptile," boomed Dumfries, whose delivery had become that of an orator haranguing thousands. "In addition to siding with these soulless lower animals against your own kind, you pursue some ridiculous ideal of freezing everything to immobility, as in fairy tales. You would stop all change and progress so you can study and admire a static picture forever, like a habitat group in a museum. But life is full of inevitable ch— Oh, I *am* sorry!''

A sweeping gesture by Dumfries had knocked over his glass of unfermented bumbleberry juice. While Mao Dai's well-drilled waiters mopped up the spillage and changed the tablecloth, Salazar used the interval to marshal his thoughts. At last he said:

"I'm afraid my motives are not quite so purely unselfish. I make my living studying the biota and reporting on it for my doctorate. If your gang ruins it, my work will go for nothing.''

"Have you no loyalty to your own species, man? To any normal human being, a reptile is loathsome, to be slain forthwith. And that includes Kooks!''

"Mere herpetophobia," said Salazar, "which parents implant in their children. Probably goes back to hunting-gathering days, when our naked ancestors couldn't tell a venomous snake from a harmless one.''

"If," retorted Dumfries, "the mere sight of these reptiles does not fill you with horror and revulsion, as it does normal human beings, then you are the victim of some congenital abnormality.''

"You're the one with the irrational phobia, not me," began Salazar, but Ritter broke in:

"Let's not argue who has the most neuroses. A shrink could doubtless find a few loose screws in each. But Reverend Dumfries, what's your ultimate objective? If your people took over Kukulcan, under your natalist doctrine they would soon fill the planet until it was as crowded and superregulated as poor old Terra. No wild country; every square meter devoted to raising food; every action regulated by a vast bureaucracy to make production and consumption match; births controlled by the Genetics Board."

"To get away from that condition is the whole idea," said Dumfries, "by furnishing an escape valve to relieve population pressure! As fast as one alien world becomes crowded, mankind should go on to open up another. In so vast a galaxy there's no danger of running out of habitable worlds in the foreseeable future."

"But your alien worlds," said Salazar, "will then become overcrowded and overregulated in their turn. From all I hear of life on Terra, it's like living in a neat, clean, humane jail, and who wants to spend his life in even the nicest jail? You're trying to turn the whole galaxy into such a jail."

"Besides," added Ritter, "your scheme will not really relieve population pressure, for logistical reasons. The most people you could move to other planets would be thousands per year, but the natural rate of increase on Terra, before the World Federation clamped down on it, was tens of millions a year. So you could never catch up."

"The Supreme God will show us a way," said Dumfries. "He will instruct his Demiurges, who will pass the solution on to us." He wiped his mouth on a napkin and rose. The chair, held to his vast bulk by the encircling arms, rose with him, but he quickly pushed himself free. He said:

"I apologize, but I find that the prospect of eating with a table full of reptile lovers has quite destroyed my appetite. Good night, and may the Demiurge—not this fee-

ble spook Metasu but our own Terran Yahveh or Allah—
grant you wisdom!''

The stout preacher marched out, leaving an embarrassed silence. Dinner arrived.

They were lingering over Mao Dai's desserts and acha
when four rough-looking Terrans appeared on the narrow
stationary ring of flooring inside the revolving floor. They
brandished pistols, saying:

"Stand up everybody, and you won't get hurt!"

"Bozhe moi!" shouted a nearby diner. Cries of alarm
and outrage came from the other tables.

"This ain't a robbery," said the first speaker. "Which
of you is Kirk Salazar?"

Nobody answered. One of the quartet stepped out and
came back dragging Mao Dai's smallest and youngest
waiter. The leader pressed his muzzle against the little
Gueiliner's head. "Now point out Salazar if you don't
want your brains spattered all over the pretty decora-
tions!"

The waiter pointed a trembling finger at Salazar.

"Okay, grab him," said the leader. Two of the quartet
holstered pistols and started for Salazar, who picked up
a chair. The leader fired a warning shot, *bang!* over Salazar's head.

Salazar swung the light chair as if he were going to hit
the nearest gangster over the head, then reversed and
jabbed the man in the belly with the leg. The man doubled up with a grunt, but then the other was upon Salazar. This man, who proved immensely strong, wrenched
away the chair and threw it across the room, where it
smashed into a table setting with a crash of glass and
flatware.

The man got a grip on one of Salazar's arms and
twisted. Salazar kicked, aiming for the crotch, but
missed.

The man released Salazar's arm with one beefy hand
to grab for support because the floor on which they were

struggling seemed to have acquired a sudden slant. The whir and creak of the floor-rotating machinery rose in pitch; mingled with it came the rhythmic crack of whips applied with furious intensity.

Salazar guessed what had happened. Mao or his crew must have hitched up the two spare kyuumeis and speeded up the rotation of the ring-shaped floor bearing the tables. Diners, gangsters, tables, chairs, and everything else slid clattering, crashing, and screaming down the centrifugal slope to the outer wall.

Salazar found his arm free and scrambled up the slope before it became too steep to negotiate. A gangster groped for his ankle, but he kicked free and gained the stationary inner ring.

On the fixed flooring Salazar leapt up, pushed past a gaggle of waiters, dashed to the cloakroom, and snatched his pistol from its hook. He returned to the stationary ring, shouting back at the restaurant personnel:

"Tell them to slow the spin!"

On the stationary ring he watched for his party and the gangsters to come past. As rotation slowed, they appeared. Salazar aimed, saying:

"Hands up, you four!"

"As soon as I—can—stand up," grunted one. As rotation diminished further, another bent and fumbled for his gun amid the wreckage along the outer wall.

Salazar sighted carefully and fired; the man collapsed amid the rubble. Mao Dai said:

"Mr. Salazar, I think you can give these people to us, including the dead one. We will see to it that they disappear without a trace."

"Okay," said Salazar. The Gueiliners seized the three surviving gangsters, twisted their arms, and tied their wrists behind them.

"What you gonna do to us?" said one of the trio, his voice rising in pitch. "We ain't hurt nobody!"

"You'll see," said Salazar.

"You gotta let me get my lawyer!" cried another. "The Settlements Constitution says I got civil rights."

"This isn't the Settlements," said Salazar. "Mr. Mao!"

"Yes, Mr. Salazar?"

"I'm pretty sure these people were hired by the Reverend Dumfries. If you could—ah—persuade them to sign confessions to that effect, the documents might be valuable back in Henderson. Be sure to question them separately so they don't have a chance to cook up a story among them."

Mao smiled. "I think we can obtain satisfactory results, sir."

Back at the inn, as Salazar and the Ritters entered, Ilya Levontin bustled up. "Oh, Mr. Salazar!"

"Yes?"

The innkeeper lowered his voice. "A Kook cop came in while you were at dinner, asking for you. Since you were not yet officially registered, I told him no, *nyet, bù shì,* and he went away."

"What did he want of me?"

"Just to answer some questions, he said. Are you in trouble?"

"Not yet, but maybe soon. Are there any such people around here now?"

"None that I know of, unless one of the Kook kitchen help is in Yaamo's pay."

"Then let me settle my bill now, and don't be surprised if I pull out at an odd hour or looking a bit different from the way I do now. Could the cook make me a sandwich?"

An hour later Salazar had recovered the rest of his baggage from storage and hauled it up to his room. After dinner he went to sleep until awakened by his poignet at midnight.

He got out the costume he had worn for passengers'

night on the *Ijumo*. This consisted of an emerald-green turban, an ankle-length pumpkin-yellow robe, and a long false beard. He rubbed a brown grease pencil on his face and hands until he looked like a native of the Terran tropics, then tied on the beard and the turban. The latter was of a prewound kind with stitching to hold it together. A real turban wearer would scorn it, but Salazar had never mastered the trick of winding a turban so that it would stay wound and not fall apart when the wearer moved.

With his duffel bag on his shoulder, Salazar went quietly down to Levontin's lobby. In this otherwise deserted area, Levontin was talking with a Kook whose authoritative bearing would have identified him as a peace officer even without the symbols painted on his torso. Levontin was saying:

"No, Officer. He came here this afternoon, but he checked out earlier and left. I don't know where he is."

Salazar walked past the pair and out. As he passed, the policeman turned a searching gaze upon him, then looked back to the innkeeper, saying:

"He would not rook rike zat, would he? I have not seen him."

"No, sir, nothing like that. For one thing, he is clean-shaven save for a small mustache."

Salazar headed for the station. He passed another Kook cop outside the inn, but this one hardly looked at him. He walked briskly, fighting down the urge to break into a run. Opposite Mao Dai's revolving restaurant he passed two more Kook policemen on night patrol. He was glad that he had not yielded to the temptation to run.

When at dawn Conductor Zuiha opened the door at the end of the soft-fare car of the Unriu Express, he stared at a bearded, turbaned, long-robed, brown-skinned Terran climbing aboard. The Terran passed over a ticket to Amoen without a word. Zuiha said:

"Never seen Terran in such croze. Where come from?"

"From the spirit plane," said a deep, resonant voice, "to bring enlightenment to my fellow Terrans." The man yawned and rubbed his eyes. Salazar had been trying to sleep on a station bench.

"Could enrighten me, sir?"

"Perchance, after I have dealt with the ignorance of those of my own kind. Forgive me."

The robed one entered the car, sat down, arranged his bag as a pillow, and prepared to sleep.

VIII.

The Prophet
Khushvant Sen

Despite his drowsiness, fear that Yaamo's police would appear to clamp scaly hands upon him kept Salazar alert. After a time, sounds implied that two more Terrans had entered the car. Salazar opened his eyes to slits to see two ordinary-looking Terrans take seats. One flipped a hand toward Salazar, saying:

"*Idhe!*"

The other replied: "*Einai Anatolikos.*"

Salazar thought the language was Greek, of which he did not know enough to speak it. In any case, nothing about these men suggested that their doings concerned him.

At last the Unriu Express stirred to life with a clank of couplings and a rattle of chains. Salazar thought he had dozed for a few minutes, but the jerk of the train awoke him from a frightful dream. Cantemir and Mahasingh had tied him to the tracks and were standing over him, laughing, as the train bore down upon him. Just as the engine reached him, he awoke.

Making sure that the Greek speakers were far enough not to overhear, he began softly dictating into his recorder the sermon he planned to give on Mount Sungara. He worked at this task for hours, now and then erasing

157

a paragraph to reword it. When his eyelids drooped, he dozed, awoke, and worked some more on the sermon. He would have written it out in pencil, but the lurching of the train would have made any handwriting illegible even to the writer.

At Torimas, the Greek speakers got off. Salazar was leaning out to buy another bladder of bumbleberry when he saw another Terran climb aboard. This was the towering, long-bearded Mahasingh, still with a lavender scarf wound around his head. Now Salazar would learn just how effective was his disguise. He sat up, holding his bladder of wine and giving Mahasingh a casual glance.

Making eye contact, Mahasingh halted. He placed his palms together with the fingers pointing up in a prayerful attitude. He nodded over his hands, saying:

"Namasté!"

"Good day, sir," said Salazar in an absentminded way.

Mahasingh's white teeth flashed through the mattress of beard. "Thank you, sir, and a good day to you. If I may take the liberty, I am Dhan Gopal Mahasingh."

"I'm Khushvant Sen," said Salazar. "I have heard of you. What brings you down here from Amoen?"

"I have been ordering supplies for the lumber camp I supervise, since the original supervisor met with an accident. The purchases are piled on the goods van in front."

Salazar said: "Sit down, pray. Who runs the camp in your absence?"

"My second, Hafiz Abdallah. I hope he conducts his office with efficiency and justice."

"Would you like a drop of this wine?"

"Thank you, sir, but I seek merit by abstaining. Now I must devote extra effort to my search to atone for the unfortunate accident of a few days past."

"Yes? Tell me," said Salazar.

"A mob of fanatics, inspired by their priestess, attacked my lumbering crew. To drive them off, I was compelled to shoot an attacker." He sighed gustily. "The path of virtue is hard. Would you believe it, my pursuit of merit drove my wife to leave me despite the fact that our union, celebrated with orthodox Shaivite rites, was supposed to be indissoluble?''

''Too much holiness?''

''Having given up intoxicants, the next logical step was to relinquish the fleshly pleasures of sex. After a few months of this she presented an ultimatum. All my arguments, such as the prospect of promotion in our next incarnations, did no good, and away she went. I hear she has found another husband, which is not difficult on this world with its surplus of men. I only hope that my grievous loss will be made up in my next life.''

''You have my sympathy,'' said Salazar.

''And which facet of the jewel of divine truth do you seek to polish, sir?''

Salazar had been bracing himself for such a question. ''I have evolved my own doctrine, to which I have not yet given a name. I have been influenced by Akbar's *Din Ilahi*.''

Mahasingh frowned. ''These eclectic cults never amount to much. I do not believe Emperor Akbar's syncresis outlasted its promulgator.''

''Ah!'' said Salazar. ''Akbar launched it on Terra, where it had to compete with a host of firmly established ancient traditions. We are on Kukulcan, where a new approach is needed. Whether Trimurti of Allah or Guan Yin concern themselves with events on this world is beyond our limited mortal power to ascertain. In any case, I'm sure Metasu would not tolerate interference—''

''You are sure *who* would not tolerate?''

''Metasu, the planetary spirit, or what the Reverend Dumfries would call the local Demiurge. Neither she nor the local spirit of the island of Sunga, Shiiko, would stand for meddling by spirits from other worlds light-years away.''

Mahasingh mused: ''I have heard the Kooks speak of these spirits, but I have not concerned myself with the locals' barbarian theologies. On the mainland they have no real gods, merely ancestral spirits. Perhaps I ought to give the local beliefs some serious thought. I have always held that the divine truth encompasses all, even though a mortal individual can perceive but a fraction of it—a single facet of a many-faceted jewel. But the locals' facets may be quite as real as my own Shaivite creed.''

Salazar unwrapped his sandwich. While he ate, Mahasingh sat with head bowed and eyes shut, apparently in deep thought. Then Mahasingh raised his head, opened large, brown eyes, and asked: "Mr. Sen, pray tell me, are you from Terra or were you, like me, born on Kukulcan?''

"The latter," mumbled Salazar past a mouthful of sandwich.

"A pity. I had hoped that you could give me a first-hand report on our mother planet."

"Oh?"

"Yes. All my life I have heard of the wonders of that world, its scientific and technological marvels, compared to which we Terrans here lead lives like those of centuries past. It were well worth seeing, although I know better than to take such gadgets and gimmicks very seriously."

"Oh?"

"Yes. Despite the Europeans' boasts of technological leadership, our ancestors in the land of Bharata mastered those material arts thousands of years ago—firearms, flying machines, atomic power, organ transplants, and so on. But they gave them all up in their quest for spiritual perfection.''

"Indeed? I'm sure an ancient Hindu skimmer or zapper would be well worth seeing. By the way, did the former supervisor survive his accident?''

"I don't know," said Mahasingh. "He left for Sungecho a few days ago and may have taken ship for the mainland. All I can say is that he brought it on himself by his flagrant scorn for the virtue of chastity." Mahasingh looked down his long, hooked nose at Salazar and spoke with the pride of a warrior who had routed an army single-handedly. "I have maintained *my* chastity since my wife left me. It was an arduous struggle, but I won!"

"The path of virtue is thorny," said Salazar, trying to match Mahasingh's sanctimony.

"It certainly is. Would you believe it, sir, that woman who rules the Kashanite sect, Alexis Ritter, came to me about some rash offer that Cantemir had made or that she said he made. It was a bribe to keep her cultists from interfering with our work. Naturally I refused, whereupon she offered to throw in my use of her body for carnal purposes! I refused that, too, albeit it was all I could do to keep my baser passions under control. My resistance to her charms so enraged her that she sent her cultists on an idiotic raid against the company's personnel and equipment."

"Very interesting," said Salazar. "Now I must beg you to excuse me; I have work to do."

Salazar was glad to get back to his sermon. On the one hand, he regretted not knowing enough history and other disciplines outside his chosen field to puncture some of Mahasingh's illusions. Life, even extended by modern medicine, was never long enough to learn everything one had to know to cope with conceivable contingencies.

On the other hand, perhaps it was just as well. Mahasingh was not one to be wantonly antagonized, and Salazar's father had lectured him on the common young man's folly of picking arguments for the sake of contention.

On time for once, the Unriu Express pulled into Amoen at dusk. Salazar hunted down Takao's juten stable and rented an animal. Behind the saddle he lashed his bundle of gear.

Salazar hiked up his robe, climbed into the saddle, and commanded, *"Uai!"* The animal lurched to its feet. When Salazar added *"Tettai!"* the juten obediently grasped its rider's ankles with its clawed forefeet as a substitute for Terran stirrups.

Holding the leading rope in one hand, Salazar guided the juten out of the yard by voice commands, along the main street, and up the trail to the top of Mount Sungara.

As the somber green of the forest closed over his head, Salazar speeded up the juten to a lively trot. He thought he was doing famously until the animal took a bend in the trail. A second too late, Salazar realized that the juten had let go of his ankles. Off he went into a bush, losing his turban and tearing his robe.

As if it had not noticed the loss of its rider, the juten trotted on up the trail until Salazar, scrambling out of the bush, yelled: *"Tomai!"*

The beast halted, and the command *"Shtai!"* persuaded it to squat. Battered, Salazar recovered his emerald turban, brushed twigs and leaves from his robe, limped to his beast, and mounted again.

They plodded on up the trail, though at a less ambitious pace. Salazar found that this juten, unless frequently reminded, now and then forgot to grip its rider's ankles, so that Salazar had to grab for the saddle.

"Who you?" said Choku in his rasping version of Terran speech. *"Kto vï? Ni shéi ma?"* He stood before the tent with a lantern in one hand and Salazar's rifle in the other.

"Just your honorable boss," grunted Salazar. *"Shtai!"* The juten squatted, and Salazar climbed painfully off.

"My honorable boss has no such bristles on his face," said Choku in Sungao. "How can you prove that you are he?"

"When I told you that I was going to Sungecho, you wanted to come along and were disappointed when I said you would have to remain here on guard. Then you said you would pack me for two overnight stops, including my pistol. Now, if you will help me to settle in and get this damned beard off, you will see plainly enough who I am."

* * *

When Choku saw Salazar's naked face, stained deep brown on the nose and forehead but pale where the beard had covered it, the ripple of his neck bristles betokened mirth. Salazar grumbled:

"The damned thing itches. Some day I shall grow a real one, like my old man's; it would be less trouble." He attacked the paint with a towel.

"Your robe has been torn, sir," said Choku, holding up the orange-yellow garment. "Let me mend the rip."

"Thank you, but I will do that myself," said Salazar. He had seen examples of Kookish attempts at needlework. Not wearing clothes, the Kooks were hardly out of the Stone Age regarding textiles. They had looms that turned out a coarse, heavy canvaslike fabric for tents, but such skills as sewing, knitting, and embroidery were beyond them. "What have the lumbermen been up to?"

"Yesterday Mr. Mahasingh left the camp and took the train."

"I know; he came back from Torimas with me."

"As soon as he was gone, the Supreme Choraga sent over a number of young females to make sexual advances to the lumberjacks. I have heard how, as a result of you Terrans' habit of covering yourselves with textiles, the sight of an uncovered female arouses the male to a frenzy of lust, like a male porondu in rut.

"The ensuing spectacle confirmed this rumor. The lumbering area was full of nude females, running, screaming, and laughing, pursued by lumberjacks shouting and fumbling with the fastenings of their nether garments. When a lumberjack caught a female, they copulated forthwith on the nearest patch of open ground. It made our yearly Intromission Day ceremonies seem a model of order." The cervical spines rippled mirthfully.

Salazar knew about Intromission Day. Young betrothed couples of Kooks assembled. At a signal the females fled; at another signal the males pursued them. Each female allowed her chosen male to catch her, whereupon they consummated their union on the spot. He asked:

"Did they get any lumbering done?"

"Nay, sir. After all the lumberjacks had taken their turns at the females, someone broke out the camp's supply of liquors, and the crew ended up dead drunk. Many copulated a second time, whilst others cheered them on, shouting and whooping.

"By midafternoon the lumberjacks were lying about in a drunken stupor, along with some of the females. Little by little the latter regained their senses and stole away toward the Kashanite village."

"Did not Mahasingh leave a deputy or substitute in command?"

"I believe he did, sir. I asked one of my fellow human beings, the cook's assistant, Hanatski, about it. He told me that a lumberjack named—ah—something like 'Badara' had been appointed to that post. But Mr. Badara proved as drunken and lustful as the rest. You Terrans—"

Salazar interpreted "Badara" as Choku's attempt to say "Abdallah," whom Mahasingh had mentioned. He said:

"It takes a strong man to be a lumberjack, and these fellows had long been without the normal—ah—outlets."

"Hanatski told me that some such camps have one or more females whose task it is to provide these outlets, as in some nations the onnifas do amongst us. Mr. Cantemir proposed to do likewise, but Mr. Mahasingh vehemently objected on moral grounds."

Salazar yawned. "It will be interesting to see what Mahasingh does with his wild gang. He seems a man of strict moral standards. Now if you can whip me up something to eat, I must get to bed to recover from a taxing journey."

Next morning, Salazar stole up to where he could see the lumber camp from cover. Mahasingh would obviously not get much work from his crew that day. The few lumberjacks in sight sat around with their heads in their hands.

Salazar waited with the patience that wildlife watching had taught him. By midmorning, a few lumberjacks had begun to stir. At last Mahasingh himself appeared at the door of his personal cabin. There were words between him and the workers, not loud enough for Salazar to hear.

Then he heard a feminine cry of "Yoo hoo!" Along the trail from Kashania came a file of young women, nude but for footgear. The somnolent lumberjacks began to rouse themselves and to call back endearments. Salazar felt his own blood stir.

"Ho!" roared Mahasingh. "What are you doing here?"

"Just come to give your boys some fun," said the woman in the lead. "Poor things haven't had any in sixtnights."

"Yeah!" chorused the lumberjacks. "It's about time."

"Abdallah!" yelled Mahasingh. "Where in Nâraka are you?" A squat, black-bearded man with a wrestler's build detached himself from the crowd and answered. The two talked back and forth, but Salazar could not make out the words.

The discussion became heated. At length Abdallah swung a massive fist. Before it landed, Mahasingh shot out ferocious straight punches, one, two, three, to Abdallah's face and body. Abdallah fell backward, rolled over, and slowly climbed to his feet.

"Does anyone else dispute my orders?" roared Mahasingh. "Shapir! You're my subforeman in place of this scum." He indicated Abdallah. "Now back to work, all of you!"

His words were not heeded as the women moved among the lumberjacks, exchanging endearments and suggestive gestures. Some lumberjacks began to unbuckle and unzip.

"Get out, you women!" bellowed Mahasingh. When none heeded his roars, he dashed to a nanshin trunk whence the branches had been trimmed. He picked up a branch by the thick end, where there were no needles. Then he rushed at the visiting women, waving it.

"This will burn holes in your pretty hides!" he shouted.

Shrieking, the women ran away at last, disappearing down the trail. Some lumberjacks looked resentful at having their fun cut short, while others found the sight a cause for laughter.

"Now," said Mahasingh, "get to work!"

The lumberjacks obeyed in a listless, lethargic way. Not much lumbering would be done that day. Salazar backed out of his blind and plodded back to his own camp.

"Choku," said Salazar, "is there a print shop in Amoen?"

"I believe there is, sir. There is a little newspaper published once a sixtnight, printed in Sungao with summaries in English, Russian, and Chinese. So there must be a press to print it. You Terrans always think yourselves so far ahead of us human beings, but we invented printing long before your Mr. Caxton or Mr. Gutembru. Why, sir?"

Salazar handed Choku a sheet of paper. "If you set out now to run to Amoen, when, think you, could you be back?"

"Depending on how long the printing takes, perhaps by tomorrow night."

Choku departed at his tireless trot. Left alone, Salazar fed and exercised his juten. He spent the rest of his time watching kusis and making notes. He was nearing the point where the quirks of kusi behavior proved new to him only at longer and longer intervals. He was nearing the end of his study and would soon have to prepare to return to the mainland.

Still, he was committed to derailing the Adriana Company's project to destroy the nanshin forest. Alexis Ritter had tried to stop it, first by sending a platoon of club-armed naturists to attack the lumberjacks, next by sending some of the shapelier young women to seduce them. Her efforts so far had succeeded only in delaying the Adriana Company's schedule by two days. So Salazar would have to see what he could do. He would begin by choosing a site for manifesting himself as Khushvant Sen.

"Here you are, sir," said Choku, looming out of the darkness. He handed Salazar a stack of sheets of paper. Salazar held one up to the light of the camp fire and read:

SAVE OUR WORLD! HEAR THE PROPHET OF THE GREAT METASU! LEARN THE WISHES OF THE PLANETARY SPIRIT TOWARD US MORTALS!
    The Reverend Sri Khushvant Sen will lecture on the evening of the thirteenth at the meeting place half a kilometer west of the Adriana Company's lumber camp and below the border of the nonvenomous vegetation. He will discourse on the disaster threatening our planet and the measures that must be taken to avert this catastrophe. Time, 2000 Terran standard. Come all! No charge!

"Now," said Salazar, "please tack these fliers up on trees around the lumber camp and the Kashanite village without letting yourself be seen. You will find a box of tacks in my tool chest."
    "Aye, aye, sir," said Choku.

The next two days Salazar and Choku spent preparing their meeting place in the lower forest, felling a few small trees and clearing a space near a large fallen tree trunk. By the evening of the thirteenth day they had it ready.
    People began straggling in before the appointed hour. There were lumberjacks from the Adriana camp and Kashanites from Alexis's village, the latter now more con-

ventionally clad. Some of the audience stood in the rear, while others sat on the ground or on tree trunks.

When the space was full, Salazar, in his Khushvant Sen makeup, mounted the big tree trunk and called out in the deep, oratorical voice he had used in his swami act on the *Ijumo*:

"Peace to all sentient beings! Peace! Peace! Peace!

"My children, the ruling spirit of the planet Kukulcan, Metasu, has sent me amongst you with the most important message that you shall ever receive. Hear and be warned!

"For many years Metasu has observed the deeds of the beings that inhabit her surface. With interest she has seen one species of her planet develop intelligence and go on to acquire speech and writing and to learn to manipulate the material world for its own benefit—in other words, to attain civilization. More recently she has witnessed the coming of another sapient species across the vast, nighted gulfs of interstellar space from a distant world."

He went on and on, mixing history, philosophy, and sheer gibberish: "And now, my dear children, we must resume the triad in unity. We must rectify the noncohesion. We must activate the benisons of our world."

He was careful not to put in too many hard facts, since in studying the art of swaying a Terran assembly he had learned that too much fact killed the audience's emotional reaction. The listeners would become bored and withdraw their attention.

"This means that we must bring the exploitation of the natural world under spiritual control. Some forms of exploitation Metasu views with approval, some with indifference, and some with alarm, such as the project to destroy the nanshin forest. She is horrified by the aliens' plan to rape Mount Sungara of its protective forest cover, warning of irreversible damage to the environment if this continues. If all else fails, she will if need be blow up Mount Sungara, destroying all life on Sunga.

"She has given me a dire warning to pass on. To her

we are as insectoids are to us, and she can stamp us out as easily as we can creeping things. Have you ever watched as a weathered log is placed in a roaring fire and the insectoids scramble out of their burrow in the wood, seeking in vain to escape? And watched them writhe and kick as they died? Such is our situation.''

Groans arose from the audience.

''And so I, unworthy as I am, come amongst you. To carry the word of Metasu's will, I shall require followers. Among these I shall designate those who can most effectively spread Metasu's word.''

Salazar finally ran out of his mixture of conservationism and rhetorical flapdoodle. He ended with ''Peace! Peace! Peace!'' as he slowly lowered his outstretched arms.

Applause spattered. The burly Hafiz Abdallah approached, saying: ''Sri Sen, don't you need someone to collect for you?''

''True, my child. For myself, I can live on wild fruits and drink the dew; but for an organization, more material means are needed. Will you kindly hold this bag open?''

The audience crowded around Abdallah, dropping into the bag United Settlements paper money and polygonal Kukulcanian coins. They called up to Salazar:

''What can we do? What do you want us to do, sir?''

Although he had aimed for this result, Salazar was amazed to find that a carefully rehearsed theatrical performance, delivered in a certain tone of voice with certain gestures, had so devastating an effect on his fellow Terrans. He had slipped in a strong message for saving the nanshins; but even if his speech had consisted entirely of orotund balderdash, it would have had an equal effect and been just as effective in collecting money. In the firelight he caught the sparkle of tears on some of the cheeks of the audience; even the tough-looking Abdallah shed a tear or two.

No wonder, he thought, that throughout human history people had been so easily seduced by grandiloquent rodomontade to follow one pied piper after another, often to their destruction! People whose private personalities were as unlikable as Alexis Ritter's had swayed multitudes, whipping their emotions to a frenzy and sending them off to conquer the world, or save the souls of the heathen, or exterminate some sect, tribe, or other group whom the leader considered evil.

Salazar was appalled to realize that he, too, had this power over his conspecifics. It was an insidious, treacherous, irrational power. He belonged to a species with a built-in and often fatal weakness, to believe anything said to it in a certain emphatic way, in a certain voice, and pushing certain emotional buttons. It worked as surely and as arbitrarily as the magical spells of children's fairy tales.

If he wished, Salazar could drop science, start a cult, make a million, and become a mover and shaker of Kukulcanian civilization, at least of the Terran part of it. He doubted that Kooks, with their robotic, coldly logical minds, would be so easily taken in. But he felt no temptation to follow such a course. Not only did he despise those who took advantage of this human weakness, but the kinds of activities it would entail—endless speeches, committee meetings, and secret intrigues—bored the spots off him.

"Mr. Abdallah!" he said. "Will you kindly take charge of this money? Metasu tells me to appoint you leader of her first group of Terran devotees. Gather them around you and set up an elementary organization, with officers and committees.

"Now I must withdraw to replenish my spiritual forces and to seek guidance from great Metasu for my next step. Good night, all!"

He hopped down from his log and walked to where his juten squatted munching leaves. Hiking up his robe, he commanded the animal to rise and then to head for his camp.

Choku had again been left in camp and was now presumably standing guard. Salazar had not worn his pistol because it would have made his costume bulge betrayingly, and with it under the robe he could probably not have gotten it out fast enough for an emergency.

Beneath the stars and two of Kukulkan's miniature moons, Salazar rode along the nearly treeless strip between the nanshin forest of the upper slope and the lower forest of mixed timber. He had covered half the distance to his camp when the rapid *thud-thud-thud* of a running juten caused him to pull up. As the pursuer drew closer, Salazar saw that the rider wore a hooded topcoat with the hood thrown back. Then he recognized Mahasingh by his head scarf and patriarchal beard.

"Sen!" roared Mahasingh. "Stop! I must talk to you!"

"Well?"

"What in Nâraka are you doing to my work? Half my lumberjacks swear they will cut no more nanshins because they have joined some new conservationist cult!"

Salazar assumed his holy prophet voice. "I merely convey to my children the truths vouchsafed me by the planetary spirit, great Metasu."

"Believe what you like," growled Mahasingh, "but I cannot let you interfere with my duties. Will you go away for good and call off this nonsense?"

"I fear that Metasu, whose voice I am on this material plane, will not permit me to withdraw from my mission of enlightenment."

"Shiv curse you!" bellowed Mahasingh. With one hand he drew his machete or brush knife from its sheath; with the other he grabbed the end of Salazar's prophetic beard, yelling in a voice thick with passion: "We shall see how much message you can utter from a mouth without lungs attached!"

Salazar saw Mahasingh's long arm fly up, swinging the knife for a decapitating blow. By reflex, Salazar jerked violently away. The beard came off with a rending sound, leaving Salazar feeling as if his lower face had been skinned.

"Ow!" he cried, putting a hand to his face. The adhesive with which he had pasted on the beard had been entirely too effective.

Mahasingh sat in his saddle, looking bewilderedly at the beard in his hand and then at the erstwhile Sri Khushvant Sen.

"Salazar!" he gasped. "By Shiv, I'll kill you for this!"

He swung the machete again. But with a yell of *"Katai! Yukki!"* Salazar put his animal into a rapid run. The blade swished through empty air.

Mahasingh's mount pounded after Salazar. Light flashed, and Salazar heard the thunderous bang of Mahasingh's big pistol. Again and again the gun roared. Salazar thought he heard the whistle of a couple of near misses, but the dim light and the jouncing of the jutens made marksmanship impossible. At least, he thought, the shots after the first seemed to be coming from farther away, as if he were gaining on Mahasingh. He could understand this, because their jutens were of about the same size, but Mahasingh must have weighed over half again as much as he, Salazar, did.

The pistol banged once more. This time, through his saddle, Salazar felt the impact of the bullet on his juten. The animal gave a piteous squall and collapsed on the stony ground. Salazar was thrown over its head to land on all fours on the soil before it.

"Ha!" roared Mahasingh, pounding toward him. "Now we shall see!" He pointed the pistol, but it only clicked.

Scrambling up, Salazar glanced around. To his left the downward slope offered little cover for another fifty to a hundred meters, where the outskirts of the lower forest, black in the starlight, began. To his right loomed the dark mass of the nanshins.

Salazar pulled out his whistle. Blowing lustily, he ran

into the venom trees. He pushed his way through, stumbling in the darkness, going to his knees, and scrambling up again, all the while blowing to burst his lungs. He heard the robe tear as it snagged. Then away went the turban.

Fainter and fainter came the yells of Mahasingh, vainly trying to get his juten into the nanshins. Smart animal, thought Salazar.

Then Mahasingh's bellows ceased, and Salazar heard the thrashing and crackle of a man forcing his way into the forest. Salazar plunged on, confident that the nanshins would treat Mahasingh as they had Cantemir.

The noise kept on and on, growing louder. Mahasingh, Salazar thought, was a stalwart man, but surely he did not have a hide proof against nanshin venom! There was nothing to do but struggle on.

Salazar soon emerged into starlight again. Ahead loomed the huge, squatty, conical mass of the volcano summit. Sounds of Mahasingh's approach came louder. Salazar had no weapon, and in any form of hand-to-hand combat the huge Shaivite would pulverize him. He could do nothing but plod on up the slope, hoping that he could wear Mahasingh down to the point of abandoning the chase.

IX.

The Crater Shikawa

Salazar threw away his tattered robe. Jogging on up the slope, he stumbled and fell again, tearing a hole in one trouser knee. His fingers felt a sticky wetness where the rock had gashed his skin. On he plunged.

He climbed and climbed. Now and then the slope became steep enough to require the use of hands. His heart raced and his breath came in gasps, so that betimes he had to stop for his laboring body to catch up. Served him right, he thought, for studying so much as not to leave time for more exercise than he had been taking!

Each time he stopped, he looked back for Mahasingh. But the starlight was too dim to make out a human form among the tumbled rocks and scanty shrubs of the slope behind him.

On he plodded, wondering what to do at the top. If Mahasingh still pursued him, should he skirt the crater and go down the other side, hoping to lose his foe in the nanshin forest? Perhaps he would have been wiser to step aside when he had entered the venom trees at first and quietly wait for Mahasingh to blunder past him.

Perhaps Mahasingh had been fatally stricken by the venom and had never emerged from the nanshins. That was probably too much to hope for, but at least he could take his hike a little more easily.

Then a deep roar killed this hope. Mahasingh shouted

from below: "I see you, Salazar! You cannot escape. I shall do you as you deserve for making me fail in my duty!"

Salazar strained his eyes through the darkness. At last he thought he detected movement. A paler patch in the darkness bobbed among the darker shapes of rock and bush. He resumed his climb, berating himself for letting his pursuer catch him against the night sky.

On and on he climbed. The next time he turned to look, Mahasingh was closer. There was something odd about his appearance, but the starlight was not bright enough for Salazar to tell what it was.

Salazar wondered why Mahasingh had not shot at him again. He was sure that with his longer legs, the giant would catch up with him, barring a broken leg or heart failure. The sheath knife at Salazar's belt had a twenty-centimeter blade, useless against Mahasingh's machete save in a clinch. He ought to have cut himself a club from a branch, but it was too late for that now.

On he went despite racing heart and laboring lungs. He remembered the fable of the rabbit who outran the fox; the fox ran for his dinner, while the rabbit ran for his life. If people had unkindly compared Salazar to a rabbit, he would follow the advice of Arjuna in the Hindu epic and be the best rabbit he could.

As they climbed, the air grew colder and mistier. Salazar scrambled over ridges of glassy black obsidian. He stumbled and fell to his knees again, gouging a cut on his palm from the glassy fractures of the lava.

The slope rounded off to a level. A glance back showed that Mahasingh was still coming. The pursuer shouted:

"I have you now, Salazar!"

The man waved his machete; the mist was too thick to make out details except at close range.

Then a puff of breeze slightly cleared the intervening air. In the starlight Salazar saw that Mahasingh was twelve or fifteen meters behind and a smaller distance below him. He also saw what was different about the man: he was stripped to loincloth, shoes, and the scarf around his head.

Evidently Mahasingh had gotten his clothes full of nanshin venom in the forest and had shed them when he emerged. If Salazar had a chance to plunge into the nanshins again, Mahasingh would follow him thither at his peril.

Salazar ran again, heading for the dim red glow in the mist ahead. Soon he neared the crater, whence came the eternal *swish-swish* of the fountains of lava. If he could lose Mahasingh in this dim, rubescent light . . .

In the pit of Shikawa, the silver-gray scum of cooling lava looked black beneath the night sky, while the zigzag cracks and the ever-rising and falling fountains shone a brilliant orange. Salazar turned to the right and jogged along the circumference, jumping obstacles dimly seen in the lava light and lifting his feet lest he trip. Behind came Mahasingh's labored breathing.

The sound receded; Salazar glanced back. Mahasingh had halted on the edge of the crater, gasping; Salazar did likewise. The biologist remembered his father's joke about the time he had dug on an archaeological site in Durango, on Terra. It got so hot there, said Keith Salazar, that when you saw a coyote chasing a jackrabbit, both were walking.

As if at a signal, both men resumed running. Again they halted and again recommenced. Salazar thought he was nearing the end of his endurance, but he suspected the same of Mahasingh. If the foreman had longer legs, those legs had to carry a lot more weight.

Something about the terrain seemed familiar; then Salazar recognized the embayment in the wall that Alexis had shown him. Of the two points of land embracing the circular void, he had previously stepped out on the farther one.

He glanced back at Mahasingh, coming on fast and

raising the machete. The lava light gleamed redly on the steel.

Salazar measured the distance between the points of rock, noting irregularities. Then he ran out on the nearer point and leapt across the gap. He came down on the farther point, teetered for a desperate second, and recovered his balance. He ran on a few steps and stopped to watch Mahasingh.

Without pause, Mahasingh launched himself on a leap like Salazar's, but he came down just short of the easterly point. His feet skidded off the edge, and with a hoarse cry he slid down the rock face. At the last instant he grabbed the surface of the point. His scarf-wound head remained above the rocky edge, while his arms scrabbled for handholds. Salazar heard the machete clink as it bounced off the rocks below.

Mahasingh grunted as he tried in vain to swing a leg up to get a foothold. Salazar felt around in the lava rock at his feet. He walked toward Mahasingh holding a lump of perhaps two kilos.

"Salazar!" said Mahasingh.

"Well?"

"If you are going to kill me, I beg a favor."

"What?"

"I pray that you crush my skull with that rock in your hand. I have a horror of falling alive into the lava, and I had rather be unconscious when I go on to my next life."

Salazar tossed the rock from hand to hand. "I don't really want to kill anybody. I'm a scientist, not a soldier or a gangster. I did scrag a couple of those lumberjacks you sent to ambush the train—"

"I did not send them! It was all Cantemir's idea. He insisted, against my advice."

"He tells a different story, but I won't try to sort it out now. In fact, I would even help you up if I didn't think you would then do me in."

"I swear by the holy Trimurti to do nothing of the sort!"

"Easy to say, but how do I know?"

"Listen, Salazar. I am through with my job for the Adriana Company. Half my lumberjacks have signed up with Abdallah as members of that new cult you started. The others have begun to drift away. Some, including Shapir, whom I made subforeman in Abdallah's place, have gone to Miss Ritter's village; others have gone back to Sungecho. With the crew I have left, it would take years to harvest the trees.

"I have tried to follow Arjuna's advice and be a good lumber-camp foreman, but I never knew the job would involve me in so many immoral, unethical actions. It has smudged my karma almost beyond repair. If you get me out of here, I shall return to the mainland, leaving Adriana's contract with High Chief Yaamo void. Cantemir never signed it; first, because Yaamo insisted on a delay because of the zuta watchers' objections. Now George is out of the picture, so Dumfries would have to sign it. Even if the company sent another gang, it could never meet the deadlines."

Salazar tossed up and caught the rock while thinking of a reply. Besides the rock, he still had his sheath knife, while Mahasingh had lost his machete, so Salazar could probably hold his own with the man. At last he said:

"All right, I'll try to get you out. But you see this?" He held up the two-kilo lump. "If you make a false move, I'll nail you with this. I was on my college baseball team, so I can kill or cripple you with this at any time."

This was a lie. Salazar had been a failure at sports, but Mahasingh need not know that. Salazar was thankful not to have betraying cervical spines.

"Baseball?" said Mahasingh. "That is the game that Terrans of American or Japanese descent play instead of cricket, is it not? I have seen them make jolly good throws and catches."

"Yes. But before I do anything more, I want some answers. First, why did you stop shooting?"

"Ran out of rounds, and in my haste I forgot to bring an extra clip. Stupid of me."

"Next, how did you get through the nanshins?"

"I was wearing a stout coat, and I drew the hood tightly and used the saddle pad from your juten as a shield. Even so, I got a few drops on my skin. When I came out of the woods, I took off the affected clothes before the venom ate through them."

"Speaking of my juten, who's going to pay the stable in Amoen for the animal?"

Mahasingh thought. "The ethical thing is for me to give you my mount. You will find it squatting where I left it, below the nanshin belt."

"How can I tell it from any other juten if it wanders off?"

"The claw on the third finger of its right hand is missing."

"Lastly, how did you survive such a long, hard climb? You must be quite an athlete."

"I practice harkat-yoga, which keeps me fit. Had I not been winded from the climb, I could easily have made that jump. I say, Mr. Salazar, if you do not do something soon, I shall fall into the lava, anyway. My arms are giving out."

"Hm. But if I give you a hand, you're likely to pull me down with you. Let's see. If I can have that thing around your head, I may be able to brace myself while holding one end, and you hold the other."

"Here you are!" With one hand, Mahasingh snatched off the scarf and tossed it.

Salazar studied the contorted surface. He picked a spot where he could brace both feet against ridges of lava rock while his free hand grasped another projection. He tossed one end of the scarf to Mahasingh and, holding the other end looped around his wrist, lowered himself into a well-braced supine position.

"Okay," he grunted.

Then began a long, sweat-beading struggle. Salazar

hoped the scarf was strong enough. It would be heart-breaking to have the fabric tear and drop Mahasingh into the inferno anyway.

Little by little Mahasingh inched his way up over the apex of the point. At last he could, with an additional pull on the scarf, wriggle one foot up the wall of Shikawa until he could get the toe of his shoe atop the edge. Then, with further grunting and heaving, he worked his way up and over. For an instant he remained on hands and knees, gasping.

Salazar stepped back, away from the edge, holding his rock at the ready. When Mahasingh finally rose to his feet, he made no move toward Salazar. His naked brown chest was scored and bleeding from the lava he had hugged.

"Mr. Salazar," said Mahasingh, "please believe me when I say that I have tried throughout to do the right thing. I admit I let that crass materialist Cantemir lure me into actions that will probably get me incarnated as a worm or a spider. Good night and good-bye, sir!"

Mahasingh walked off into the misty dark. Salazar thought, I could almost like that fellow if he weren't so self-righteous. Then he saw that the other had left his scarf on the rocks. He started to call out but choked off the call. The article might come in handy, so Salazar pocketed it.

For some minutes Salazar remained where he was, breathing hard and thinking. He preferred to see no more of Dhan Gopal Mahasingh. If he went back down the mountain with the man, he would have to keep his rock ready in case Mahasingh should change his mind and try to kill him after all, an act for which he would doubtless have worked out a lofty-sounding self-justification.

True, Mahasingh managed to sound like a high-minded, naively idealistic man trapped by circumstances in the role of villain. But as his father was wont to say, one could never be sure. The sensible thing would be for Salazar to keep his distance.

* * *

A quarter hour later Salazar stood on the base of the point from which he had rescued Mahasingh, taking a last look at Shikawa. The fountains sounded their steady *swish-swish, swish-swish*. Salazar had heard that at intervals the molten lava either rose and spilled out over the top of the mountain or sank down out of sight. In the latter case, pieces of the wall cracked off and went thundering down to the depths.

"Kirk!" barked the commanding voice of Alexis Ritter. "Are you alive? Silly question. Where's Mahasingh? Fall into the crater?"

"No, he's alive and well. At least, he was a few minutes ago, when he started back down the mountain. What are you doing here?"

"Somebody saw Mahasingh chasing Sri Sen, both mounted. I sent my Kooks to investigate, and they found one juten dead of gunshot and another squatting quietly without its rider. A long false beard lay on the ground between them." She looked hard at Salazar. "I thought there was something familiar about that phony prophet. He must have been you in a beard.

"There were also signs that someone had gone through the nanshins, hacking away the branches. So I collected Hatsa and Hagii and came up to see what happened." A wave indicated her rifle-bearing bodyguards, barely visible through the mist. "Your Choku said he would come, too, as soon as he secured your camp. I haven't seen him since. Did you say Mahasingh did *not* fall into Shikawa? And that you didn't push him in?"

"Absolutely not! The last I saw of him, he was headed down slope, scratched and battered but otherwise functional."

"You look a bit scratched and battered, too. But Shiiko shall have her due, never fear!"

Alexis drew her bowie knife and rushed upon Salazar, holding the weapon out in an upward-stabbing position. The action was so unexpected that Salazar was almost caught unaware and stabbed. At the last instant he threw his rock, but between his haste and his lack of skill the missile went wild.

When the relentless woman was almost upon him, he turned, ran three steps to the apex of the point, and leapt.

He came down on the solid ground of the opposite point. Alexis pulled up with a scream of rage.

"What the hell do you think you're doing?" Salazar shouted.

"Fulfilling my contract with Yaamo!" she shouted back; then in Sungao: "Hatsa! Hagii! Seize that man and throw him into the crater!"

As Salazar braced himself to flee, one of the bodyguards said: "We cannot, mistress."

"What mean you, you cannot? I command!"

"We dare not slay Mr. Salazar, because he is also Sri Khushvant Sen, the holy man, who has influence with the planetary spirit Metasu. Besides, it is illegal to attack Terrans save to prevent a crime. He threatens us not at the moment."

"So I was right about your being two-faced!" said Alexis. "It was you, then, who lured a score of my Kashanites away for your silly conservationist cult! Hatsa! Hagii! He is no holy man but a Terran scientist who donned that costume and manner to thwart the Adriana Company's program. He has also disrupted my community and if not stopped will destroy it. Then I shall not be able to continue you in my service. Would not depriving you of your livelihood be a crime which you are entitled to forestall?"

"Now that you put it that way, mistress . . ." said Hagii, scratching his scaly skull.

"Then seize Salazar!"

Hatsa said: "Mistress, you have raised a deep moral problem for us. We must go a little away to reason it out before we can decide whether to obey you."

Both Kooks turned their backs and faded into the mist. Alexis screamed and stamped her foot.

Salazar had a flash of superstitious fancy. What if at that instant some genius loci caused the point of rock to collapse beneath Alexis, dropping her into the lava? There would be a brief flare as her clothing flamed and then, no more Alexis. It would make a fine, dramatic end to her career.

Nothing of the sort happened. Alexis looked around and called: "Hagii! Hatsa! Come back! You can hold him whilst I slay him!" She screamed the bodyguards' names again, without response.

"I'll get you yet!" she shouted at Salazar. She started to run around the embayment, holding her knife at the ready. Salazar ran along the circumference of Shikawa, keeping a comfortable lead on Alexis, who was too plump to be a good runner.

She tripped and fell so that the knife skittered over the rock. At her yell of pain and dismay, Salazar turned back. With three long bounds he reached the knife.

Alexis sat up, nursing a bleeding knee. Tears streamed down her soot-smeared face. "What are you going to do, Kirk? Kill me? Rape me?"

Salazar allowed himself a grin as he picked up the knife. "Neither, my dear. But I'll keep this; you're not to be trusted with weapons."

"Oh, fuck you!" she spat, climbing painfully to her feet. "I'll get even with you yet. Hey, here come my Kooks back." She dropped into Sungao. "What have you twain decided?"

"Mistress," said one, "Hagii and I have concluded that your arguments are sound enough to overbear those against them. So command us and we shall obey."

"Then grab that man!"

Salazar wondered for a flash if he could outrun the Kooks over the tumbled lava in the dark, trusting to their poor night vision to give them as many falls as he would probably incur. He was still limping from the bash he had given his knee.

But the two bodyguards were already upon him with

clawed hands outspread. Salazar gripped Alexis's knife
and aimed an underhand thrust at the nearer Kook, a
long, upward-sweeping lunge that would have disemboweled a Terran opponent. But Kooks' reflexes were faster
than men's. Before Salazar's thrust sank home, a scaly
hand gripped his wrist and stopped his attack. The other
Kook seized his other arm, while the first assailant
twisted the knife out of Salazar's grip. The two then
dragged him toward the edge of the crater. Alexis cried:

"Good-bye, Kirk! No hard feelings!"

Stupid, stupid, he thought, for not starting to run as
soon as he had picked up the knife! He had had a perfectly good chance to escape and had muffed it. Why?
Because of curiosity to see how the Kooks would decide,
because of his intellectual's weakness for reasoning everything out instead of acting instantly by reflex, and because of masculine resentment at being chivied about the
country. He hoped that death in the lava would be quick.

Two strides more brought Salazar and his captors to
the rim. Instead of throwing him over the edge forthwith,
the Kooks halted. One asked:

"Mistress, which is the correct way to perform this
act? With the victim facing the crater or away from it?"

"It matters not," she said. "Go ahead, throw him!"

"Hold!" said another Kookish voice. "Put the honorable Sarasara back on his feet forthwith and release
him or you will be shot!"

Choku was standing over the Kooks' two rifles, which
they had laid down to seize Salazar. He cradled Salazar's
rifle and aimed at Hagii and Hatsa, swinging his muzzle
toward Alexis to include her in the threat. In his free
hand he held a lantern.

"What's all this?" said a deep, powerful voice in English. "Whatever it is, stop it at once!"

The heads of Salazar, Alexis, and the three Kooks
swung to peer into the firelit murk. Out of the mist came
a litter made of lengths of bamboolike cane, like that
wherein Alexis's Kooks had carried Salazar from Amoen

to Kashania thirty-odd days before. Two Kooks bore this litter, one fore and one aft. They halted and put down the carrying chair. Out climbed the bloated body of the Reverend Valentine Dumfries, holding a lantern.

Choku spoke in Sungao: "Sir, this Terran woman and her helpers—"

Dumfries waved a hand. "I don't understand a word. Can you speak English or at least some Terran tongue?"

"A ritter," said Choku. "Zis woman and her Kooks were about to srow Sarasara in crater. He is my boss, so I muss protec' him."

"Is this true, Mr. Salazar?" said Dumfries. He rolled ponderously toward the other group, helping himself along with his crutch-headed walking stick.

"You bet it's true, Reverend." Walking toward Choku, Salazar picked up the two rifles laid down by Alexis's Kooks. He exchanged one with Choku for his own fire-arm, since each weapon had a stock adapted to its own-er's species.

"What about this other?" asked Choku.

"Best gotten rid of," said Salazar. Staying well clear of Alexis and her Kooks, he walked back to the brink and tossed the extra rifle over the edge. There was a brief, sharp crackle as the cartridges in the magazine exploded.

"Ha!" cried one of Alexis's Kooks. "That was my gun! You must pay me for it!"

"So sue me!" said Salazar. "After you tried to give me a bath in lava, I do not think your magistrates will pay you much heed."

"But what on Earth," asked Dumfries, "or on Ku-kulcan, for that matter, possessed Miss Ritter to attempt so foul a deed?"

"Don't believe a word he says!" cried Alexis. "He was trying to push *me* into Shikawa, and my Kooks saved me."

"Well, Mr. Salazar?" asked Dumfries.

"She's got it backward, Reverend. She has a deal with

Chief Yaamo to sacrifice one human being a year by tossing him into Shikawa to propitiate the volcano spirit. If you don't believe me, ask Choku here."

"My honoraber emproyer tess ze truce," said Choku. "Awr us human beings know about zis."

"Don't believe that Kook, either!" cried Alexis. "He would of course stand up for his employer!"

"Then," said Salazar, "ask Miss Ritter's Kooks. If you don't know, Kooks are the cosmos's worst liars; they hardly know how."

"Well, you two?" said Dumfries.

Hagii and Hatsa put their heads together; then Hagii spoke: "Prease, we wir not answer, because it would be disroyar to our emproyer."

"There you are," said Salazar.

"Anyway," Alexis burst out, approaching Dumfries, "neither Kook nor Terran law touches what we do in the outback. And where's that money Cantemir promised for keeping my people from interfering with the lumbering?"

"What did George promise?" asked Dumfries.

"Twenty thousand in gold. When I took it up with Mahasingh, he refused to honor the promise and referred me to the higher officers of the company. Well, since you're board chairman, I couldn't go any higher."

"Is that promise in writing?"

"No; I trusted Cantemir's word."

"It seems to me that by setting your people on the lumbermen to disrupt their schedule, you haven't done anything to be paid for."

"When Mahasingh welshed on Cantemir's promise, I had to show I wasn't to be trifled with. But if you'll make an agreement now, I'll tell my people to lay off."

"No!" said Dumfries. "We do not pay people for letting us do what we have a perfect right to do. George was foolish to make the promise in the first place, assuming of course that you are telling the truth about it."

"I'll settle for half."

"No again. Anyone who pays an extortionist is merely asking for more of the same."

"I can throw in a night of pleasure if you wouldn't mind being on the bottom."

"Great Demiurge, what an idea! Look, young woman. Get it through your pretty red head that I am not interested in fornication, and that I would never pay a penny to anyone who would make a deal with a slimy reptile—sacrificing a human being to the mythical spooks of a race of vile, slithering beasts. You are a traitor to your species!"

During this talk Alexis had quietly moved past her two Kooks and towards Dumfries, who stood near the rim with his back to the crater. Now she gave a scream of:

"Then go to Shiiko yourself, you fat monster!"

She threw herself upon Dumfries, giving a fierce push to his bulbous belly. The push sent him back a step, but when he put his foot down, it was upon the thin air inside the crater.

The sect leader gave a roar for help, and for an eye-wink his arms windmilled. Then down he went. Salazar was not close enough to see Dumfries strike the lava below, but he heard the piercing scream and the smack of the body hitting the scum.

A bright yellow flare from below lit up the rosy, misty murk, then swiftly subsided as the combustible parts of Dumfries and his garments were consumed. Salazar would have liked, as a scientist, to watch this instant cremation, but that would have meant leaning over the edge, and with so many unfriendly presences around, he did not care to risk following Dumfries into Shikawa.

"Oh!" said Alexis, as if talking to herself. "I didn't really mean . . ."

One of Dumfries's litter bearers cried: "This Terran has slain our livelihood! We can sue her for loss of income! Seize her to hale before a magistrate!"

The speaker started toward Alexis, whose two Kooks stepped forward as if to protect her.

"Enough!" shouted Salazar in Sungao, covering the Kooks with his rifle. "That will do! All of you, return whence you came, forthwith!"

"You are being as foolish as a Terran, in any case," added Choku, also covering the group with his rifle. "It is a well-established law that a human being who works for a Terran does so at his own risk!"

The four other Kooks put their reptilian heads together, argued briefly with much flicking of forked tongues, then turned away from the crater. Their backs faded into the ruby mist. The two who had borne Dumfries carried the litter; the lantern had gone into Shikawa with Dumfries.

"Kirk," said Alexis, "since you've won, how about calling off the war? Come back to Kashania with me and I'll give you another night to remember!"

Salazar grinned. "No thanks! Do you offer free cunt to everybody you have an argument with? Anyway, I've had enough to remember all my life already.

"And by the way, doesn't your cult believe in reincarnation?"

"Yes, but what of that?"

"I know what you must have been in your last life. There's a voracious Terran freshwater fish called a piranha, which—"

"Oh, go to hell!" she snarled, and stamped off into the darkness after her Kooks.

"Let us go, Choku," said Salazar, stooping to pick up Alexis's bowie knife.

"Are you all right, sir? I see that you limp."

"Not entirely. I have been run almost to death and put through enough—how would you say, 'melodrama'?—put through enough crises to last three lifetimes."

Choku slung the Kookish rifle over one shoulder by its sling. "You have been physically harmed as well, sir. You bleed. Do you wish to return to the camp?"

"Certainly! How got you up here without my neutralizing whistle?"

"Through a gap in the forest, sir."

"Show me the way, please."

Salazar started limping around the rim of the crater, in which the fountains continued their play. He declined an offer by Choku to carry him, fearing that with a Kook's poor night vision, his carrier might stumble into Shikawa. Choku asked:

"What befell your beard, sir?"

"Mahasingh seized it to try to cut off my head. When it came off, he was too surprised to strike again before I got away."

"You aliens!" muttered Choku. Salazar could imagine the Kook's neck bristles fluttering in wonder and disdain. "This evening, sir, after you left in disguise for the meeting, a human being came asking for you. He said he was a scientist who wished to learn of your investigations, but I knew better. He bore upper-caste professional symbols, but under those I could faintly see an earlier set identifying him as a member of the high chief's police."

"Hm. Perhaps I had better get back into my Sri Sen outfit and clear out. Does the Unriu Express run tomorrow or the day after?"

"The day after, I believe. Tomorrow is already today."

"I lost my robe and turban on the flight up the mountain."

"Perhaps we can improvise substitutes, sir. Not wearing those coverings, we human beings are easily deceived by those alien disguises."

Emerging from the nanshins, Salazar said: "If my reckoning be right, we should be near the place where my juten was slain."

Choku flicked out his tongue. "I am sure you are right, sir. I detect the odor of juten."

As they neared the place where Salazar had begun his flight afoot, Salazar heard animal sounds. He said:

"Choku, pray hand me the lantern."

Limping, Salazar led the Kook towards the source of the sounds. When they came within range of the spotlight, Salazar saw a pair of poöshos tearing at the carcass of his juten. There was no sign of the other riding animal, which must have fled when the nocturnal predators had approached.

Salazar raised his rifle, sighted as best he could in the dark, and fired. At the bang, the poöshos fled with ghostly wails. One snatched up something from the ground and vanished into the darkness.

"Damn it, it's got my beard!" cried Salazar. "I can't chase it with my bum knee."

"Get on my back, sir," said Choku.

Mounted piggyback, Salazar endured the Kook's jouncing run. The poöshos fled along the open strip below the nanshin belt. As Choku began to overhaul them, Salazar said:

"Stop an instant, Choku!"

While Choku directed the spotlight at the fleeing animals, Salazar fired over Choku's head. The shot seemed to have missed, but the poösho bearing Salazar's beard abandoned it. Back on the ground, Salazar collected it.

The sky was paling when Choku and Salazar returned to their camp. Salazar caught a few hours of sleep and made last-minute observations of the nearby kusis. As the sun went down in a glory of crimson, gold, and azure, he said:

"I think the time has come to return to Henderson. Additional observations would add but little to my thesis."

"And your cult, sir?"

"Abdallah is in charge; and Mahasingh says he, too, is leaving. The Adriana lumbering appears to be collapsing, at least for now."

"But sir, suppose the lumber company recruits another crew to complete the job?"

Salazar shrugged. "If I come back, it will be as Doctor Sarasara, with more authority than I now have. I cannot stay on forever as unpaid guardian of the nanshin forest. So let us pack."

They toiled through half the night. Salazar, after putting his notes in the best order he could, stuffed them and his recorder reels and rolls of film into his large, waterproof plastic case with a lock.

"This," he told Choku, "is more important than all the rest of my gear together. If it be a choice betwixt saving the case and all the other baggage, save the case. I could get a new tent, rifle, cameras, and so forth, but I could not replace these records until I get home and duplicate them."

The sky was still a star-spangled black when Choku roused Salazar, who set to work, yawning, to transform himself into Sri Khushvant Sen. The beard was a little the worse for wear but could still be combed out and affixed.

Making Mahasingh's scarf into a turban proved more obdurate. After two unsuccessful attempts by Salazar, Choku said:

"I can help, sir."

Salazar sat while Choku expertly wound the scarf into an authentic turban and tucked the free end in. This time Salazar found he could move and even shake his head without the headgear's coming apart. "How did you ever learn that, Choku? I never heard of a Kukulcanian's wearing a turban."

"I worked for Mr. Kashani, sir, before Miss Ritter came. He taught me the trick, since he wore it in leading his cult. He said very few Terrans on his home world wore them nowadays, save cult leaders."

"Why are you not still working for the Kashanites?"

"Miss Ritter dismissed me, I suppose because of my

reluctance to comply with some of her more extreme commands.''

For the discarded robe, Salazar's yellow slicker was pressed into service. The color was not quite right, but there was no time to correct it.

Around midday Salazar set out for Amoen. Choku toted the baggage, in which Cantemir's big-game rifle was packed. Salazar wore his pistol and carried the case with his notes and records beneath his arm.

Arriving before sunset, they sought Amoen's nearest thing to an inn. This was a small house, a blocky concrete affair like most Kook houses, with a couple of extra rooms equipped as bedrooms. The owner, Geshukya, let out the extra rooms to Terrans.

Other Kooks never stopped there. Having a remarkable indifference to comfort and bound by complex rules of kin and caste, Kooks had no native equivalent of ''hotel'' or ''inn.'' When nightfall caught one away from home with no kith or kin, he simply sat on the ground with his back against something and went to sleep.

On the way to Geshukya's, Salazar clapped a hand to his forehead. ''Oh, my God!''

Choku turned. ''Sir, I believe that English expression denotes agitation. What, pray, is amiss?''

''We shall have to walk past Takao's juten stable to get to Geshukya's unless we make a wide detour through the woods. At this time of day, that strikes me as unwise.''

''Well, then, sir?''

''If Takao sees me, he will ask after the juten I rented from him, which Mahasingh shot. If I tell the truth, there will be an inquiry and we shall be stuck here for sixtnights.''

''Well, then, sir? Do you wish to remove your disguise?''

''But if I show my bare face, one of Yaamo's constables is looking for me. In a one-street town like this he would probably find me. So either way I am likely to be intercepted.''

''If, sir, you could assume a third personality . . .''

"Exactly! We will go behind that barn and cut off most of this beard. Then get my regular sun hat out of the bag."

When they emerged on the town's main street again, Salazar was still brown of skin but wore a short, close-cut black beard. On his head was a Terran sun helmet. His father had imported several of them from a Terran land called India, claiming they were the most practical headgear for persons of north European ancestry forced to work under tropical suns.

They passed Takao's stable. In front, a trio of Kooks surrounded a juten, arguing. Takao called out:

"O Terran! Pray pause. May your health be good!"

"And may your health be likewise good," replied Salazar automatically.

"May your ancestral spirits guide you to success!"

"And may your ancestral spirits save you from errors and perils!"

"May you overcome all obstacles."

Salazar finally said: "Very well, my friends, what is it?"

Takao said: "You see here the juten hired two sixt-nights ago by a Terran named Maasinga or something like that, saying he worked for the Adriana Lumber Company. Earlier today this same beast wandered back to our stable without its rider. Know you Mr. Maasinga? He has facial bristles like unto yours, but longer."

"I have met him," said Salazar cautiously. "I hear he means to return to Sungecho."

"We have heard of disturbances up this mountain, with riots and other Terranisms. Know you aught of this?"

Salazar studied the juten. Sure enough, the third right foreclaw was missing. Mahasingh had sounded noble in giving Salazar his mount in trade for the slain one, as if it were his to give. In fact, this looked like the start of convoluted litigation. Mahasingh could claim he owed Takao nothing because Takao had his hackney back. Salazar could claim he did not owe Takao for the dead juten because Mahasingh had killed the beast, not he. He answered:

"True, there was a disturbance. I went thither—"

"Excuse me, sir, but who are you?"

"Hasan Misri," said Salazar, giving the first name that popped into his head. "I went up the mountain to see if there was a place to set up a trading post to sell sundries to Terrans. Finding conditions unfavorable, at least for now, I shall return to Sungecho."

"Another thing, sir," said Takao. "Another Terran, giving the name of Sen, also rented a juten. He had somewhat of your appearance and seemed to be the leader of some Terran religious cult. We have heard naught of him since."

"I have met Mr. Sen," said Salazar gravely. "He said he wished to consult the hermit Seisen; that is all I know. May all paths lie smooth before you!"

"And may all your paths run straight and level."

Salazar emerged from Geshukya's house next dawn in his Arab businessman getup, with his pistol holster beneath the slicker. He had touched up his makeup; the real beard, sprouting beneath the false one, itched. Choku, who had slept with his back against Geshukya's house, joined Salazar, taking over the duffel bag, while Salazar carried the record case.

As they neared the station, Salazar touched Choku to detain him, saying: "Is that not Mahasingh?"

"Indeed it is, sir."

Mahasingh was handing his ticket to Conductor Zuiha. Salazar muttered: "That will not do. He knows who I am. Wait a moment, please!"

Salazar hastened back to the juten stable, where a Kook stable boy was feeding the animals. Salazar sent him in to rouse the owner. Takao appeared with his neck spines rippling displeasure.

"What would you, alien, at this hour?" he snapped.

"You wished to speak to the Terran Mahasingh, did you not?"

"Aye."

"I just now saw him boarding the express at the terminal. If you hurry, you can catch him."

"Oh, that is different! Thank you, sir!"

Takao departed at the Kooks' jouncing run. A few minutes later Salazar, strolling toward the station, saw three figures approaching: Takao, Mahasingh, and a Kook whom Salazar took to be the constable.

Salazar found a recessed doorway to a shop and stepped into the niche, studying the merchandise through the windows. It was junky stuff made for Terran tourists, but Salazar focused his attention on it until, reflected in the glass, he saw the two Kooks and the tall Terran pass by. The constable's scaly, clawed hands firmly gripped Mahasingh's arm. The latter volubly protested:

"But why should you detain me if the honorable Takao has his animal back? I shall miss my train. I will in due course pay the excess over the deposit!"

Salazar waited until they were past and then hurried back to Choku. Together they marched to the station, where Choku piled Salazar's bag on the baggage flatcar. Salazar bought soft-fare tickets for both.

"Honorable boss," said Choku, "that is unnecessary extravagance. I am perfectly comfortable on the open car, though I understand that it is different for you delicate aliens."

"It is not your comfort but my own skin whereof I think," said Salazar. "I need you as a bodyguard."

"You aliens!" said Choku. "Ever quarreling and feuding like infants! How you ever coöperated long enough to organize voyages between the stars I shall never understand."

They entered the soft-fare car. Salazar pulled out his copy of Yorimoto's *Pithecoidea of Kukulcan*. Now and then he glanced nervously toward the end of the car, watching for Mahasingh in case the ex-foreman talked his way out of his predicament. Sounds implied another arrival. Salazar, bracing for another confrontation, choked back an exclamation.

The person entering was Alexis Ritter.

X.

Sungecho Harbor

Salazar quickly looked down at the pages of Yorimoto. After Alexis, a Kook climbed into the car bearing a bag like Salazar's record case. Alexis sat a few seats away from Salazar; her Kook attendant handed her the case, bowed, and departed. Mahasingh did not appear.

Salazar tried to return to his reading, but soon he realized that he was reading the same paragraph for the third time and had not taken in any of it. Then Alexis spoke:

"Hey, you're Kirk Salazar! The hat's different and the whiskers are shorter, but I still know you. Well?"

"Well, what?"

"What have you to say for yourself? What's the point of going around in that outfit when I know you anyway?"

"Why should I say anything? I needn't excuse myself to the murderer of a friend of mine."

"What do you mean? Dumfries? I never did!" Alexis rose and stepped toward Salazar.

"No, I mean Jean-Pierre Latour. I suppose he dove into the crater on his own?"

"Oh, you mean that Frenchman? I never heard of him! And where's my knife?"

"What knife?"

"The knife I—you know the one! It's mine, and I want it back!"

197

"It's like the Gnome King's magic belt, which Dorothy confiscated when he tried to use it on her."

"Dorothy? Gnome King? What the hell are you talking about?"

"If you don't know, your education's been neglected."

"Oh, you're impossible!" Her arm went up, swinging her loaded handbag. Salazar started to duck, but Choku shot out a scaly arm and caught Alexis's wrist in a steely grip. The handbag flew across the aisle and landed on a seat with a clank.

"Naughty, naughty!" said Salazar, retrieving the handbag. "I ought to keep this, too, on the same principle."

"It's not fair, two of you against one!"

"Life is unfair, as my father quotes some politician as saying." Salazar hitched his pistol holster around within easy reach. "I must say, you've added a lot to my education in the last month."

"If you don't give me back my money, I'll have you arrested for robbery! That'll sure add to your education!"

Salazar handed the coin-weighted bag to Choku. "Hold this, please. Alexis, if you're a good girl all the way to Sungecho and don't give me away, I'll return your money."

"How do I know you will? Why should I trust you?"

"You don't know. You'll have to trust me because I have the firepower."

She spit an expletive and returned to her seat. Conductor Zuiha put his head in the door. "Tickets, prease!"

"Conductor!" said Alexis in Sungao. "I demand that this Kook be removed. His smell makes me ill."

The conductor looked from passenger to passenger. To Salazar he said: "Have you any objection to this human being's presence, sir? This is, after all, our planet."

"On the contrary," said Salazar, "he works for me, and I brought him here. As you see, his ticket is in order."

Alexis fell silent. Zuiha took the tickets, returned the stubs, and left the car. Choku said:

"If I may say so, sir, I think you handled that rather well. But you aliens' minds are so complex and devious that one never knows."

"You are right about our minds, Choku. Perhaps in another century I shall get the hang of them myself."

The locomotive whistled, Zuiha whaled his gong, the conductor and his trainkooks shouted, and the Unriu Express pulled out with a clank and a clatter.

"Kirk," said Alexis, standing in the aisle, "I'm sorry I lost my temper. Let's be friends."

Salazar looked up. "Okay."

"Will you be stopping at Levontin's again?"

"Sure. It's the only choice for us effete Terrans."

"Well, perhaps we could get together." She touched a plump hip against his shoulder, and the lurching of the car made it rub back and forth. He felt the familiar hypogastric thrill, but he sternly told himself that it would be safer to take a venomous boshiya to bed. She continued:

"Perhaps I could add some more to your education. But I wouldn't make it a heavy date with all that spinach on your face. What's the point of it, since I know who you are anyway?"

"Good idea," said Salazar, thinking: This woman is unshakably convinced that if all else fails, she can infallibly get what she wants from any male by offering the hot notch in her crotch. "Might as well change back to myself. Choku, have you the solvent for taking off the beard?"

A quarter hour later he emerged from the toilet compartment with the beard in his hand and the greasepaint scrubbed from his face and hands.

"That's better," said Alexis, "though you could do with a shave."

"Thought I'd grow the real thing. Some people, in-

cluding your luscious self, said I reminded them of a
rabbit with my poor little chin. A beard might help.'' He
sat down and took up his book.

She said: "We'll have a great time together. Now, how
about giving me back my money?''

"Not till we get to Sungecho.''

"I'll tell people you are also the swami Sen!''

"Then I'll tell how Val Dumfries met his timely end.''

"What I did was no more illegal than your taking my
money!''

"Maybe so, but Dumfries has fanatical followers, and
at least some of them would come after you for revenge.''

She cursed him with a verve that would have roused
envy in a longshoreman and stamped back to her seat.
Salazar resumed reading.

As they alighted at the Sungecho terminal, Salazar
handed over the handbag. Alexis looked at it as if she
could not believe her eyes. "Jesus, you really meant what
you said, didn't you?'' She turned and called: "Hey,
Matt!''

The large, sandy-haired man down the platform turned.
In the twilight, Salazar thought he had seen this man
before.

The young man and Alexis threw themselves into a
passionate clinch. When they untangled, Alexis said:
"Kirk, this is my friend Matthew Peters. Kirk Salazar,
the up-and-coming scientist.''

Peters put out a hand the size of a gorilla's. Salazar,
by applying pressure first, got his hand back intact. Peters took Alexis's traveling case, and the two walked off
arm in arm. The young man was the one she had been
with in Levontin's breakfast room on Salazar's first morning in Sungecho.

Salazar wondered what would have happened if he had
taken Alexis up on her latest advance. Would she have
had Peters lying in wait, to pounce just as Salazar prepared to dip his wick? Or had she planned a mini-orgy,

with Peters and Salazar mounting seriatim? It would be interesting to attend an orgy once in his life; but on the whole, this was a mystery of the sort he was willing to leave unsolved.

On the way to Levontin's, Salazar and Choku encountered Hilbert and Suzette Ritter. After greetings, Salazar said:

"Alexis came down on the train with me, but she went off with Peters."

Suzette sighed. "Not surprising. She avoids us, saying she can't bear to be preached at. Peters is her local fancy man, whom she comes down more or less monthly to quote see unquote. Oyodo says he's got his cranky engine fixed and, Metasu willing, the *Ijumo* will sail tomorrow night.

"Meanwhile I've been studying the phonetics of Sungao. Some call it a dialect of Feënzuo, while others consider it a separate language."

"I know these endless arguments," said Salazar, "which boil down to questions of definition. In my field it's about questions like: Does the extant hurato belong to the same species as the fossil hurato one of my colleagues dug up last year? The only way to settle it would be to put a male of one kind in a cage with a female of the other and wait to see if they were interfertile. But there's no way you can cross-breed a fossil with a living animal, or anything else, for that matter. Has Levontin an empty room?"

"I'm sure he has. He says rumors of disturbances on Mount Sungara have damaged his tourist trade ever since that boatload of Suvarovians was here."

Choku helped Salazar settle in his room at Levontin's Paradise Palace. As usual, Choku declined Salazar's offer to share the room, saying that his kind did not feel comfortable in alien dwellings, wherefore he would sleep against the outside wall as usual. Then a loud knock was followed by a demand in Sungao:

"Open in the name of High Chief Yaamo!"

The speaker proved a Kook with the painted insignia of Yaamo's constabulary. "Both of you!" he said. "You are commanded by the High Chief to appear in the conference room forthwith!"

"What now?" muttered Salazar. Soon he found himself back in the converted game room, as at the end of the trip to the Michisko Bush. He sat facing Chief Yaamo, with a translator and a squad of subordinates.

Those summoned, besides Salazar and Choku, were the elder Ritters, Alexis Ritter, and her friend Matthew Peters. The last two had evidently been snatched from bed at an inopportune moment. Peters had a sheet wrapped around his otherwise unclad torso, while Alexis was nude but for slippers. Her defiant glare said that nobody had better comment on those facts if he knew what was good for him.

"May aw your heth be good," said Yaamo slowly and with effort. "We wi' do wizzout ze perim—preliminaries."

He turned to his interpreter and spoke rapidly in Sungao. The interpreter translated:

"The High Chief has received reports of violence on Mount Sungara among Miss Ritter's followers and the employees of the Adriana Company. This has shut down the lumbering. Most of the lumbermen have departed, leaving too few to carry on.

"In addition, there is a tale of a Terran, a holy prophet, who stirred up this trouble. His name is reported as Sen. After arousing many to form a group to oppose the lumbering, he vanished, leaving the former subforeman in command. We have been unable to find him despite close watch on transportation facilities.

"A local Terran, who lives by selling other Terrans predictions of their futures, told us that some Terran holy men have the power of making themselves invisible. We shall doubt this until we see a convincing demonstration. Can any of you Terrans vanish whilst we watch? Nay? We thought not.

"Furthermore, we have a complaint from one Takao, owner of the juten stable in Amoen, of the disappearance of a juten rented by this alien Sen without payment for the animal. The remains of a carcass, mostly devoured by wild animals, were found on the edge of the nanshin forest, and it is suspected that this is the beast in question." The interpreter looked at Salazar. "You are Mr. Salazar, are you not?"

"I am."

"What have you to say about these matters?"

"The Reverend Khushvant Sen came by my camp on the juten in question. Later he returned afoot, saying that Mr. Mahasingh, enraged by his teachings, had pursued him and shot his animal dead. Sen escaped by hiding in the nanshins, where the spirit of Metasu protected him from the venom. So if anyone owes Takao for the animal, it is Mahasingh."

"Where is Mahasingh now?"

"This morning he meant to take the train to Sungecho with me. But questions about the missing juten detained him in Amoen until after train time."

Yaamo muttered to one of his subordinates; Salazar caught the word 'Maasinga.' The Kook hurried out, doubtless to alert the police to watch for Mahasingh.

So began an hour of questioning and tale telling. Salazar's heart was in his mouth lest Alexis blurt out that he was also Khushvant Sen. But she held her fire, probably, he thought, because of his counterthreat to expose her murder of Dumfries, whose name did not come up. Salazar wondered what she would do if it did. Yaamo would think nothing of the fact that she had sacrificed Dumfries to Shiiko to pay the rent on her lease; but if she confessed to this in open court, she would arouse fierce hostility among other Terrans.

She said that she had seen Salazar; in fact, they had

climbed Sungara to the crater together for a picnic. Afterward, all she saw of him was glimpses as he went about his research. She attended Sen's meeting but had no idea whence he came or whither he went. When she finished, Salazar drew a breath of relief.

Even riskier was the chief's questioning of Choku, since every Kook had a built-in lie detector. When his turn came, Choku merely said that he had brought Sen down from the crater and had seen him as far as Amoen. If the high chief had asked about the true identities of Sen and Salazar, the fat would have been in the fire, but that question seemed not to have occurred to the inquisitors.

At last Yaamo said through his interpreter: "The more we look into this affair, the more tangled it becomes. Trust Terrans to complicate matters beyond human understanding! When we locate Mahasingh and Sen, questioning may make some sense of the story. Meanwhile the Terrans Salazar and the young female Ritter shall remain in Sungecho until these matters be clarified.

"Like a sensible person, we avoid interference in disputes amongst aliens. Know, however, that all this business of strange Terran cults, crimes, conflicts, and riots is intolerable to us human beings. The next such outbreak, we shall order *all* aliens off Sunga, even if it means that we shall have to send real human beings to Shikawa to keep Shiiko well disposed. We are sure that as a result of the bad example set by you Terrans, we shall have enough human criminals to satisfy the volcano spirit.

"While the aliens' presence brings us some small advantages in manufactures and trade goods, they are not worth these disturbances and interruptions of the island's orderly activities. Your crimes against one another we do not deem our proper business, but lately there have even been Terran offenses against human beings. We will not put up with that!

"From all we have seen of Terrans, we conclude that whilst you have pretensions to an advanced civilization, based upon your precocious technological progress, you are actually primitive organisms, evolved but little beyond the kusi stage. You are still driven by the sort of instincts that adapted you to a life of wandering about the wilderness in little bands and foraging for anything edible.

"You are not, however, at all suited to a civilized life of order and reason. You require an elaborate apparatus of law, government, and supernatural belief to keep you in a barely tolerable state of order. Remove these restraints, as by letting you roam at large in human lands, and you run wild, assaulting, robbing, and slaying one another and sometimes even molesting real human beings."

It sounded to Salazar much like what the hermit Seisen had said. Yaamo continued: "To tolerate many of you in our midst were like giving a band of kusis the run of one's house. Kusis make amusing and even affectionate pets. But they also go on rampages, destroying everything breakable and biting you if you try to stop them.

"That is all we have to say for the present, save that, we repeat, at the next outbreak of Terranism, off to the mainland the lot of you go! What our fellow authorities on the mainland choose to do with your turbulent, irrational species is their affair. May your health remain good!"

The next day Salazar drew his money out of the bank, got a haircut, and returned the book on Asian religions to the library. He visited Doctor Deyssel to see if he needed treatment for any of the cuts, scrapes, sprains, and bruises that he had lately suffered, and he took care of other needful chores. From the physician he learned that George Cantemir was still undergoing treatment for the repair of his member and would not be ready to return to the mainland on the *Ijumo*'s next voyage.

At seventeen by Terran clocks, trailed by Choku, Salazar walked to Mao Dai's with the record case beneath his arm. At the retsuraan, he counted notes out of his wallet. When he handed the wad to Choku, the Kook riffled through them, detached three, and handed them back, saying:

"Honorable boss, you miscounted. You owe me these not."

"That is a gift for taking such good care of me. Without you, I would have been dead several times over."

"Thank you, sir, but I cannot accept. We had an agreement as to how much a day you should pay me, and I have served you for precisely forty days. I should be most unhappy to receive either more or less than my exact due."

"Oh, all right," said Salazar. "Would you like to continue as my assistant back to Henderson? I find you invaluable."

In the dimming light, while Choku's turtle-beaked face remained impassive, his neck spines rippled. "Thank you, sir, but I will not now leave Sunga."

"Why not? Are you not fain to see more of the world?"

"Nay, sir. I was born on the mainland and have traveled about the continent. For another thing, I have not seen my wife in forty days, and I begin to feel somewhat as those lumberjacks did when the Kashanite females flaunted their persons at them."

"I knew not that you even had a wife!"

"You never asked me, sir. A wife, named Dzucho, and three small human beings. Now, if you wish, I will carry your bag aboard the ship whilst you and your Terran friends consume your dinners."

Later, accompanied by Choku, Salazar approached the pier to which the *Ijumo* was moored. Under his arm he tightly gripped his case of records, which now included the confessions of the three gangsters in Dumfries's pay. As the men had disappeared without giving their testimony in open court, the confessions were of flimsy legal value, since they might have been extorted by torture. Still, Salazar was glad to have them in case someone should raise questions back in Henderson.

Suzette and Hilbert Ritter followed Salazar and Choku. As they neared the pier, Salazar said:

"Choku, I see what I think is one of Yaamo's policemen at the foot of the gangplank. I suspect that he is there to make sure that I stay in Sungecho, as the High Chief commanded."

"Then must you remain on shore, sir?"

"Belike you could approach him and tell him that there has been a disturbance, with shooting, at Mao Dai's retsuraan."

"Very well, sir," said Choku doubtfully. He walked out on the pier and spoke to the sentry. The Kook slung his rifle over his shoulder and set off at a run, passing Salazar and the Ritters without pause.

Choku came back. "It is fortunate, sir, that in the darkness the officer could not clearly see my neck bristles or he would have known that I lied. You aliens!"

Salazar mused: "I am sorry to run out on the High Chief, leaving the Takao case in the air, but I have my own work to do. Besides, Yaamo might decide, from the loftiest motives, that I was next in line for Shikawa. Or Alexis might hire another gang from the local underworld, as Dumfries did, to do me in."

Walking up the gangplank, Hilbert Ritter said: "Kirk, I agree that Alexis deserves to 'go to Shiiko' herself. But one can't take quite so cold-blooded an attitude with a daughter. She'll doubtless go on and on, pulling one outrage after another, until someone equally ruthless does the same to her. As some ancient Greek said, the best equipment for life is effrontery."

"She and Abdallah will fight it out," said Salazar. "He's a tough customer."

Hilbert Ritter said: "There's a rumor that Dumfries is dead."

"So I hear," said Salazar. "Some say his heart just

stopped, not surprising in one so overweight. Others say he tripped over a lava rock and fell into Shikawa. At least that's one threat to the local environment eliminated.''

"For the present," said Ritter. "But don't be surprised if someone else, hoping to profit from that conquer-the-universe message, picks up Dumfries's torch and runs with it. It's not a war you can win by overrunning the enemy's lands but a battle for people's minds, which never ends.''

"I think I know the true story of Dumfries's death,'' said Suzette quietly.

"What?" cried Hilbert. "Why didn't you tell me, darling?''

"I didn't think it safe until we were aboard the ship.''

"What is it?''

Suzette narrated the successive confrontations at the crater much as Salazar remembered them. He said: "How did you hear that?''

"Kooks are great gossips. Some were at the crater, and one passed the word to one of my phonetic informants. I also heard about that meeting called by Sri Something, which started the anti-Adriana movement. Mr. Something sounded remarkably like Kirk Salazar doing his burlesque swami act on the *Ijumo*.''

"Well?" said Salazar.

"You could be a hero to the environmentalists if you let it all come out.''

"Thanks; I'd rather be a live scientist than a dead hero. Some fanatical cultist would probably bump me off. I told your daughter that if she didn't blow the gaff on Sri Khushvant Sen, I'd keep quiet about her sending the reverend to his Gnostic heaven. And that's what I shall do.''

On the fantail Salazar said to Choku: "Good-bye, and may your health remain good.''

"May your health be better than ever,'' replied the Kook.

"May your ancestral spirits adroitly guide you.''

"And may your ancestral spirits protect you from all contingencies."

Feeling that this time he ought to show his best Kukulcanian manners, Salazar continued the formulas as long as he could remember them. When he ran out of well-wishes, Choku said:

"Farewell, honorable boss."

The Kook walked down the gangplank and disappeared. Captain Oyodo bawled:

"Aw passengers on board, prease!"

Then he shouted in Sungao. Deckhands seized the gangplank to haul it aboard. Others cast off mooring lines. Forward, the engine puffed and the paddle wheels began slowly to turn.

With a quick thud of feet, Matthew Peters, Alexis's local bed partner, dashed up the plank. Salazar had been facing forward and was unprepared when the case of his research materials was snatched out from beneath his arm. Peters whirled and sprinted aft. The gangplank was dropped to the deck with a bang, but the pier was still within easy jump. The captain shouted.

Salazar could have drawn his pistol and shot Peters, but then Peters would have fallen into the sea, document case and all. Instead, Salazar launched himself in a flying tackle. He was no expert at that athletic feat, but his life in the outback had hardened him, and the surge of adrenaline at the prospect of losing his research gave him abnormal strength and adroitness. He and Peters slammed to the deck together.

The case, which Peters had clutched to his bosom, flew out of his grasp, skittered across the deck, and vanished into the water astern.

Damn, thought Salazar, I might as well have shot the bastard, after all! He reached the fantail, where the deckhands had not replaced the movable section of rail. The case bobbed ghostly on the slight swell. Salazar dove in, came up spitting dirty harbor water, and struck out f the case. His garments hampered his swimming, but he grimly plowed on until he had a grip on the case.

Peters, too, rose. He took two steps and launched himself in a leap toward the pier. But the distance had widened since Salazar had downed him. Peters struck the edge of the pier with his shins and, with a yelp of pain, fell into the water near Salazar.

Salazar swam a one-armed back stroke toward the receding *Ijumo*. At a shout from the captain, the paddle wheels stopped turning and a rope was thrown from the deck. Salazar looped the end of the rope around the case and tied the loop.

"Pull that up first!" he sputtered.

When Salazar was finally hauled aboard, Ritter said: "Kirk, I wish I were on the committee you'll take your orals from! If there ever was a dedicated scientist, you're it!"

Salazar shrugged. "I couldn't waste a season's research." He glanced astern, where a pair of Kooks were hauling Peters up on the pier. "I could pick him off . . . but better not. Things are complicated enough, and my gun's wet. But why the devil should that woman want to get her hands on a mass of records of the ethology of *Cusius brachiurus*?"

Ritter shrugged in turn. "Maybe in hope of luring you back on shore, where her boys could grab you, or to extort something from you. She knows you value it." He spread his hands. "I suppose you could go back to Sunga and ask her."

"I'll do that when Kashani comes back from the dead! As Choku says, with Terrans one never knows what crazy thing they'll do next." He sneezed. "Now excuse me. I need to get dry."

he pier at Oöi, the Ritters watched as a small, oung woman and Kirk Salazar threw themselves h other's arms. When they came up for air, Sa-
d:

"Do you know Calpurnia Fisker? These, darling, are the Doctors Ritter, Hilbert and Suzette. My best friends on the trip."

"Delighted," said Ritter. "Miss Fisker, this young man is remarkable. He's not so big as some or so handsome as others, but he has something more important in the long run."

"I know he's smart!"

"No, though that's also important. I mean he has *character*. Inside that modest, mousy fellow is a hero struggling to get out."

"Oh, I've known that all along," said Calpurnia. "He looks years older with that sprouting beard. He even looks taller."

"Sunga matured him," said Ritter. "He'll have lots of adventures to tell you."

"Oh, bilge!" said Salazar. "Flattery will get you everywhere. I'm just another apprentice professor and would-be scientist, trying to do his job." To himself he added: There is one adventure that I won't even mention!

Ritter continued: "How did you happen to be here to meet the ship?"

"Kirk wrote he would probably come on this one," said Calpurnia. "He said he had something important to say, so I—I . . ."

"Came four days by train to make sure he said it." Ritter turned to Suzette. "Come on, darling. They want us in the customs shed."

Watching Salazar and Calpurnia walk off with arms around each other, Salazar pressing his record case firmly under his other arm, Suzette said: "I hope they make it."

Ritter replied: "Nobody knows the future, but I'd say their chances were as good as anybody's. Let's find the table with the R's."

About the Author

L. Sprague de Camp, who has over ninety-five books to his credit, writes in several fields: historicals, SF, fantasy, biography, and popularizations of science. But his favorite genre of literature is fantasy.

De Camp is a master of that rare animal called *humorous fantasy*. As a young writer collaborating with the late Fletcher Pratt, he set forth the world-hopping adventures of Harold Shea and the delightfully zany *Tales from Gavagan's Bar*, a book that has remained in print for forty years.

In 1976, at the thirty-fourth World Science Fiction Convention, he received *The Gandalf–Grand Master Award for Lifetime Achievement in the Field of Fantasy*. The Science Fiction Writers of America presented him with their *Grand Master Nebula Award of 1978*. Alone, and with his wife and sometime collaborator, Catherine, de Camp has been a welcome guest of honor at fan conventions throughout the United States.

The de Camps live in Texas. They have two sons: Lyman Sprague and Gerard Beekman, both of whom are distinguished engineers.

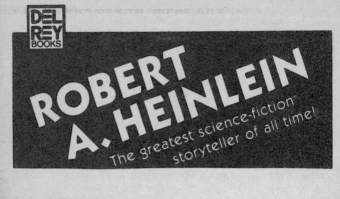